PATRICIA WENTWORTH
THE COLDSTONE

PATRICIA WENTWORTH was born Dora Amy Elles in India in 1877 (not 1878 as has sometimes been stated). She was first educated privately in India, and later at Blackheath School for Girls. Her first husband was George Dillon, with whom she had her only child, a daughter. She also had two stepsons from her first marriage, one of whom died in the Somme during World War I.

Her first novel was published in 1910, but it wasn't until the 1920's that she embarked on her long career as a writer of mysteries. Her most famous creation was Miss Maud Silver, who appeared in 32 novels, though there were a further 33 full-length mysteries not featuring Miss Silver—the entire run of these is now reissued by Dean Street Press.

Patricia Wentworth died in 1961. She is recognized today as one of the pre-eminent exponents of the classic British golden age mystery novel.

By Patricia Wentworth

The Benbow Smith Mysteries
Fool Errant
Danger Calling
Walk with Care
Down Under

The Frank Garrett Mysteries
Dead or Alive
Rolling Stone

The Ernest Lamb Mysteries
The Blind Side
Who Pays the Piper?
Pursuit of a Parcel

Standalones
The Astonishing Adventure of Jane Smith
The Red Lacquer Case
The Annam Jewel
The Black Cabinet
The Dower House Mystery
The Amazing Chance
Hue and Cry
Anne Belinda
Will-o'-the-Wisp
Beggar's Choice
The Coldstone
Kingdom Lost
Nothing Venture
Red Shadow
Outrageous Fortune
Touch and Go
Fear by Night
Red Stefan
Blindfold
Hole and Corner
Mr. Zero
Run!
Weekend with Death
Silence in Court

PATRICIA WENTWORTH

THE COLDSTONE

With an introduction by
Curtis Evans

DEAN STREET PRESS

Published by Dean Street Press 2016

Cover by DSP

First published in 1930 by Hodder & Stoughton

ISBN 978 1 911413 19 6

www.deanstreetpress.co.uk

Introduction

BRITISH AUTHOR Patricia Wentworth published her first novel, a gripping tale of desperate love during the French Revolution entitled *A Marriage under the Terror*, a little over a century ago, in 1910. The book won first prize in the Melrose Novel Competition and was a popular success in both the United States and the United Kingdom. Over the next five years Wentworth published five additional novels, the majority of them historical fiction, the best-known of which today is *The Devil's Wind* (1912), another sweeping period romance, this one set during the Sepoy Mutiny (1857-58) in India, a region with which the author, as we shall see, had extensive familiarity. Like *A Marriage under the Terror*, *The Devil's Wind* received much praise from reviewers for its sheer storytelling élan. One notice, for example, pronounced the novel "an achievement of some magnitude" on account of "the extraordinary vividness...the reality of the atmosphere...the scenes that shift and move with the swiftness of a moving picture...." (*The Bookman*, August 1912) With her knack for spinning a yarn, it perhaps should come as no surprise that Patricia Wentworth during the early years of the Golden Age of mystery fiction (roughly from 1920 into the 1940s) launched upon her own mystery-writing career, a course charted most successfully for nearly four decades by the prolific author, right up to the year of her death in 1961.

Considering that Patricia Wentworth belongs to the select company of Golden Age mystery writers with books which have remained in print in every decade for nearly a century now (the centenary of Agatha Christie's first mystery, *The Mysterious Affair at Styles*, is in 2020; the centenary of Wentworth's first mystery, *The Astonishing Adventure of Jane Smith*, follows merely three years later, in 2023), relatively little is known about the author herself. It appears, for example, that even the widely given year of Wentworth's birth, 1878, is incorrect. Yet it is sufficiently clear that Wentworth lived a varied and intriguing life that provided her ample inspiration for a writing career devoted to imaginative fiction.

It is usually stated that Patricia Wentworth was born Dora Amy Elles on 10 November 1878 in Mussoorie, India, during the heyday of the British Raj; however, her Indian birth and baptismal record states that she in fact was born on 15 October 1877 and was baptized on 26 November of that same year in Gwalior. Whatever doubts surround her actual birth year, however, unquestionably the future author came from a prominent Anglo-Indian military family. Her father, Edmond Roche Elles, a son of Malcolm Jamieson Elles, a Porto, Portugal wine merchant originally from Ardrossan, Scotland, entered the British Royal Artillery in 1867, a decade before Wentworth's birth, and first saw service in India during the Lushai Expedition of 1871-72. The next year Elles in India wed Clara Gertrude Rothney, daughter of Brigadier-General Octavius Edward Rothney, commander of the Gwalior District, and Maria (Dempster) Rothney, daughter of a surgeon in the Bengal Medical Service. Four children were born of the union of Edmond and Clara Elles, Wentworth being the only daughter.

Before his retirement from the army in 1908, Edmond Elles rose to the rank of lieutenant-general and was awarded the KCB (Knight Commander of the Order of Bath), as was the case with his elder brother, Wentworth's uncle, Lieutenant-General Sir William Kidston Elles, of the Bengal Command. Edmond Elles also served as Military Member to the Council of the Governor-General of India from 1901 to 1905. Two of Wentworth's brothers, Malcolm Rothney Elles and Edmond Claude Elles, served in the Indian Army as well, though both of them died young (Malcolm in 1906 drowned in the Ganges Canal while attempting to rescue his orderly, who had fallen into the water), while her youngest brother, Hugh Jamieson Elles, achieved great distinction in the British Army. During the First World War he catapulted, at the relatively youthful age of 37, to the rank of brigadier-general and the command of the British Tank Corps, at the Battle of Cambrai personally leading the advance of more than 350 tanks against the German line. Years later Hugh Elles also played a major role in British civil defense during the Second World War. In the event of a German invasion of Great Britain, something which seemed all too possible in 1940, he was tasked with leading the defense of southwestern England. Like Sir Edmond and Sir William, Hugh Elles attained the rank of lieutenant-general and was awarded the KCB.

Although she was born in India, Patricia Wentworth spent much of her childhood in England. In 1881 she with her mother and two younger brothers was at Tunbridge Wells, Kent, on what appears to have been a rather extended visit in her ancestral country; while a decade later the same family group resided at Blackheath, London at Lennox House, domicile of Wentworth's widowed maternal grandmother, Maria Rothney. (Her eldest brother, Malcolm, was in Bristol attending Clifton College.) During her years at Lennox House, Wentworth attended Blackheath High School for Girls, then only recently founded as "one of the first schools in the country to give girls a proper education" (*The London Encyclopaedia*, 3rd ed., p. 74). Lennox House was an ample Victorian villa with a great glassed-in conservatory running all along the back and a substantial garden-- most happily, one presumes, for Wentworth, who resided there not only with her grandmother, mother and two brothers, but also five aunts (Maria Rothney's unmarried daughters, aged 26 to 42), one adult first cousin once removed and nine first cousins, adolescents like Wentworth herself, from no less than three different families (one Barrow, three Masons and five Dempsters); their parents, like Wentworth's father, presumably were living many miles away in various far-flung British dominions. Three servants--a cook, parlourmaid and housemaid--were tasked with serving this full score of individuals.

Sometime after graduating from Blackheath High School in the mid-1890s, Wentworth returned to India, where in a local British newspaper she is said to have published her first fiction. In 1901 the 23-year-old Wentworth married widower George Fredrick Horace Dillon, a 41-year-old lieutenant-colonel in the Indian Army with three sons from his prior marriage. Two years later Wentworth gave birth to her only child, a daughter named Clare Roche Dillon. (In some sources it is erroneously stated that Clare was the offspring of Wentworth's second marriage.) However in 1906, after just five years of marriage, George Dillon died suddenly on a sea voyage, leaving Wentworth with sole responsibility for her three teenaged stepsons and baby daughter. A very short span of years, 1904 to 1907, saw the deaths of Wentworth's husband, mother, grandmother and brothers Malcolm and Edmond, removing much of her support network. In 1908, however, her father, who was now sixty years old, retired from the army and returned to England, settling at Guildford, Surrey with an older unmarried sister named Dora (for whom his daughter presumably had been named). Wentworth joined this household as well, along with her daughter and her youngest stepson. Here in Surrey Wentworth, presumably with the goal of making herself financially independent for the first time in her life (she was now in her early thirties), wrote the novel that changed the course of her life, *A Marriage under the Terror*, for the first time we know of utilizing her famous *nom de plume*.

The burst of creative energy that resulted in Wentworth's publication of six novels in six years suddenly halted after the appearance of *Queen Anne Is Dead* in 1915. It seems not unlikely that the Great War impinged in various ways on her writing. One tragic episode was the death on the western front of one of her stepsons, George Charles Tracey Dillon. Mining in Colorado when war was declared, young Dillon worked his passage from Galveston, Texas to Bristol, England as a shipboard muleteer (mule-tender) and joined the Gloucestershire Regiment. In 1916 he died at the Somme at the age of 29 (about the age of Wentworth's two brothers when they had passed away in India).

A couple of years after the conflict's cessation in 1918, a happy event occurred in Wentworth's life when at Frimley, Surrey she wed George Oliver Turnbull, up to this time a lifelong bachelor who like the author's first husband was a lieutenant-colonel in the Indian Army. Like his bride now forty-two years old, George Turnbull as a younger man had distinguished himself for his athletic prowess, playing forward for eight years for the Scottish rugby team and while a student at the Royal Military Academy winning the medal awarded the best athlete of his term. It seems not unlikely that Turnbull played a role in his wife's turn toward writing mystery fiction, for he is said to have strongly supported Wentworth's career, even assisting her in preparing manuscripts for publication. In 1936 the couple in Camberley, Surrey built Heatherglade House, a large two-story structure on substantial grounds, where they resided until Wentworth's death a quarter of a century later. (George Turnbull survived his wife by nearly a decade, passing away in 1970 at the age of 92.) This highly successful middle-aged companionate marriage contrasts sharply with the more youthful yet rocky union of Agatha and Archie Christie, which was three years away from sundering when Wentworth published *The Astonishing Adventure of Jane Smith* (1923), the first of her sixty-five mystery novels.

Although Patricia Wentworth became best-known for her cozy tales of the criminal investigations of consulting detective Miss Maud Silver, one of the mystery genre's most prominent spinster sleuths, in truth the Miss Silver tales account for just under half of Wentworth's 65 mystery novels. Miss Silver did not make her debut until 1928 and she did not come to predominate in Wentworth's fictional criminous output until the 1940s. Between 1923 and 1945 Wentworth published 33 mystery novels without Miss Silver, a handsome and substantial legacy in and of itself to vintage crime fiction fans. Many of these books are standalone tales of mystery, but nine of them have series characters. Debuting in the novel *Fool Errant* in 1929, a year after Miss Silver first appeared in print, was the enigmatic, nautically-named *eminence grise* Benbow Collingwood Horatio Smith, owner of a most expressively opinionated parrot named Ananias (and quite a colorful character in his own right). Benbow Smith went on to appear in three additional Wentworth mysteries: *Danger Calling* (1931), *Walk with Care* (1933) and *Down Under* (1937). Working in tandem with Smith in the investigation of sinister affairs threatening the security of Great Britain in *Danger Calling* and *Walk with Care* is Frank Garrett, Head of Intelligence for the Foreign Office, who also appears solo in *Dead or Alive* (1936) and *Rolling Stone* (1940) and collaborates with additional series characters, Scotland Yard's Inspector Ernest Lamb and Sergeant Frank Abbott, in *Pursuit of a Parcel* (1942). Inspector Lamb and Sergeant Abbott headlined a further pair of mysteries, *The Blind Side* (1939) and *Who Pays the Piper?* (1940), before they became absorbed, beginning with *Miss Silver Deals with Death* (1943), into the burgeoning Miss Silver canon. Lamb would make his farewell appearance in 1955 in *The Listening Eye*, while Abbott would take his final bow in mystery fiction with Wentworth's last published novel, *The Girl in the Cellar* (1961), which went into print the year of the author's death at the age of 83.

The remaining two dozen Wentworth mysteries, from the fantastical *The Astonishing Adventure of Jane Smith* in 1923 to the intense legal drama *Silence in Court* in 1945, are, like the author's series novels, highly imaginative and entertaining tales of mystery and adventure, told by a writer gifted with a consummate flair for storytelling. As one confirmed Patricia Wentworth mystery fiction addict, American Golden Age mystery writer Todd Downing, admiringly declared in the 1930s, "There's something about Miss Wentworth's yarns that is contagious." This attractive new series of Patricia Wentworth reissues by Dean Street Press provides modern fans of vintage mystery a splendid opportunity to catch the Wentworth fever.

Curtis Evans

Family Tree showing Anthony Colstone's Descent

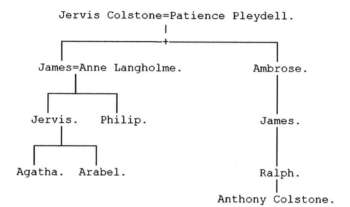

```
        Jervis Colstone=Patience Pleydell.
                        |
        ----------------+----------------------
        |                                     |
   James=Anne Langholme.                  Ambrose.
        |                                     |
    ----+----                                 |
    |       |                                 |
 Jervis.  Philip.                          James.
    |                                          |
 ---+----                                      |
 |      |                                       |
Agatha. Arabel.                             Ralph.
                                               |
                                    Anthony Colstone.
```

Prologue

SIR JERVIS COLSTONE lay in his bed propped up with pillows and looked across the room and out of the window. He was close upon a hundred years old, and the world was slipping away from him. He looked out of the window, and who can say what he saw? What other eyes might have seen was a green picture of tilted fields running slantwise up a hill. The June grass stood high in the fields, and high above the June grass of the midmost field two tall grey stones stood pointing up to the blue June sky. Perhaps Sir Jervis saw more than just two stones. Perhaps he saw a great full circle, and in the midst of the circle a stone of ancient sacrifice. Perhaps he saw a pillar of fire and smoke that went up into a midnight sky. Perhaps he saw other things.

He stirred, shifted his right hand in a groping fashion, and said, "Susan—"

The old woman who sat at the bed foot leaned forward and put her hand on his. She was older than he by three months. Her black eyes were indomitably alive and courageous. She wore a decent black gown, a black silk cap, and a little black apron with pockets. A handkerchief lay in her lap; but she had not wept, nor would she weep. She touched his hand and said,

"Jervis—"

He said, "Safe—" and then, with a sudden energy, "You'll not tell him."

Old Mrs. Bowyer patted the big bony hand. All the Colstones ran to bone—big men, hard to move.

"You'll not tell him," he repeated, stumbling a little over the words.

Old Mrs. Bowyer's look deepened.

"And what am I not to tell him, my dear?"

"Not—anything."

"He's your own flesh and blood—he'll be Colstone when you're gone. There've been a plenty of Anthonys afore him, haven't there?"

He gave an impatient groan.

"Don't—trust—anyone. Don't—tell—anything." A pause, and then, *"Promise."*

Susan Bowyer patted his hand again.

"Don't you fret, my dear."

She felt the hand twitch. The wraith of the old passionate frown darkened his face.

"Promise."

Perhaps he saw her shake her head. Perhaps he only saw the picture which filled his mind. Perhaps he saw the tilted fields and the two grey, watching stones.

The door opened and Nurse Collins came in, very bright and neat.

"He's been talking all the time, I suppose—never stops, and not a word of sense. It's a pity you troubled to come, really. There—just listen to him!"

The frown had deepened. A rapid mutter came from the pale parted lips—words, sentences, but all in confusion, as if the thread on which they were strung had snapped and left them split abroad.

"No use your staying." Nurse Collins was brisk and patronizing. "The daughters will be back in a minute, though there's nothing they can do. He won't know them any more than he knows you."

Old Mrs. Bowyer's black eyes rested on her with an odd sparkle somewhere deep down in them.

"What some folks knows is worth knowing," she said.

Chapter One

ANTHONY COLSTONE sat forward in his chair. He looked at Mr. Leveridge with a kind of alert sparkle in his eyes.

"What?" he said.

Mr. Leveridge prepared to repeat what he had just said. A solicitor becomes accustomed to repeating himself. He coughed, set a sheet of blotting paper straight, and said, raising his voice a little,

"Sir Jervis desired that you should give a solemn undertaking."

Anthony slapped his knee.

"But the thing's absurd!"

"Well—" said Mr. Leveridge.

"Absurd! Look here—I never expected to come into the place. Why, I hardly knew of its existence—never heard it talked of—never thought about it. But if I've come in for it—well, I *have* come in for it. And the first thing you ask me to do is to give a solemn undertaking that I won't do this and I won't do that—all for no reason at all." He fixed a fleeting glance, half merry, half appealing, upon the solicitor's square, guarded face. "I say—it isn't reasonable—is it? I mean you do think it a bit thick yourself to have a condition like that tacked on to a place."

The square, guarded face did not respond at all; the eyes remained dull and a trifle superior, the mouth hard and indifferent. Anthony remembered interviews with his headmaster, and felt abashed and then angry because he had let old Leveridge make him feel like a schoolboy. He reminded him of Roberts at his prep school.

Leveridge was speaking. He said drily,

"It is not a condition. As I was telling you, Sir Jervis counted on seeing you, and when he realized that you could scarcely reach England in time, he sent for me—"

"Yes?"

Mr. Leveridge had paused. He did not immediately respond to this eager prompting. He lifted the pencil, balanced it, set it down again.

"You realize, of course, that the property was entirely at Sir Jervis' disposal. There has never been any entail. He could have left everything to his daughters if he had wished to do so, or—"

"Why didn't he? I'm only—what sort of relation am I? I'm hanged if I know. Something pretty far away, isn't it?"

"You are the great-grandson of Sir Jervis' uncle, Ambrose Colstone."

Anthony held his head.

"Ambrose Colstone was the younger brother of James Colstone, Sir Jervis' father. Sir Jervis leaves two daughters, Miss Agatha and Miss Arabel Colstone. Ambrose had a son, James, who was your grandfather."

"Yes, I know."

"As I was saying, Sir Jervis could have left everything to his daughters."

"Then why didn't he? It seems a bit unnatural."

"Well"—again that pause—"he had not a great opinion of women, and the old ladies—"

"Oh, they're old?"

"Well, oldish—round about seventy. Sir Jervis was just on a hundred. They are a very long-lived family. Well, Mr. Colstone, Sir Jervis has left you everything. In return, he expected this pledge from you. At the last he would, I think, have made it a condition, but there was not time. I assured him that I would put the matter to you as strongly as possible."

Anthony felt himself stiffening a little. He was having his duty pointed out to him; a superior eye directed him towards it; he was being pushed. He stiffened. No one likes being pushed. He said,

"Why was he so keen about it?"

Mr. Leveridge looked at a picture on the wall.

"Sir Jervis disliked changes of any sort. He had a very strong feeling for the place and everything belonging to it. The property is a very old one, you know. Parts of the house are very old. I have heard Sir Jervis say—" He broke off with a slight frown.

Anthony had a sense of something withheld. He felt irked and out of his depth.

"Yes, but you can't tie and bind people like that—it's not reasonable." He too paused, and then said, "If there's no reason, I won't bind myself. And if there is a reason, I should like to know what it is."

Mr. Leveridge withdrew his gaze from the picture, let it fall a thought weightily upon this young Colstone, and found something that gave him food for thought. He had seen, up to now, just a good-looking young soldier, boyish for his twenty-six years; now, all of a sudden, he looked older and spoke as if he were sure of himself. There was no likeness to Sir Jervis, but he was much mistaken if there were not something of the same stubborn strain.

He said, "I can't give you any reason. Sir Jervis expected the undertaking to be given. I don't think he would have left you the property if you had refused to give it. I can't say any more than that— it's not my place to say any more. I assured him that I would put it to you as strongly as possible. I can do no more than that."

Anthony fixed a steady gaze on his face. Damping old blighter this. Awfully like Roberts.

"But there must be a reason," he said.

"Sir Jervis had the greatest possible dislike of intrusion."

"I don't follow you."

"The Stones are of interest from the archæological standpoint, I believe. I think Sir Jervis had a horror of possible excavations. He once said something on those lines. I think he had an idea that the whole place would be turned upside down—natural features obliterated or spoiled—tourists too. He would never show the house, you know."

"It's a ring of stones—like Stonehenge?"

"Oh, nothing as important as Stonehenge. They call it the Coldstone Ring, but there are only one or two stones, I believe—that is, there are only one or two remaining so far as I know. I have never seen them myself."

"And I'm to give an undertaking that I won't move them, or allow them to be moved?"

"For any purpose whatsoever."

"Come to that, why should anyone want to move them?"

Mr. Leveridge's faint air of superiority became less faint.

"The local archæological society will certainly apply to you for permission to excavate. At intervals they have approached Sir Jervis, with, I may say, most unfortunate results. He had not been on speaking terms with Lord Haverton for more than ten years in consequence of the last attempt. Lord Haverton is the president of the society. He will probably approach you. Sir Jervis feared it, I know, and desired you to be safeguarded by a definite promise."

Anthony Colstone squared his shoulders and threw back his head.

"That's treating me as if I were a child! I think the whole thing's damned unreasonable." He flushed a little and went on more quietly, "I never expected to come into the place. I always understood that there'd been no end of a family quarrel—though I don't know what it was about."

"Your great-great-grandfather, Mr. Jervis Colstone was, I believe, very much annoyed with your great-grandfather, Ambrose, on account of his refusal to enter the army—he was the second son, and the second son invariably entered the army. Mr. Ambrose Colstone not only refused to do so, but further incensed his father by taking up art as a profession."

Anthony burst out laughing.

"He painted some of the worst pictures in England! It's the only thing I knew about him till now. You see, my father died when I was three, and my mother a year later; but the aunt who brought me up—my mother's aunt—kept the whole collection of mouldy old pictures because she said they were heirlooms."

"Er—yes. Well, that was the reason for the breach. Sir Jervis carried on the feeling about it—he carried it on very strongly. You know, of course, that he served with distinction in the Crimea, and was awarded the K.C.B. for his services during the Mutiny. It was when you entered the army that he made the will under which you inherit. By the way, I suppose you mean to send in your papers?"

"Oh—I don't know. I've got eight months' leave. I thought I'd go down and have a look round."

"Sir Jervis hoped you would go into Parliament. He himself left the army and went into Parliament when his father died."

Exasperation mounted in Anthony. He was to do this, and he was not to do that. He had been left the property because he had pleased Sir Jervis by going into the army; and now he was to leave the service and take up politics because Sir Jervis had left the service and taken up politics about a hundred years ago.

"I shan't decide anything at present."

"Unless you have private means—"

"I haven't."

"You may find the place too expensive to keep up. Sir Jervis found it difficult, and now, what with the death duties and a charge on the estate of eight hundred a year for Sir Jervis' daughters—"

"I won't decide anything till I've had a look round. By the way, the old ladies, the Miss Colstones—I thought of running down to-morrow. They won't mind, will they?"

"You won't find them at Stonegate. They were anxious to move as soon as possible."

"I say, that's rather beastly for them, isn't it?"

"It was their own wish. You will find them very pleasantly installed in what is called The Ladies' House. And they particularly desired me to say that they were looking forward to making your acquaintance."

Anthony got up.

"That's awfully nice of them. What are their names again?"

"Miss Agatha, and Miss Arabel. Their grandmother, a Miss Langholme, claimed descent from the Lady Arabella Stuart. They are very proud of the fact, especially Miss Arabel. And—about this undertaking, Mr. Colstone—you are not inclined to give it?"

"Not without a reason," said Anthony.

Chapter Two

Anthony Colstone went down to see his new possession next day.

The station was Wrane, but he had to drive seven miles to reach Ford St. Mary; at first through low-lying pasture land dotted with an occasional farm; then up into hilly country, open, arid, lonely to a degree he would hardly have believed possible; and then down once more to where a little river moved between pollarded trees, with the village of Ford St. Mary straggling beside it on the hither side.

A sharp bend hid everything. They passed into a black shade of over-arching trees. It was strange to be in bright sunlight one moment, and then to lose it. The wood was very thick, and full of a dense undergrowth. Another turn, and they were out of it, running between high banks that hid the view. Then the first house—a cottage, crooked with age, asleep under its heavy thatch, with a neglected garden full of knee-high weeds.

Something pricked him sharply. If this was Ford St. Mary, he was on his own ground. The fields across the river were his—this old cottage his. The secret pride of possession flared up into an intense flame. He had always wanted land; but not till this moment had he known what it would feel like to look at water, and fields, and trees, and say, "These are mine."

He pulled up his thoughts with a jerk. He wasn't going to let the place knock him off his feet. He tried to see it all dispassionately. More cottages, all thatched; some with bright gardens—hollyhocks, marigolds, snapdragon, and climbing roses, with a sultry drowsy August sunshine over all. Then the village street, and a high stone wall rising sheer on the right; no house visible, only the long towering wall. In the middle of it a heavy oak door flanked by stone pillars, and between the pillars a shield with an almost obliterated device.

The taxi stopped. Anthony put his head out.

"Can't one drive in?"

He got a shake of the head; and opening the door, he jumped out and rang the bell.

It wasn't in the least like what he had expected. He had thought that there would be an entrance gate and a drive; a park perhaps; big grounds. This high blank wall challenged his imagination. It made the place seem like a castle. He liked it.

Then the heavy door opened and he saw that a glazed passage led from it to the real door of the house. There were a few plants in tubs, things with striped leaves, a palm or two, some gawky geraniums. He stared past them through the glass, trying to get a view of the house, and had a confused impression of grey stone and formal windows. Somehow he had expected something older—gables, old beams, something more in line with those thatched and timbered cottages.

The butler, Lane, met him at the door—a pale, stoutish man, just perceptibly nervous. Behind him, Mrs. Hutchins, the housekeeper—large, rubicund, jolly. Behind them, the house—his house. He desired ardently to get rid of them and to make its acquaintance.

The grey stone front was like a mask; it hid beauty. The eighteenth century had built on to and covered up the original Elizabethan Stonegate. The old hall remained, rising to the height of the second storey, with a stair that swept nobly up to a carved gallery. The great chimney measured ten feet across. On the dark panelling hung pictures almost as dark.

He went up the stair and along the gallery, Mrs. Hutchins a little in advance, talking about which room he would have, and what a hot day it was—"Though to be sure, sir, you'd make nothing of that, coming from India. And if you please to mind the step. Built everything with steps up and down in the old days, and I'm sure I don't know why. There's another one here, sir—up this time—and then just a half step down again."

She flung open a door and stood aside for him to enter.

"This was Sir Jervis' room, sir."

Anthony came into it with a sense of intrusion. It was a fine room with three large windows, and paper, not panelling. The whole room had a surprisingly modern air; the furniture Victorian mahogany, the paper very faded and hideous beyond belief—olive green whorls on a ground of yellow ochre; the bed a plain old-fashioned brass affair of the same period as the huge dark wardrobe on the opposite side of the room. Two of the windows looked upon a green lawn set with cedar trees. The high stone wall lay on the left. It had fruit trees trained against it, and a narrow border at its foot, somewhat empty and neglected.

Anthony walked to the other window. It looked to the hilly country through which he had come; a patch of dark trees on the right—the wood where he had lost the sun; fields all on the slant; not many trees; hedges; cows grazing. And straight in the line from where he stood something grey that caught his eye. He turned quickly to Mrs. Hutchins.

"Are those the Stones?"

"Yes, sir."

He looked round at her quickly. She had been so voluble—and now only two words, and her mouth set as if she didn't mean to open it again. He had thought her a jolly old thing, but as he looked round she seemed formidable, and her little grey eyes cold; the whole of her big red face was like a slammed door. He looked back at the hillside.

"How many stones are there? I can see two. Is that all there are?"

"I don't know, sir."

He swung round impatiently.

"Why? How long have you been here? I thought Mr. Leveridge said—"

"I've been here thirty years, sir—housekeeper for fifteen."

Her face relaxed a little. Pride in her long service was evident.

Anthony gave a short, half stifled laugh.

"Thirty years! And you don't know how many stones there are?"

"No, sir. Will you be having this room, may I ask, sir?"

"Never been up to have a look at them?" He ignored the question of the room. He was puzzled and intrigued.

"No, sir. About the room, sir—"

He walked to the window and stared out. Straight maroon curtains framed the green fields that were his—green fields all on the slant of the hill. He wondered if he could farm the land and make it pay. He had always wanted to farm really. He looked at the two grey stones, like grey sheep feeding on the green slope a long way off—two of them. And Mrs. Hutchins didn't know if there were any more. She had been here thirty years, and she didn't know.

He turned, smiling; and when he smiled he looked like a schoolboy.

"And how long has Lane been here?"

"Forty years. Shall I have this bed made up, sir?"

"No—I don't think so. I don't think I'll have this room."

"It's the best room."

"I don't think I should ever feel as if it were mine. Is there another room that looks up the hill? I'd like that."

He thought that Sir Jervis had liked it too; he could lie in bed and look across the brass knobs of the footrail at the green fields that climbed the hill, and the grey stones that broke the green.

They went along the passage, through a door, up a step, and down three more. Anthony began to wonder how long it would take him to find his way about the house.

Then Mrs. Hutchins flung open a thick oak door.

"It's one of the old rooms, sir, if you don't mind that."

He had to bend his head a little, because the doorposts were not quite six foot. The room pleased him immediately. It had panelling to about his own height, and then clean whitewash crossed with timber. Two heavy beams ran overhead, and all the narrow end of the room looked through a long casement at the green, tilted fields. The bed was a four-poster stripped of its curtains, the fluted posts as bare and graceful as winter trees. On the floor a faded Persian carpet, and the bare oak boards polished and blackened by the passing feet of many generations.

"I'll have this room," said Anthony with decision.

Chapter Three

AN HOUR LATER he stepped across the village street to pay his respects to the Miss Colstones. The Ladies' House had a little square paved garden in front of it; there was a low stone wall, and a high stone gate. The house itself crossed the back of the garden and sent out two wings that enclosed it. There was a square bed of scarlet geraniums in each corner of the paved place, and a round bed, with a large lavender bush and an incongruous edging of lobelia, in the middle. The path led up to the round bed, divided in two to encircle it, and then ran straight up to a worn grey step and a dark green door.

Anthony was shown into a white panelled room with a glass door open to a miniature lawn. On either side of the door there were casement windows very deeply recessed. He stood in the middle of the pale flowered carpet and looked about him. The furniture exhibited a pleasing mixture of periods. There were three gimcrack gilt Empire chairs, some dignified oak, a round table with a wreath of flowers inlaid upon its edge and a marvellous erection of wax fruit under a glass shade standing in the middle of it, flanked by photograph albums with gold clasps and edges. One of the albums was bound in crimson plush, and the other in faded red morocco. Over the fireplace a lady in a ruff looked sadly at her own long thin fingers, her hair drawn tightly back beneath a jewelled cap, her eyebrows raised in strained interrogation.

The door opened, and there came in a little lady, very point device, with pretty white hair rolled back over a cushion, and scraps of old lace at the neck and wrists of her mourning gown. She had a wisp of a white Shetland shawl about her shoulders. Her eyes were a clear pale blue, her cheeks round and pink, her mouth the cupid's bow of a Victorian book of beauty. She had pretty little hands and pretty little feet, and a fluttered manner that was pretty too in its suggestion of timid welcome. The small outstretched hand trembled just perceptibly.

Anthony took it, and found it cold.

He said, "How do you do, Miss Colstone?"

"Oh, not Miss Colstone! Indeed I hope you will call us Cousin. And I am not Miss Colstone—I am Miss Arabel—your Cousin Arabel. Agatha is Miss Colstone, and—won't you sit down?"

He chose one of the stronger chairs, moving it nearer to the frail gilt sofa with its faded brocade cushions which made Miss Arabel's cashmere look so dead a black.

She gazed at him earnestly and said,

"You are not at all like dear Papa. Did you have a pleasant journey? We would have sent to meet you, but we have no carriage. Have you come alone?"

"I'm expecting a friend to-morrow."

"That will be pleasant for you. It is a big house to be alone in."

"I feel as if it would take me ages to find my way about in it. Do you know if there's a plan of the house at all?"

"A plan?"

"Yes. I'd like to get it into my head."

"I—don't know." She looked a little alarmed. "Oh, here is Agatha."

Miss Agatha Colstone came in through the open door from the garden. She wore a wide straw hat tied under her ample chin with a bit of rusty black ribbon. Her skirt was short, her shoes very sensible. She held a garden fork. The hand she offered Anthony had obviously been weeding.

"There!" she said in a deep voice. "I've finished that border, thank goodness! So you're young Anthony. Let me have a look at you. Who are you like?"

"He isn't like poor Papa," said Miss Arabel rather plaintively.

"Why should he be?"

"Must I be like someone?" said Anthony with a twinkle.

Miss Agatha fixed her rather prominent eyes upon him. They were brown and round like little bullseyes, but not unfriendly.

"H'm—I can't see any likeness."

Then she sat down, fanned herself with the fork, and began to ask him all the questions that Miss Arabel had already asked. For the second time, he had had a pleasant journey, and a friend was coming to stay with him. Then, with relief, to new ground. The friend's name was West—about his own age—he hadn't seen him for four years because he had been in India—they used to be great pals—he was a junior master at Marfield.

Miss Agatha was a vigorous questioner. She elicited in a swift competent manner that Anthony was twenty-six, disengaged, a golfer, a fair shot, six foot in his socks, and of no particular brand of politics. This appeared to shock her a good deal. Sir Jervis had obviously ranked politics with religion—and the greater of these was politics.

Anthony hastened to change the subject. He wanted to talk about Stonegate. But Miss Agatha did not.

"Your father died—"

"When I was three. I hardly remember him or my mother. Her people brought me up—an aunt and her husband. He farmed his own land. I think I'd have gone in for farming if he'd lived; but he died when I was sixteen. My aunt wanted me to go into the army. She said farming was no good without capital."

"Quite right."

"I was wondering—" He broke off. He didn't want to embark on plans. The word sent him back to the question he had asked Miss Arabel. "I suppose there are plans somewhere—of the house and everything? I want to know my way about. And perhaps you can tell me what's my best way up to the field where the Stones are. I thought I'd walk up and have a look. Fancy—I asked Mrs. Hutchins about them, and she couldn't tell me how many there were. She said she'd never even been to have a look at them. Isn't it amazing?"

Miss Agatha had been fidgeting with the dusty fork, to the detriment of her black serge skirt. When Anthony said "Amazing," she dropped the fork and stooped frowning to pick it up again. Miss Arabel said "Oh!" in a helpless, fluttered sort of way.

"She couldn't even tell me how many stones there were," pursued Anthony cheerfully. "And by the way, of course you can tell me all about them. I'm fearfully interested. How many are there?"

There was one of those silences that follow the worst kind of *faux pas*. He had dropped a brick—most undoubtedly he had dropped a brick. He would have liked to drop a few more, noisily, with a crash; to heave, say, the plush photograph album through the left-hand casement window; or to catch Miss Arabel round the waist and swing her across the room to the latest tango.

He smiled charmingly at Miss Agatha's blank frown and repeated his question.

"How many are there?"

"I don't know," said Miss Agatha. Her voice was deep and reluctant, heavy with things unsaid.

She got up, moved to the window, and pitched her weeding fork out on to the lawn. Then she came back, untying the strings of her hat. Miss Arabel sat quite still. She looked frightened. Her plump little hands clasped one another in her black cashmere lap.

Agatha Colstone removed her hat and began to fan herself with it—it certainly made a better fan than the fork. She sat on the edge of a solid mahogany chair with claw-and-ball feet. Her iron grey hair was drawn almost as tightly away from her face as that of the lady with the ruff. The back of her head was covered with flat rigid plaits. She looked angry and nervous. She said, in a loud voice that shook a little,

"We don't talk about the Stones."

Anthony felt better. The brick had at least broken the awful hush.

"Why don't you talk about them?" He nerved himself and added, "Cousin Agatha?"

Miss Arabel made a little fluttered movement. She said, "Poor Papa—" and then stopped as if that explained everything.

"I don't understand," said Anthony. He understood very well that the old ladies were trying to hush him up; but he felt very resolute about not being hushed. He looked at Miss Agatha with a sparkle in his eyes.

"What's the matter with the Stones? Don't you think I'd better know and have done with it? After all, if I'm going to live here—"

Miss Agatha let her hat fall on to the floor. She spoke in a slow, considering manner:

"I cannot tell you how many stones there are, because, like Mrs. Hutchins, I have never been to look at them. Everyone does not take the same interest in these things that you seem to. And if you wish for an additional reason, I can give it you very simply. The village people have some foolish superstitions connected with the Stones, and my father did not wish us to become associated with them in any way." She shut her mouth firmly.

Miss Arabel said, "Dear Papa—" and then stopped again because Miss Agatha turned a forbidding eye upon her.

Anthony felt pleasantly stimulated. He had drawn her to the extent of admitting that there were superstitions in connection with the Stones. He wanted very badly to know what they were. He thought he would ask, and risk a snubbing.

"What sort of superstitions? It sounds awfully interesting."

"I am afraid I can't tell you, Anthony." She rose to her feet. "And now, I think, we will change the subject. Perhaps you would care to see the garden. I hope Mrs. Hutchins is making you comfortable. She is a valuable servant, and so is Lane."

They passed out on to the sunny lawn.

When Anthony had taken his leave, Miss Agatha waited until she heard the front door shut. Then she turned to Miss Arabel and said,

"Well?"

"He is very agreeable, Agatha."

Miss Agatha said "H'm!"

"And very good-looking."

Miss Agatha said "H'm!" again.

There was a pause. Then Miss Agatha spoke in a forced, jerky voice:

"Susan Bowyer has got that girl here again."

A faint colour came into Miss Arabel's face.

"That girl Susan?"

"Yes."

"It is very awkward, Agatha," said Miss Arabel. "What will people say?"

Miss Agatha drew herself up.

"What can they say? She's Robert's grand-daughter—Robert Bowyer's grand-daughter—she's Susan Bowyer. There isn't anything that anyone can say. Why shouldn't Susan have her son Robert's granddaughter to stay with her?"

"It is very awkward," said Miss Arabel.

Chapter Four

ANTHONY WENT UP the hill with the feeling of adventure strong in him. The Stones appeared to be the subject of some extraordinary taboo. Miss Agatha was round about seventy years of age; she had lived seventy odd years in this delightful, benighted, mediævally rustic spot—and she had never bothered to cross three fields and look at the Stones. Mrs. Hutchins had also lived here all her life—Miss Arabel had informed him that her father had been sexton for some vast number of years. The "Mrs." was apparently in the nature of a brevet. She also had never troubled to climb these gently tilted fields. Going to see the Stones wasn't done in Ford St. Mary; you didn't go and see them, and you didn't talk about them. The villagers entertained vain superstitions about them. Now he wondered a good deal whether Sir Jervis had not entertained them too.

He crossed the last field and came to an apparently impenetrable hedge. There was no pathway, and there was no stile; there was nothing you could climb over or under.

Anthony began to break a way through the hedge with the oddest sense of guilt. He had to go on reminding himself that it was his own hedge and his own field. He felt exactly as if he were eight years old, breaking into an orchard to steal plums. In the end he pushed his way through a tangle of sloe and thorn, and got clear of the hedge with a jagged tear in his coat and a scratch on the cheek from a blackberry trail. There was going to be a jolly good crop of blackberries here if the weather held. He disentangled another trail from his left ankle and looked about him.

The field was almost waist-high in flowering grass, hemlock and sorrel, with a few late moon-daisies and patches of purple thistle. The other fields had been mown, and had their second crop of grass drying off in the sun. It was scarcely knee-high. But this field had not been touched. Its hedges closed it in like prison walls. There was no way into it except the way that he had broken for himself.

He looked about him and saw the Stones, two of them, separated by almost the whole width of the field, the nearer one not twenty feet away, a tall, misshapen monolith of roughened grey stone stained with orange fungus. He walked up to it, wondering whether it had been one of a pair like the great uprights of Stonehenge. There was no sign of anything but this one pillar. He judged it to be about fifteen feet high, narrower than the stones at Stonehenge.

He cut across the field diagonally towards the other monolith. It did not seem to be quite so tall, and it leaned sideways a little, like the leaning tower of Pisa. The grass and the sorrel were up to his waist as he walked. Everything smelt very sweet. There was red clover amongst the grass, and camomile. The sun was going slowly down the hazy slope of the sky. Everything was very still, and hot, and sweet. The only sound was the swishing of the ripened grass as he pushed through it.

And then all of a sudden the grass came to an end and he saw the third Stone. It lay flat in a bare space. First the long grass ceased, then the short, sparse, weedy straggle. The Stone lay flat, and for a yard all round it there was not so much as a green blade.

Anthony came out on to the open place and looked down at the Stone. It was not quite so big as the others. It was wider, flatter. It was sunk, so that only a hand's breadth of its worn grey sides showed above the earth. It looked as if it had been laid there. He wondered whether it had been laid there, or whether it had fallen hundreds of years ago. The place gave him a curious feeling.

He walked all round the Stone, and just as he came to the east side of it, he saw the marks upon its surface. The low sun caught a faint, worn tracery. Right in the middle of the Stone there was something that looked like interlaced triangles. It was very much rubbed and worn;

two of the points were gone. But there it was. He wondered who had done it, and how long ago; and he wondered what it meant.

He looked up towards the other standing Stone, and saw a man's face watching him. The Stone was up in the left-hand corner of the field, not half a dozen yards from the hedge. The man's face looked out of the hedge. He must have forced his way into the middle of it and pushed his head between two branches of leafy elder, for only his head was visible—a head with smooth black hair, pale oval face, and black staring eyes. The eyes were fixed on Anthony, but the moment that Anthony's own eyes met them the head vanished. One minute it was there, and the next minute it wasn't there. It was all so very sudden that just for a moment Anthony wasn't sure whether his imagination had been playing him tricks.

He pelted off up the field, reached the hedge, and parted the elder branches. There was no one there. There was nothing to be seen in the field beyond except some placidly cropping sheep. The grass was short, thanks to the sheep, but there were four hedges. Anthony was blowed if he was going to scramble through another thickset hedge to search for the gentleman with the staring eyes. He had a look at the standing Stone, and then walked back across the field to the gap he had made in the lower hedge.

As he walked, he couldn't help thinking about the face. It was odd. Why was it odd? There wasn't anything odd about it. Someone was having a look through the hedge—and why not? On the other hand, why? It wasn't a village lad. Now how on earth could he be sure of that? He didn't know. But he *was* sure. He began to produce reasons. The fellow had a sort of high-brow look, well brushed, well shaved. He kept seeing the pale oval face with the smooth lip and chin and the black hair brushed away from the pale high forehead. Well, anyone can look through a hedge. So they can—but they needn't glare. This fellow had most undoubtedly glared. No, glared wasn't really strong enough. "He looked as if I was poison—rank bad poison." Very surprising to be looked at like that. Anthony gave it up.

He reached the gap he had made in the hedge, and received a second surprise. A girl in a blue cotton dress was standing in the gap, looking past him up the field. She must have heard him coming, but she did not move until he was within a yard. Then she let go of the thorny trail which she had pushed on one side and sprang back. He followed her. His visit to the Stones seemed to be attracting quite a lot of attention.

As he emerged from the hedge, he was aware of her, quite close. She wore a blue sun-bonnet that matched her dress; her skirts were a good deal longer than the skirts of the girls he knew. She held her hands together in front of her, as if she was shy. She bobbed a little curtsey and said in a breathless, pretty voice with a marked country accent.

"I'm sure I beg your pardon, sir."

Anthony supposed that she was one of the girls from the village—his village. He wasn't quite sure how he ought to talk to her. She was a pretty girl, and she looked fearfully shy, and as if she was afraid she had made a break of some kind. It was rather embarrassing.

He said, "Why should you beg my pardon?" and he smiled, because he always smiled when he felt shy.

The girl bent her head so that the wing of the blue sun-bonnet hid her face. He didn't know village girls ever wore sun-bonnets now. They were awfully becoming.

He said, "Do you live here?"

"No," said the pretty voice. There was a pause "I'm visiting my granny." The head began to lift again. "I've heard tell of the Stones, and I wanted to see them."

He found himself looking into a lovely pair of eyes. He had never seen any eyes quite like them. They were just the colour of sea water when it is rather green; they were blue, and yet not blue. They had a sparkle in them which he found hard to reconcile with her rustic shyness. The lashes were black, and fine, and soft.

Anthony removed his gaze with an effort. It was possible to do this because the black lashes had swept down suddenly and covered the sparkle.

"Haven't you seen the Stones before?"

"No," said the girl. Then quickly, "No, sir."

"Do you want to go in and look at them?"

"No, sir—I'll be getting back."

They began to walk along side by side. Anthony felt rather worried about it. If they walked back together into Ford St. Mary, the whole village would probably talk—he hadn't been brought up in a village for nothing. On the other hand, he didn't want to be rude. She might think it most awfully rude if he turned back now. Besides, there was the fellow who had glared.

He had got as far as this, when the girl said,

"I'll be getting back now."

"Yes, of course," said Anthony easily. "You—you're visiting your grandmother, you said. Does she live in Ford St. Mary?"

"Yes, sir. You're Mr. Colstone, sir, aren't you?"

"Yes. I don't know anyone in the village yet—I only came to-day. I expect I shall meet your grandmother. What is her name?"

"Mrs. Bowyer. And now I'll be getting back, sir."

What was she driving at? He suspected a convention of some sort.

"Yes—rather."

The sun-bonnet hid the face rather suddenly. He felt a most uncommon ass. The girl stopped dead and spoke without looking at him:

"I'll be getting along by myself, sir. Folks'll talk if you walk with me, and Gran'll be in a way."

"Look here," said Anthony, "that's all right. But there was a man in the hedge just now, up at the top of the field where the Stones are. I didn't like the look of him. That's why I thought I had better walk with you."

There was a quick lift of the blue sun-bonnet.

"A man?"

"In the hedge—staring at me."

"What sort of a man?" A complete change had taken place in her manner; she spoke only just above her breath, yet with a certain force that pressed for an answer.

He found himself speaking as if to someone whom he knew well.

"Awfully odd sort of fellow. I couldn't make out what he was up to."

"What was he like?"

This wasn't the embarrassed village girl he had been walking with. He looked at her in astonishment. He had thought her pretty, and gauche. She was self-possessed enough now, and it wouldn't have occurred to him to call her pretty; the word didn't seem to have anything to do with her. It suggests something commonplace, and there was nothing commonplace here. The lovely eyes looked out of an almost colourless face; the lips took an odd irregular curve.

He said, "Oh—queer—very pale—black hair and staring eyes. He looked as if he'd like to do me in." He broke off with a short laugh. "That's nonsense of course. But I thought I'd better see you across the fields."

She looked away. He caught her profile. Her nose had a sort of ripple in it—rather nice. She walked on in silence to the edge of the field. Then she turned with downcast eyes and fingers catching at her dress.

"And now I'll be getting along, thank you kindly all the same, sir."

Chapter Five

ANTHONY WENT BACK to Stonegate across the remaining field and in at a door which took him through a brick wall into the vegetable garden. He did not, therefore, see Mrs. Bowyer's grand-daughter come down the village street and enter the cottage immediately opposite his own front gate. It was the oldest house in the village, and old Susan Bowyer was the oldest inhabitant.

The front door opened straight into the living-room. It was empty. The girl in the blue dress went to a door on the far side and opened it, calling "Gran!"

When there was no answer, she went through the kitchen, which was spotlessly clean and neat, and passed out into the garden. There was a border with bright flowers, and a strip of orchard with plums and apples ripening. All along the fence there were bee-hives. Mrs. Bowyer was bent over the nearest hive.

The girl called "Gran!" again, and she turned and came in, walking briskly, just a little bent, in a black dress with a small alpaca apron and a white net cap with lappets. She was small, and her face was covered with multitudes of tiny lines. A little fluffy white hair showed under the cap. Her dark eyes were full of an amazing dancing vigour.

"What were you doing, Gran?"

"Doing?" she said. She gave a little pleased laugh. "I were telling the bees—that's what I were doing. Now I suppose you'll say you never heard tell of that."

Young Susan put her arm about old Susan's waist.

"What were you telling them? Mind the step, Gran!"

Mrs. Bowyer freed herself.

"Look you here, Susan! I've lived in this here house a hundred years come Christmas. Did I ever tell you as I was a Christmas child? They don't fear hail, nor snow, nor winter blow. Did you ever hear that? And, as I were saying, if I don't know there's a step there by now, I'll never know it."

"What were you telling the bees, Gran?"

Mrs. Bowyer passed into the living-room and sat down in the oak rocking-chair by the right-hand window. The windows were set on either side of the door. They had latticed panes, behind which bloomed the finest geraniums in Ford St. Mary.

"What should I ha' been telling the bees?" said Mrs. Bowyer. Her voice had lost its ring, but it was still full of energy. "Colstone is master here, and when Colstone comes to Stonegate, that's the master coming home. And when the master comes home, you're bound to tell the bees. If you don't, they'll turn cross on you. Bees has got to be told when things happen to their folks, and if you don't tell 'em, they goes contrary. And that's why all these new-fangle folk make such a muck of bee-keeping."

Susan stood by the hearth. There was no fire there. The wide black chimney made a background for the pale blue of her dress. She said,

"I've seen him."

Mrs. Bowyer's dancing eyes looked at her with eager interest.

"What? Colstone? You've seen him?"

"Yes, up in the fields."

"And what were you doing up in the fields?"

"I went up to see the Coldstone Ring."

"You never!"

"Why shouldn't I?"

A very curious expression came over Mrs. Bowyer's face.

"And you met him there—Mr. Anthony Colstone? Oh Lord, 'tis funny to say it! Anthony Colstone! Son of Ralph—son of James—son of Ambrose—" She stopped with a quiver of laughter. "Sir Jervis' uncle he was—I can remember him. I was a little maid of six when he quarrelled with his father and went away. Jervis and I were playing in the garden—there wasn't any Sir about him then—three months younger than me, and a limb. We were playing, and we were quarrelling, and Mr.

Ambrose come out to us looking like a bit of blued linen, and he says, 'It's a pity to quarrel, children. My father's quarrelled with me.' And he kissed us and said good-bye, and nobody never saw him any more—and that's more than ninety years ago." She began to rock herself slowly. "Ninety-four years ago come Christmas—no, 'twas in the summer, for we were making daisy chains." She rocked again, her hands folded on the black alpaca apron, then asked suddenly, "What's he like? Mr. Ambrose wasn't nothing to look at, but Mr. James, his brother that was Jervis' father, he was a fine-looking man, six foot and a bit over. What's the lad like?"

"Oh, he's big enough."

"Don't you go and tell me he's one of they long weeds!"

Susan laughed softly.

"Oh, he's wide enough," she said.

"Well, what's wrong with the lad?"

"I didn't say there was anything wrong with him. He's a very nice, discreet, polite young man, and quite as good-looking as is good for him."

"H'm—" said Mrs. Bowyer. "I like 'em bold meself, but not to say outrageous bold. What colour's his eyes, deary?"

"Oh, just no colour at all."

Mrs. Bowyer sat up straight and stopped rocking.

"Are you telling me you're the kind of maid that don't notice what coloured eyes a lad has got?"

Susan tilted her chin. The corners of her mouth took an upward quirk, a dimple showed in the curve of her cheek.

"Of *course*, Gran. I'm very, very modest." She broke into a laugh at Mrs. Bowyer's expression. "Now, Gran, don't you look like that! Personally I think no-coloured eyes are quite good business. They make a sort of weather gauge, because if he's in love with you they'll be blue, and when he's angry they'll go grey, and when he starts thinking about somebody else they'll be hazel. Hazel eyes are the fickle eyes, aren't they, Gran? And black—" She broke off and shivered.

"You'd best keep clear of the black, my girl. And Anthony Colstone—have you seen his eyes look blue or grey? For if you have, it's early days. He didn't talk bold to you, Susan?" Her voice sharpened.

"Not a bit of it—he was shy. I could see him wondering how he could get rid of me without hurting my feelings. I told you he was a discreet young man."

She took off her sun-bonnet and swung it by the strings. The bare head was beautifully shaped and beautifully held. The shingled hair was very dark and very soft; it curled a little where it was long enough to curl.

"And you think the worse of him for it?"

"I don't."

"Maids are all alike! If he'd ha' kissed you, you'd ha' thought him a fine fellow."

Susan's lip lifted a little.

"People don't kiss me unless I want them to, Gran." The soft voice was a little haughty.

Mrs. Bowyer rocked with inward laughter. She made no sound at all; she quivered and put a little wrinkled hand to her side. After a moment Susan laughed too.

"Gran, you're a fiend! I wish you'd been there. I did it beautifully. I copied Mary Ann Smithers—you know the way she holds her hands and sort of gives at the knees. And I made him a perfectly lovely bob, and I said 'sir' at least once in every sentence."

Mrs. Bowyer stopped laughing with great suddenness.

"The Coldstone Ring's no place for a lad to meet with a lass," she said; and then, very sharply, "What took him there?"

"How should I know? What's the matter with the Stones, Gran? Why won't anyone go near them?"

Mrs. Bowyer gazed abstractedly at her geraniums.

"Gran, you might tell me!"

"There's those that's best not talked of."

Susan knelt down by the rocking-chair and coaxed.

"In a whisper, Gran!"

"What's a whisper to *Them*?" Susan felt a tingle of excitement.

"Gran—you might tell me! You told me about the passage."

Old Susan Bowyer turned on her sharply.

"And you promised sure and certain you'd never name it to a living soul."

"Yes, I did, Gran—and I won't."

She was holding one of the work-worn hands. Her own were brown, and smooth, and beautifully shaped. Mrs. Bowyer put her other hand down on them. It pressed them, trembling.

"You promised sure and certain before I told you. And I wouldn't ha' told you, only there's no one left of all the Bowyers but you. Thomas' girl I don't count—she's Bowyer by name, but she's Dickson by nature, and a Dickson is what I never could abide, not from the days when Cis Dickson that was her mother's grandmother made her great sheep's eyes at my William. No—Jenny's a Dickson through and through, if she was Thomas' daughter ten times over."

"All right, Gran, next time she comes to see you, you just call her Jenny Dickson and see what happens."

"You're a wicked maid!" said Mrs. Bowyer enjoyably. "I don't count Jenny, and I don't count Robert's grandchildren, if so be he's got any, because they be all 'Mericans, and it stands to reason I can't tell what's got to be told to 'Mericans on the other side of the world. So there's only you, my dear. And I told you because Bowyers ha' lived in this house just so long as Colstones ha' lived at Stonegate, and there's bound to be a Bowyer that knows the secret—and if I don't count Jenny and all they 'Mericans, there's only you, my dear."

"Then tell me about the Coldstone Ring," said Susan in a whisper.

Mrs. Bowyer became remote. She took her hand away from Susan's. Her voice was brisk and matter of fact.

"Least said, soonest mended," she said.

Chapter Six

ANTHONY DINED in a dark, low room that would have accommodated forty people with ease. Lane's hushed voice, proffering sherry or murmuring "Certainly, sir," hardly seemed to break the silence. The old-fashioned oil lamp hanging down over the table hardly seemed to break the darkness. Anthony thought he would have electric light put in if there was any money at all. Oil lamps were bad enough in an Indian bungalow where the whitewashed walls gave the light a chance, but one old lamp hanging low in a dark panelled room was a bit too much of a bad thing.

He ate his dinner sitting just on the edge of the circle of yellow light cast by the lamp. Lane went to and fro in the outer darkness. Over by the door behind him an even older and less efficient lamp smelled to heaven. It was most frightfully depressing.

"Will you take coffee here, sir?" said Lane. He had the tray in his hand, an old heavy silver tray.

Anthony swung his chair sideways and put an elbow on the table.

"Yes, please—just put it down. And look here, sit down yourself—I want to talk to you."

"I can stand, sir."

"No, sit down. I want to talk, and I can't talk unless you sit."

Lane took a chair under protest. As he sat down on the edge of it, the circle of light just touched his cheek. He drew back from it, but Anthony received a momentary impression of a worried elderly face.

"Now!" he said, but for a moment no more came. Then he asked quickly, "Who is Mrs. Bowyer?"

He had an idea that Lane relaxed, and he wondered whether he had been afraid that he was going to be asked about the Stones.

"Mrs. Bowyer, sir?"

"Yes."

"She's Sir Jervis' foster sister, sir. That is to say she's older than Sir Jervis was, but her mother nursed him. She's close on a hundred, and very much respected, sir, by the gentry and all."

Anthony thought about that for a moment.

"I say, people seem to live to a good old age at Ford St. Mary!"

"Yes, sir. Mrs. Bowyer's grandfather, old Tom Bowyer, he lived to be getting on for a hundred too, and so did his father before him, sir. Mrs. Bowyer she was a Bowyer born, and married her cousin. And she'll tell you how he died young through an accident at no more than seventy-five. She felt it a bit of a disgrace, sir, because Bowyers always reckon to pass ninety. I beg your pardon, sir."

Anthony laughed.

"I'd like to meet Mrs. Bowyer."

"She'd take it kindly if you stepped across, sir. She's only just over the way."

"Does she live alone?"

"She does, and she doesn't. There's a girl goes in and does for her—Smithers' daughter—he's gardener, sir—Mary Ann Smithers. She looks after her, and when there isn't anyone there she sleeps in."

"When there isn't anyone there?"

"She has her granddaughter—that is, I should say, her great-granddaughter—that's come on a visit a couple of times since Sir Jervis died. She's there now, I believe."

There was a silence. If he were to ask questions about Mrs. Bowyer's granddaughter, Lane would think it odd. Or would he? There were a whole lot of questions he would like to ask—where she lived, and what she did; and why she had two voices, a slow drawling country voice, and that quick breathless whisper. She puzzled him very much, but he couldn't ask Lane about her.

He threw back his head with a jerk and said abruptly,

"Why won't anyone talk about the Coldstone Ring, Lane?"

Lane was caught off his guard. His chair went back with a grate. He got up and stood there, well back in the shadow.

"Sir Jervis—" he began, and then stopped.

Anthony prompted him.

"Sir Jervis didn't like people to talk about it. Was that what you were going to say?"

"Yes, sir." Lane was relieved and eager.

"Yes. But why? It's no use, Lane—you might as well tell me."

"There's nothing to tell—not that I know about, sir." He sounded very unhappy.

"Well, let's take it that you don't know anything, but you've heard something. I'm asking you what you've heard about the Stones."

"I can't say, sir."

"Hang it all, what's the good of saying you can't say? It's senseless, man! I don't ask you to vouch for anything—I only want to know what's said. There are the Stones, and a field you can't get into. The hay isn't cut there. Nobody'll talk about them. People who've lived here all their lives have never walked a quarter of a mile to see them. The Miss Colstones say there are superstitions about them. Well now, Lane, I'm asking you straight out, as an old family servant, to tell me what those superstitions are. You've been here forty years, and you can't pretend you don't know."

Lane made a curious unintelligible sound of protest. Then, as Anthony moved, he said in a low, hesitating voice,

"Sir—sir—I'd rather not. I—I don't know anything."

"I'm asking you what is said."

Lane looked over his shoulder. The room was not so dark but that it held darker shadows. He took a step towards the lighted circle.

"Ask Mrs. Bowyer, sir—don't ask me. She knows a deal more about the Stones than anyone else do. Her great-grandfather he saw things with his very own eyes—" He broke off in some agitation.

"What did he see?" said Anthony, laughing.

"I don't know, sir."

"But Mrs. Bowyer knows?"

"That's what folks say. And if she don't know, there's nobody that does. I can't say more than that."

He came forward as he said the last words, took up the coffee tray, and went out, moving a little more quickly than usual.

Chapter Seven

FORD ST. MARY went to bed early; by the time the church clock struck eleven there was not, as a rule, anyone awake to hear it. On this particular night two people heard the last stroke die away in the soft, warm dark. The silence came back again, flowing in softly, dreamily, drowsily.

Susan yawned and thought that she had better get into bed. She had put out her light more than half an hour ago and set the casement window wide. There was no breeze, only a faint stirring of the clear dark air. She sat on the wide window ledge in her nightgown, a surprisingly modern affair for the girl who had worn an old-fashioned blue print frock and sun-bonnet that afternoon. The nightgown was also blue; but it had pink ribbon shoulder-straps and no sleeves, and it showed as much of Susan's very pretty neck and shoulders as if she had been going to a ball in Queen Victoria's day. It was made of something silky and diaphanous.

Susan reached out her bare arms and stretched. Then she got up and left the window with reluctance. It was really awfully hot, and the heavy old-fashioned bed was over on the other side of the room. She sat down on the edge of it and wished that she could lift the roof off. Then she laughed. Gran in the next room was sleeping peacefully under two blankets and an eiderdown, with her pet patchwork quilt neatly folded at the foot of the bed!

"Marvellous old dear!" said Susan, and stretched again. "Well, here goes!"

There was only a sheet on her own bed. She folded it back, piled up the three pillows—which Gran considered so destructive to the figure—and settled herself against them. "A flat bed makes a flat back." She could just hear Gran quoting that.

She began to think about Stonegate, and Anthony Colstone, and the man who had looked through the hedge. If Anthony hadn't walked through the fields with her, she would have gone back and had a look at the man who had been watching him. She wondered if she had given herself away. It couldn't have been Garry; and if it were Garry, was it possible to do a more senseless thing than to give the whole show away to Anthony Colstone? It couldn't have been Garry, because Garry was in Ireland. No, Garry had *said* he was going to Ireland. But, being Garry, that might quite easily mean that he hadn't the slightest intention of going there.

She thought of Garry with an exasperation that became rather blurred, rather uncertain. The pillows were comfortable. She began to slip into the shallow waters that lie on the edge of sleep. A faint dream of Garry hovered—Garry frowning; Garry smiling; Garry whistling.

She woke with a start, bewildered because part of the dream seemed to have been left behind, caught in the darkness. She sat bolt upright and listened with startled ears. Someone was whistling under the window. Her heart gave a great thump. It was Garry. No, it couldn't be Garry—Garry was in her dream. Her heart thumped again. It *was* Garry. There wasn't anyone else in all the world who would be whistling *Garry-owen* under her window at this ridiculous hour. She went hot with rage and bounded out of bed.

With a knee on the window-seat she leaned out and tried to pierce the darkness. There was someone there, but it might have been anyone—only it wasn't; it was Garry.

Susan said "Ssh!" in a furious whisper, and hoped ardently that Mrs. Smithers on the one side, and the entire household at the Ladies'

House on the other, were sleeping the sleep of the pre-fresh-air period behind hermetically sealed windows.

The whistling stopped. A voice said *"Susan"* in a melting whisper— Garry's voice.

"Go away at once!" said Susan in a fierce undertone. Then she added, "What on earth are you doing here?"

"Come down!" said Garry.

Susan gritted her teeth with rage. She would have to go down, because if she didn't, he would certainly say whatever he wanted to say standing in Gran's front garden. She only trusted that he wasn't standing on the lobelias, or the geraniums, or anything that was going to show a compromising foot-print. Garry was capable of *anything*.

She said "All right" in a tone as near inaudibility as she could compass, tiptoed to her trunk, rummaged out a black chiffon frock, and hitching up her nightgown, slipped the frock over it and groped for shoes and stockings. If the stairs creaked, all would be over; or the bolt—bolts have a fiendish way of creaking.

She came down, lightly, lightly, and nothing stirred. The bolt ran smoothly back, the door let her through. And there was Garry with his heel on a broken geranium.

Susan took him by the arm and pinched really hard.

"Ssh!" Her lips were at his ear. "We can't talk here—I shan't have a rag of character. Follow me! I'll go first."

She was out of the gate and over the street in a flash. Under the Stonegate pillars the shadow was as black as ink. She stared out of it at the dark houses opposite, all asleep, all close and still and dreaming. "I bet mine's the only open window of the lot," she said to herself.

And then Garry's hand touched her, groping.

She said, "Not here!" and slipped along in the shadow until they were clear of the houses and the road turned uphill.

Where the stile led into Anthony Colstone's fields she stopped.

"Now what on earth does this mean, Garry?" she said.

Garry's voice sounded sulky.

"Is that what you're asking me?"

"Yes, it is."

"Then there are two of us, for it's what I've come here to ask you."

Susan laughed, not out loud but in her own self, because that was Garry all over—attack's the best defence. Yes, that was Garry. She said,

"That's no good. I'm doing the asking, and you've got to explain. If anyone saw me slip out just now, I'm done for as far as Ford St. Mary's concerned. This isn't London, you know."

"What are you doing here?" said Garry.

"Visiting Gran."

"Again?"

"Why not?"

"Why? *Why?* I want to know why."

Susan did not answer. She took him by the arm and closed her hand hard.

"What are you doing here, Garry? What were you doing in that field this afternoon? And why were you watching Anthony Colstone?"

He wrenched his arm away.

"Did he tell you I was watching him?"

Susan laughed again.

"Did you think he was blind? He isn't, you know. He can see across a field. He saw you watching him—at least I suppose you were watching him."

"What did he tell you?" said Garry fiercely.

Susan answered him lightly. The lightness was like something moving over deep water.

"He told me there was a man in the hedge—an awfully odd sort of fellow. He said you stared. He said, my dear Garry, that you looked as if you would like to do him in. What it is to have an expressive face!"

It was Garry's turn to take hold of her. He caught her roughly by the shoulder, and she said,

"Don't do that!"

"Do him in? Yes—if he asks for it. What were you doing talking to him at all?"

"Garry, let go of me!" said Susan in a steady whisper.

"I will not. You are to tell me what you were doing up by the Coldstone Ring talking to Anthony Colstone."

"Garry, if you don't let go of me—" She paused.

"Well?"

"I was just thinking," said Susan.

"Thinking?"

"What you'd like least."

"And have you made up your mind?"

"Yes—I think I shall scream and give your description to the police. You wouldn't like that a bit—would you?"

He laughed and let go of her.

"I'd rather finish our talk first."

"There isn't going to be any talk, my dear, unless you tell me what you're doing here—"

"And have you tell Anthony Colstone—"

"Don't be silly, Garry!"

"Will you swear you won't tell him?"

Susan said, "No," and then, "What are you up to? I won't make any promises, but you'd better tell me for your own sake. What are you doing here?"

There was a moment's hesitation.

"I'm on my own business—not that it mightn't be your business too if it came off. Can I trust you?"

"You ought to know, Garry."

He flung out an arm as if to clasp her, but she stepped back.

"Garry—it's not that stupid business of the Sikh treasure?"

"And why is it stupid?"

"You know your great-grandfather was off his head."

"I do not."

"But, Garry, your Aunt Emma always said the whole thing was a delusion. He had sunstroke, and imagined he'd been cheated out of a fortune."

Susan felt rather bewildered. She remembered old Major O'Connell, very dried up, very old, always talking; and Miss O'Connell, changing the subject whenever it came round to India or the Mutiny.

"Who said he imagined it?"

"Your Aunt Emma."

"And where did she get it from? From Sir Jervis Colstone—Sir Jervis who cheated him. It's so easy to say that a man who's had sunstroke doesn't know what he's talking about. That's what Sir Jervis said—and everyone believed him. I've read his letters, and they make me sick. Damn hypocritical denials, full of soft sawder—didn't know what his 'dear O'Connell' was driving at—begged him not to excite himself, and trusted he'd soon be restored to health. And my grandfather had written across the signature, 'A black liar' on one letter, and 'Judas' on the other."

"It sounds *mad*, Garry," said Susan frankly.

"Well, and wouldn't you be mad if you'd been cheated like that by your best friend?"

Susan shrugged her shoulders.

"If you're looking for your great-grandfather's treasure, you're just wasting your time, for I don't believe it ever had any existence, except in his dreams."

Garry came quite close to her.

"Then why wouldn't Sir Jervis let anyone go near the Cold-stone Ring?"

"I don't know."

"I do then. It's because the treasure's buried there."

"Garry, how ridiculous! It's not that at all. There's some old superstition. Gran knows about it."

"Village gossip! You're not going to tell me Sir Jervis would believe it? It suited him well enough because it covered up what he'd been doing."

"But good gracious, Garry, if he *had* buried the treasure, why should he leave it there?"

"My great-grandfather was alive till ten years ago. I say Sir Jervis didn't dare dig the stuff up until his 'dear O'Connell' was dead, but by that time he was too old. He couldn't do it himself, and he hadn't got anyone he could trust. And if he couldn't have it himself, he didn't want anyone else to have it, so he tried to get his heir to promise not to shift the Stones."

"The Stones?" said Susan. A little cold shiver went over her.

"The treasure's there," said Garry with cold finality.

Susan shivered again. She hated the whole thing—the Stones, the treasure, the old mad O'Connell—and Garry. No, she couldn't quite hate Garry. But she wished most desperately that she was in bed and asleep. As a first step towards getting there, she smothered a yawn and said,

"Is that all?"

And in a moment Garry was off into one of his rages. It was like something blowing up, and it always frightened her, deep down under her self-control. If there had been any light, she would have seen his face quite, quite colourless, lips drawn back from the pointed, irregular teeth, eyes frightfully black, a ring of white showing all round the iris. Gran had been right when she said "Keep clear of the black." But she didn't know Garry. Susan did; and she was frightened for herself, and for him, and for Anthony Colstone.

"All?" said Garry. His voice was quite soft. He began to pour out a medley of frightful words very slowly and deliberately. It wouldn't have been nearly so frightening if he had shouted. He never shouted when he was angry; he said blood curdling things softly, slowly, deliberately, with pauses between the words as if he were dwelling on them.

Just when Susan felt as if she were really going to scream, he stopped.

"No, it isn't all," he said in his usual voice—"not quite. Sir Jervis had a nurse when he was ill—and Sir Jervis talked."

Susan stood quite still. All this seemed very unbelievable. Thin sort of stuff to be keeping one out of one's bed at midnight. She was so tired that she didn't care how much treasure was buried in the Coldstone Ring, or anywhere else. Garry's rages were very depleting. She wanted to get away and shut herself up in her safe dark room and go to sleep. She didn't believe a single word about old Major O'Connell and the treasure. She wondered whether Garry really believed it either. It didn't seem possible to believe a story like that.

"I ran across the nurse in Wrane." There was a note of triumph in Garry's tone. "Sir Jervis talked—and she told me what he said."

"What did he say?"

"He said, 'It's safe. No one will ever find it,' He was talking in his sleep, you know, the night before he died. Then he woke with a start, and said 'Did I say anything?' And the nurse told him what he'd said, and he said, 'So it is—quite safe. And nobody will find it, because nobody knows it's there.' And presently he went to sleep again, and when he was asleep he talked some more."

There was silence—warm, drowsy silence.

"Is that all?"

"It's all I'm going to tell you," said Garry.

Chapter Eight

"ALL RIGHT," SAID SUSAN. Then she said, "Good-night, Garry," and ran past him down the hill.

She heard him swear under his breath, and she heard him follow. She wondered if she could run faster than he could, and a little breath of excitement just touched her and went past. She took hold of herself and stood quite still, and he came up with a rush and caught her round the waist.

"You're not going like that!"

"I was."

"You can't now." His arm tightened.

"I shall have more luck than I deserve if I can get back without being seen. By the bye, where are you getting back to?"

"Wrane. I've got a motor bike. There's no hurry. Kiss me, Susan."

Susan heaved a weary sigh.

"My good Garry, I don't want to be made love to—I want to go to sleep."

Garry held her closer.

"Susan!"

"I'm dead sleepy."

"Bored with me, I suppose."

"Frightfully bored with you."

"If I thought you meant that—"

"I do mean it."

"I'd—"

"Well, my dear?"

The movement with which he let go of her was so violent that she nearly lost her balance. She said,

"Really, Garry!"

"Sometimes I think I could kill you," said Garry.

"Think again!" said Susan. Then she laughed. "You're being most frightfully silly. Good-night."

This time she did not make the mistake of running. She walked away briskly and lightly, and after a moment's pause she heard him go running back up the hill. She came into the warm hush of the village street and looked up at the blank windows again. Not a glimmer, not a sound. Old houses, dreaming old, confused dreams of all the things that had ever happened in them. Old drowsy houses, slipping back into the past out of which they had come.

She lifted the latch of the garden gate, skirted the lavender bush, slipped into the dark living-room, and slid the bolt. She couldn't see anything at all, it was so dark. "Black as the inside of an oven," Gran would say.

She felt her way to the stairs and went slowly, slowly up, each step solid under her foot without a creak, and the heavy rail smooth as glass under her hand. Hundreds of years of polish had made it as smooth as that—just the slipping of hands going up and down for three hundred years.

She reached the top, felt for the wall—and heard her name: "Susan—" It made her pringle all over. She hadn't made a sound.

"Susan—"

Susan pushed open the door of old Mrs. Bowyer's room and went in.

"What is it, Gran?"

"Where ha' you been?" The voice came out of the dark very composedly.

Susan didn't know what to say. Gran was the limit. She laughed, because that was easiest, and Mrs. Bowyer said,

"It's no laughing matter."

"Gran dear, I went out for a breath of air. It's so hot."

"You needn't trouble to tell me lies, my dear."

"*Gran!*"

There was the splutter of a match. Mrs. Bowyer sprang into view in a white frilled nightcap, leaning over on her elbow to light a candle in an old candlestick that was rather like a shovel with a piece of metal to grip the candle. When the wick had caught, she pulled herself bolt upright against the head of the bed and looked at Susan. Her eiderdown covered with red turkey twill was drawn up to her waist. She wore a flannelette nightdress trimmed with crochet of her own making. Her eyes rested with sarcasm upon Susan's uncovered neck and the diaphanous black of her dress with its long floating sleeves.

Susan burst out laughing.

"It's a fair cop!" she said. "But you're not going to ask me a lot of questions, are you?"

"You've been meeting a lad."

"I didn't want to, Gran—*honest injun*. He came and whistled under my window, and I thought of Mrs. Smithers putting out her head to listen, or Miss Agatha, or Miss Arabel, or their awfully proper cook. So I just went out to tell him he must go away. You see, Gran darling, it really was most frightfully compromising for you. I don't know what Mrs. Smithers would say if she thought young men came serenading you."

"Come here, Susan!" said Mrs. Bowyer.

Susan came reluctantly. She sat down on the red eiderdown, and Gran's black eyes bored through and through her.

"Was it Anthony Colstone?"

"Good gracious, no! What a frightfully amusing idea, Gran! I wish it had been!"

"Wishes come home to roost," said old Susan Bowyer. She picked up a fold of the thin black dress. "What d'you call this stuff, eh?"

"*Georgette*, Gran." Her cheeks grew hot. "I dragged it out of my box because it was black, and I should have hated to frighten Mrs. Smithers or the cook by being all white and ghostly."

"You've a good tongue, my girl. Who ha' you been meeting?"

"I can't tell you." Susan put her hand down on the old fingers and stroked them. "You needn't worry—I can look after myself."

"I never knew a maid that couldn't—until 'twas too late. Are you in love with him?"

"Of course I'm not."

"Is he in love with you?"

"He's a nuisance," said Susan, frowning. Then she jumped up. "I do want to go to sleep so badly."

She bent forward and blew out the candle.

"Good-night, Gran."

Mrs. Bowyer's voice followed her on to the landing:

"If I don't ask no questions, I won't be told no lies. Is that your meaning?"

Susan's laughter came back to her, and the sound of the closing door.

Mrs. Bowyer lay down flat on her one pillow and straightened the sheet. She liked to wake tidy in the morning. She thought about Susan, and the core of her heart was warm. She thought about an earlier, softer Susan, pretty, gentle, sweet—Susie, so pretty-spoken—William's darling. He never spoilt the others, but he spoilt Susie. She could see William now, ever so big and strong with his little maid on his shoulder, ducking his head to come in at the door, and Mr. Philip behind him laughing—"I say, you might let me carry her for a bit!"

She fell into a dream of her own courting. William, too shy to speak, snatching a kiss in the dusk. And then it wasn't her and William, but Susie with her floating curls crying bitterly at her mother's knee: "Oh, Mother, I love him true—I love him true!" And again, Philip, on the threshold, looking at them.

Young Susan lay awake in the dark, three pillows heaped behind her and only a sheet for covering. It had been in her mind that she would fall asleep at once. But she lay awake. It was just as if she had come up against a smooth, blank wall. There was a door in it somewhere, but she couldn't find it, though she kept feeling for it with groping hands.

In the end, the wall melted and let her through, and she saw Garry, with a face like a demon, hurling a great stone down upon her from the top of a high black mountain. The stone broke into three pieces and fell into the sea, and three rushing fountains sprang up from where the fragments had fallen. Only they were not fountains of water, but fountains of fire.

Chapter Nine

BERNARD WEST ARRIVED next day. Anthony dug out the aged Daimler and drove into Wrane to meet him. It was four years since he had seen West. He found him the same, but yet not the same. Small, lean, dark, opinionated, intolerant, he was everything that West had been, only there was more of it. In the four years he had intensified to such a degree that another four at the same rate would land him in caricature.

By the time they had covered the seven miles back to Ford St. Mary, Anthony began to wonder how they were going to get on. He had been a good deal peeved because West was only sparing him a couple of days on his way to join a walking tour, but already two days seemed to be rather a long time.

West talked a great deal. He always had talked a lot; but in those days one said "Shut up!" and hove things at him. He had developed a scholastic eye and a manner of competent authority. One could no longer throw things at him, and he remained unresponsive to the politer ways of saying "Shut up!"

Anthony walked him up to see the Coldstone Ring, and he had plenty to say about it. It wasn't his subject, but he could quote Karnak, and Stonehenge, and Avebury—dolmens—sun and serpent worship—and the Bronze Age.

He immediately propounded a theory that there had been an inner and an outer circle of stones, and that the prostrate stone had not fallen, but was a true altar stone, occupying the central position and lying east and west, so that the officiating priest might face the rising sun as he stood to sacrifice. All this from a cursory and casual glance at two upright stones and one lying flat in a bare stony space ringed about with high, ripe meadow grass. Then, still talking, off again down the hill, turning every now and then to admonish Anthony with lifted hand as if he addressed a class.

"If we postulate a double ring, the missing stones have to be accounted for, and I expect to find them here there and everywhere in this village of yours. Your own gates—have you thought of that?—are, in all probability, cut from one of these monoliths. But of course your local archæological society may have some information—not that these local people are to be relied upon, but still they might be able to furnish some data."

Anthony got a word in edgeways.

"Sir Jervis wouldn't let them see the Ring."

"What?" West had the air of having been contradicted by a small boy.

"He wouldn't let anyone see it. You saw the hedge. I had to break my way through."

"Why on earth?"

"Can't tell you—a kink I should say."

"Oh, but that's all nonsense. You must change all that. Get into touch with experts. I wouldn't trust local people to do any excavating, but the whole thing ought to be thoroughly and carefully investigated.

Ah now! Here! What did I say? What did I tell you? That gate of yours—look at the pillars! The stone is undoubtedly the same. Vandals! We shall probably find bits of these archaic stones built into half the houses of the village. This doesn't look like a stone country, but of course anyone who wanted stone for a gate-post, or a well-head, or a doorstep simply went and looted from the Coldstone Ring. By the way, what's the origin of the name?"

"I don't know."

"Your family name obviously derives from it."

"I suppose so."

"Suppose so? Of course it does! Have you asked about the origin of the name? Someone ought to be able to give you some information. Have you tried the parson? Parsons are very often a mine of information on this sort of subject. Have you tried your local man?"

"We haven't got a resident parson. We go shares with two other villages, and the present man is a retired Indian chaplain who has only been here a few months—at least so the Miss Colstones say."

Mr. West pounced on the Miss Colstones.

"Ah! And what do they say about the Ring?"

"Nothing," said Anthony. Somehow it gave him great pleasure to say "Nothing" like that to West. He grinned, and West frowned portentously.

"*Nothing?* Have you asked them?"

"They don't talk about the Ring. No one in Ford St. Mary talks about it—it's a great taboo."

"Since when? There wasn't any taboo when they set these gates and built this wall. That garden opposite too—look at those flagstones. Look at them—look at them! And the doorstep! The house is Elizabethan. There wasn't any taboo in those days, whatever there may be now." He darted across the street and hung over Mrs. Bowyer's gate, discoursing upon the stones that paved her garden.

He proceeded to discover fresh evidences of vandalism in the Smithers' well-head, and in the wall of the churchyard. At least a dozen of the oldest tombstones he declared to be portions of the Stones from the Coldstone Ring.

After a tour of the village he returned full of energy to the Ring itself. This time each Stone was minutely examined. He made copious notes as he talked. Then, at the prostrate Stone, he stiffened, knelt down, and began in great excitement to trace the worn markings which Anthony had already discovered.

"What's this? What's this?"

Anthony cheered up a little. He had begun to feel rather like one of those small tags which adorn the tail of a proud, erratic kite, and have perforce to follow its soarings and plungings. He found it a boring rôle. Now he cheered up a little. These marks, at any rate, he had discovered for himself. He said so:

"Oh, those triangles? I found them the other day. I suppose they are triangles?"

Mr. West threw a scornful glance over his shoulder.

"Triangles? It's a pentagram. That's very interesting—that's very interesting indeed. I don't remember any other instance—I don't believe there's any other instance."

"Well," said Anthony, "anyone might have put it there, any old time. And—er—isn't a pentagram a thing with five points? This has six."

West was on his knees beside the Stone. He turned now and looked up with an arrested expression.

"Yes," he said, "yes—put on afterwards—perhaps as a charm—to ward off evil. I can't see six points. I believe I'm right in saying that the pentagram, or pentacle, was freely used in mediæval magic. Magic's not my subject, but I seem to remember that."

They went on to the standing Stones, but there were no more marks. West talked about the pentacle, about Solomon's temple, about free-masonry, about mediæval magic, about Friar Bacon, and about Michael Scott. Anthony wondered how much he really knew about any of them, and he thanked his stars for the walking tour that was going to absorb West the day after to-morrow—only the day after to-morrow was the deuce of a long way off. By the time it came, he never wanted to see West again. The fellow was possessed of a perfect demon of energy. He wanted to interview everyone in the village on the subject of the Stones. He cross-examined Lane and Mrs. Hutchins; and the gardeners, and the maid-servants and the boot-boy; and a cowman whom he caught in a field; and the postman, who came from Wrane and said he didn't know nothing about any of it; and the sexton, who grunted, spat on his hands, and went on digging; and three village boys, two of whom were inarticulate, and the third impudent.

No one told him about old Mrs. Bowyer, so he did not interview her. The people he did interview displayed that dense ignorance with which the peasant in every country in the world knows how to shield the knowledge which he does not intend to impart. No one knew anything about the Coldstone Ring. The Stones were "great old stones." They had always been there. They hadn't been to see them themselves. Sir Jervis didn't hold with people going into his fields—and, to all the flood of voluble suggestion made by Mr. West: "You don't say so!" or "Like enough you're right, sir."

Anthony did his best to keep him out of the Miss Colstones' way. He had a perfectly clear vision of West with a note-book in the white panelled room—West sitting on the edge of a gim-crack gilt chair, rattling off questions at Miss Agatha and Miss Arabel like a human maxim, whilst he himself perspired in the background. As far as the village was concerned, he hoped to live West down; but he felt it would be hard to live him down with the Miss Colstones.

It is fatal to try and keep people apart; anxiously placed obstacles seem merely to defeat their own ends. To Bernard West, earnestly copying the inscriptions on some of the older tombstones in the little churchyard, there appeared from the church, where she had been arranging flowers, Miss Arabel; and, as it so chanced, Miss Arabel was feeling faint, and accepted with gratitude the arm and the escort of Anthony's friend. She could do no less than ask him in, and as Miss Agatha was busy in the garden, they had what Mr. West considered a very pleasant conversation in the white panelled drawing-room, with the portrait of the Lady Arabella Stuart looking down on them with her unsmiling dignity. Miss Arabel no longer felt indisposed.

Bernard West found Anthony a little cold on the subject of his Cousin Arabel's charms. He did not want to talk about his cousins at all. He only hoped to goodness that West had kept his mania for asking questions within decent bounds. After a chance meeting with Miss Arabel he abandoned this hope. At the mention of West's name the little lady changed colour, fluttered, and began to talk about the weather. The man was really a most infernal nuisance.

He turned from Wrane station and drove away with this thought in his mind. He had seen West off with decently suppressed joy, and he was wondering why he had ever thought Stonegate lonely. It wasn't going to be lonely; it was going to be peaceful. He felt exactly as if he were going home for the holidays after a strenuous term.

He was passing through the outskirts of Wrane and thinking vaguely what hideous outskirts they were, when his eye was caught by a little lady who was about to enter one of the houses. He slowed down, and recognized Miss Arabel, her air of exquisite finish rather startlingly out of keeping with her surroundings. The street was narrow and mean. The dull little houses were all exactly alike; they had yellow brick walls and grey slate roofs, and their windows were entirely obscured by Nottingham lace.

As Anthony approached, the door in front of which Miss Arabel was standing opened and let her in. He drove on, and had just a glimpse of a young woman in nurse's dress—just an impression of fluffy hair, butcher's blue, and white starched linen. Then the door shut, and he made haste out of Wrane.

Miss Arabel sat on the edge of a horsehair sofa and talked to the fluffy-haired young woman, whose name was Mabel Collins, but whom she addressed as "Nurse." She talked to her for about ten minutes about what a fine August it was, and how nice it was for the farmers to have it so warm and dry, but didn't Nurse find it just a little oppressive in a town like Wrane?

"What's she *want*?" said Miss Collins to herself. "You *bet* your life she didn't come out here seven miles—and they're as mean as misers—just to talk about the weather." Aloud, she agreed with Miss Arabel in a tone of deferential sweetness.

Miss Arabel passed from the weather and began to talk about her father's illness—"As if I wasn't fed to the teeth with the whole thing," Miss Collins commented inaudibly. "Oh, get on, you old fool! If you've come here to say anything, for goodness sake say it and get out!"

Miss Arabel sat a little more upright. Her feet, in their very small shoes, were pressed down hard upon the bright green Brussels carpet. All the while that she talked about "poor Papa" she saw, not the dreadful little room with the bright walnut furniture, but the room at Stonegate where Papa sat propped against pillows looking across the footrail of the bed at the field where two tall grey stones stood amongst the high grass.

She said how good Nurse Collins had been, and how grateful they felt, and how much she hoped Nurse had not found her next case as trying. And all the while she saw that room, and Papa looking past her, and talking, talking, talking in a low mutter that sometimes made words and sometimes lapsed into mere sound. Her little black-gloved hands held one another very tightly as she said,

"I would have come to see you before, because there was something that I wanted to ask you about. You know, you went off in such a hurry."

"Baby cases won't wait," said Miss Collins in a brisk, decided voice.

Miss Arabel fluttered a little. This girl—she seemed so young—it didn't seem quite nice. She returned to "dear Papa" with the sound of his muttering voice in her ears. She must ask—she must find out.

"What did you want to know, Miss Colstone?" said Miss Collins. "And for the Lord's sake hurry up!" she added to herself.

Miss Arabel hesitated, opened her little button mouth, half closed it again, and said suddenly,

"My father talked a good deal—"

"Yes, he did." ("And so do you, you silly old maid.")

Miss Arabel proceeded with difficulty:

"On the afternoon—the last afternoon—the afternoon before he died, the—the *Monday*—"

"Yes, Miss Colstone?"

"You may remember that I sat with him whilst you went to your tea."

Miss Collins nodded. What a rigmarole!

Miss Arabel found it very hard to go on, because she could hear Papa's muttering voice so plainly—just a smudge of sound, and then her own name, "Arabel." And then things, frightening things, forbidden things, that were not to be talked about, by Papa's own especial order. And yet here was Papa talking about them in that low terrifying mutter. It made her heart beat so hard that she missed the next words. And all of a sudden he was looking at her and saying the things that he had said fifty years ago. It was only for a minute. If it had lasted more than a minute, she was sure she would have fainted. But half way through a sentence he stopped; his hand lifted from the sheet and fell again; his voice changed. "Well—well—it's a long time ago—you can have them now—I kept them—" And then, whilst she leaned forward terrified, his eyes closed and he leaned back against his pillows, and an awful endless silence closed down upon the room. Neither of them moved until Nurse came back.

Miss Arabel felt as if that silence was weighing on her now. She made the greatest effort she could.

"My father was telling me something—and he stopped—I think he was tired. After you came back, did he—talk any more?"

"Oh yes—he talked." Miss Collins tossed her fluffy head a little.

"Can you tell me what he said, please?"

The hard blue eyes stared.

"But, Miss Colstone, he talked all the time—you know he did. I couldn't tell you what he said."

Miss Arabel squeezed her hands together very hard. What was she to say? She must find out. But how could she find out without saying things? Her voice became an agitated thread of sound.

"There was something he was talking about. If he mentioned any name—or anything about papers—letters—" The word hardly sounded.

"I don't think he did. Was it something you wanted to find?" There was frank curiosity in the tone.

"No," said Miss Arabel quickly. "I'm afraid I'm not at liberty. If—if he said anything—afterwards—I should be very grateful—"

Miss Collins sat thinking. She wanted to get rid of Miss Arabel, because she was expecting a friend to tea. She was, in point of fact, expecting Mr. Garry O'Connell, and she wanted to change her nurse's uniform and put on the new rose-pink jumper which she had bought in the sales. She was quite unaware of the fact that when she took off her uniform most of her claims to prettiness went with it.

"Did he—say anything?" said Miss Arabel with a little gasp.

Miss Collins frowned. Mr. O'Connell would be here in half a shake.

"Well, he did say something." Miss Arabel turned perfectly white. "He said something I thought queer—and I don't know if it's what you want or not, but he did say your name." She looked sharply at Miss Arabel's little pinched face. "He said 'Arabel' two or three times, and then he said 'Never,' and stopped. And after a bit he said it again quite loud. And after a bit he said, 'Nobody'll ever find it.' And he said, 'Safe—

safe—quite safe.' Now would that be likely to refer to what you wanted to know about?"

"Yes," said Miss Arabel faintly, "it might."

"Well, he said a lot of things like that."

"If you could tell me—"

"But, Miss Colstone, he talked for hours, and it was that sort of thing on and off the whole time. He said one awfully odd thing though. Is there anyone called David in your family?"

"No—no."

"Well, that's funny. He said it several times."

"What did he say?"

Nurse Collins laughed.

"It sounds quite off it unless you've got anyone by that name in the family—but then he wasn't talking sense most of the time."

"What did he say?"

"He said, 'Under the shield of David.' He kept on saying it—but perhaps it was just a religious way of talking."

"Yes—oh yes—and was that all?"

"All you could make any sense out of," said Nurse Collins decidedly. She had heard a ring at the bell.

Miss Arabel got up. She was very pale.

"Thank you," she said gently. "I think I must go now."

On the way downstairs Nurse Collins recollected another of those disjointed sentences. "She can have it now she's going," she said to herself. The bell had just rung for the second time, and she believed in keeping gentlemen waiting. She kept Mr. Garry O'Connell waiting whilst she told Miss Arabel what she had just remembered.

Chapter Ten

MISS ARABEL WALKED a little way up the street. It had been cloudy when she came, but the clouds had all slipped down into the east, where they lay in banks of a heavy grey, flecked with white and barred with indigo. All the rest of the sky was a bare dusty blue. The air between the houses shook in the heat.

Miss Arabel felt quite dazed with the light, and the glare, and the thing which Nurse O'Connell had just said to her. She walked with small, hesitating footsteps, and though her eyes were wide open, she did not really see where she was going until her shoulder struck hard against a lamp-post and brought her up short with a gasp. As she stood there trying not to cry—it would be too dreadful if she were to cry in the open street—she looked very small and frail.

Anthony Colstone stopped the car and jumped out. He was most frightfully glad he had thought of coming back. He put a hand on her arm and said,

"Cousin Arabel—"

She looked up at him with swimming eyes.

"The heat—" she murmured. And then she was being helped into the car, and the fresh air began to blow in her face. She heard Anthony talking, as one hears some pleasant sound a long way off.

"I saw you go in, and I went on a bit. And then I thought I'd come back and find out if I couldn't drive you home, and then—"

Miss Arabel sat up with a cry. "Oh, the keys!" she said. "I forgot!"

"What is it? Do you want to go back?"

"Oh no—I couldn't ask you. So careless! But Agatha—Oh dear me, what will Agatha say?" She presented a little pale picture of dismay in her old lady's bonnet and black silk cape.

"Look here, we'll go back, and then there won't be anything for Cousin Agatha to say."

Miss Arabel fluttered, protested, thanked him profusely, and kept up a persistent twitter of explanation as he turned the car and drove back.

"It was only—it was the keys—Lane has been so put out about them. But perhaps he didn't like to speak of it to you. And Agatha said—you see she was called away—Nurse Collins was called away immediately—the very day Papa died—and Agatha had let her have the keys—the front door key and the gate—Papa's own keys—so that she could go out and come back without ringing—because Lane had been up all night. And she went off suddenly like that and forgot to give them back. And when we wrote, she said she was sorry but she must have left them packed up in her box and she couldn't let the landlady open it, so I promised Agatha—"

The car stopped and Anthony jumped out.

"I'll get them. Sit still."

He had to ring twice. Then the door opened, and Miss Collins got what she called a start.

"Blessed if I didn't think the old lady had come back to begin all over again! I could see her there in the car with her mouth open all ready—and Mr. Colstone."

"What does he want?" said Garry O'Connell.

"Ssh! He'll hear you—he's at the door. Wanted to come up, but I wouldn't let him." She came quite close to him and dropped her voice. "I say, he wants those keys—you know—what you borrowed. Have you got them? I was on thorns for fear the old lady'd ask for them while she was here."

Mr. Garry O'Connell dived into his trouser pocket and fished up two large keys. She held out her hand, but he turned them over in a leisurely fashion, looking at them closely.

"Oh, hurry up! What are you doing?"

Mr. O'Connell was scraping a tiny ball of wax from between the wards of one of the keys. He took his time, scrutinized them again, and handed them over.

Mabel Collins ran downstairs with a heightened colour.

"They were right at the bottom of the box," she explained. "Quite *safe*, Mr. Colstone."

He put the keys into Miss Arabel's lap and started the engine.

"I say, it's hot!" he said, and looked up for a moment.

The sun swept all the windows on that side of the street. Mabel Collins was closing her front door. The lace curtains in the room above did not quite meet. From between them someone looked down at the car, at Miss Arabel and himself. Anthony saw dark hair brushed back from a pale high brow, black eyes in a smooth oval face. He had seen the face before, looking out of a hedge. This time the eyes didn't glare; they looked superior—they looked beastly superior. He thought he preferred the glare.

The whole thing passed in a moment. He drove on.

As he drove, he thought; and the more he thought, the more certain he felt that he would be a mug to waste Miss Arabel. There were a lot of things that he wanted to know very badly. If Miss Arabel couldn't tell him all these things, she could certainly tell him some of them; and here she was, dropped upon him from the skies, positively fluttering with gratitude and unhampered by Miss Agatha's presence.

He drove into a nice patch of shade and stopped the car.

"Cousin Arabel—" he said.

Miss Arabel looked into his pleasant sunburnt face. She thought how nice it was to be driven like this by a kind and attentive young man who behaved really as if she were his aunt instead of a distant cousin. She felt that she had it in her to become a very much attached aunt.

"Cousin Arabel—" said Anthony; then he smiled. "I do want to ask you some questions so badly."

Miss Arabel thought what very white teeth he had. He was a very fine young man, and credit to the family.

"Oh, yes—anything, my dear Anthony."

For a fleeting moment the smile changed to a grin. "Anything" was a tall order.

"Well then—I want you to tell me about the Coldstone Ring."

Her complacent expression instantly broke up. She looked away and said in a confused voice,

"Oh, I don't think I can."

"Why can't you?" He turned in his seat so as to face her, and leaned forward, resting his hand and arm on the wheel. "Look here, Cousin Arabel—can't you see my point of view? Sir Jervis has been most awfully good to me leaving me this place, and I don't want to go against his wishes or hurt your feelings or Cousin Agatha's, but I do want to know where I am. Only this morning I had a letter from Lord Haverton, very polite, asking me to lunch. He left a card yesterday when West and I were out. Well, he's president of the County archæological society—"

"Oh yes—Papa quarrelled with him—oh *dear*!"

"Well, I want to know where I am. I'm not such an absolute fool as to suppose that Sir Jervis took up the position he did without having some reason for it, and I think I ought to know what the reason is. Don't you think so yourself? Honest injun now?"

"I don't know," said Miss Arabel in a distressed voice. "It sounds as if—"

Anthony pursued his advantage.

"Cousin Agatha said something about village superstitions. Now that's one of the things I want to know about. If there are superstitions, what are they? There can't be any harm in telling me that."

"No—oh no," said Miss Arabel. She took a fine white linen handkerchief out of a shabby beaded reticule and dabbed her chin with it.

"What's the story about the Stones?" said Anthony quickly. "Why won't anyone go near them?"

"Oh"—the hand with the handkerchief in it shook—"Oh, I don't know. They're afraid."

"What are they afraid of?"

Miss Arabel had also turned in her seat; she had her back to the road and the high bank which rose above it. There were trees on the bank, heavy with dusty summer green. The shade was dense; here and there it deepened into an olive dusk. She looked over her shoulder and whispered through the folds of the handkerchief:

"They're afraid—"

"Yes, but what are they afraid of?"

Miss Arabel leaned nearer. Her voice trembled on the verge of inaudibility.

She said, "The devil," and sat aghast at her own words.

"What?" said Anthony.

The loudness of his voice shocked her very much.

"Oh, I don't think I ought."

"Oh, but you must—you can't stop now."

"We were never allowed to talk about it."

Anthony laughed.

"Then you're bound to know all that there is to know. There's nothing makes you get to the bottom of a thing quicker than being told you're not to talk about it."

"Of course it's only a superstition," said Miss Arabel. She looked over her other shoulder and shivered.

"Well, tell me about it. What do they think?"

"They used to take the Stones. It is a very long time ago, of course—hundreds of years. They took them to build with because there isn't any stone round here. Oh, I don't know whether Agatha would think I ought to tell you this."

Anthony put a hand on her knee.

"Oh, Cousin Arabel, do go on!"

She let her hand drop on his. Her fingers were cold. The handkerchief tickled him.

"Susan says there were two rings of Stones—old Susan Bowyer, you know. Her great-grandfather remembered them—or was it his father? All the Bowyers live to be very old. There were two rings, only they didn't quite meet. And there was a big stone in the middle lying flat, that they called the Coldstone."

"Why?" said Anthony quickly.

"Because—oh, I don't know. Our name comes from it."

Anthony patted her.

"Well, the people took the stones—and then what happened?"

"I don't quite know—something dreadful. It was a long, long time ago the first time it happened. They went to lift the Coldstone—and the devil came out!" She leaned right forward and said the last words with a gasp. The effort made her whole body tremble. Then she drew back, breathed quickly, and said, "Of course that's just what the village people believed."

"Of course. And then what happened?"

"There was an old wise man, and he helped them, and the Stone was laid down again. And he put a mark on it—"

Anthony started. He drew back the hand he had laid on Miss Arabel's knee.

"What was the mark for?"

"To keep the devil down," whispered Miss Arabel. "And after that no one moved the Stone for hundreds of years—but they went on taking the other stones. And at last they began to move the Coldstone again, and they say—"

"Yes—go on!"

"They say fire came out of the ground and burnt up all the grass round the Stone—and they dropped it quickly, or they would all have been burnt up. And they say no grass will grow round it even now—but I don't know if it is true."

She looked timidly and yet curiously at Anthony.

"There isn't any grass round it," he said.

He had a picture of the great grey Stone lying across a ring of bare stony earth; and beyond this rim, grass waist-high. He thought the story was a very odd one.

"And after that," said Miss Arabel, "no one ever moved the Stone again. And Papa wouldn't allow us to talk of it or to go there." She sat back and put the handkerchief to her lips. "Just village talk of course," she said. Her eyes asked him what he thought. "Poor Papa had such a horror of gossip—and there is a game called Russian Scandal which we used to play when I was young—Papa considered it quite instructive. So perhaps I ought not to have repeated all this foolish talk—and I don't know what Agatha—"

Her anxious gaze was met by a friendly grin.

"We won't tell Cousin Agatha," said Anthony cheerfully.

Chapter Eleven

ANTHONY CAME BACK to Stonegate with a good deal of zest. In some curious way West's departure had given him a sense of possession; he really felt for the first time that Stonegate was his. He got Lane to go round with him and tell him about the portraits that hung here and there on the panelled walls. Jervis, Ambrose, Anthony, Ralph, Philip— the names came again and again. Philip, in a ruff, with a jewel on the stiff, pale hand that fingered it—"Fought against the Spanish Armada, so Sir Jervis said, sir." Ralph, with a falling collar of lace over half armour—"Killed at Naseby." Jervis, with long love-locks, a slender youth of seventeen, his hand on a greyhound's head and blue ribbon looping the fair hair. Ambrose, in a scholar's gown. And then the names again. Ralph in a periwig. Ambrose in pearl-grey satin. A little Ralph of ten, holding by the hand an infant Anthony with apple cheeks and a stiff white frock. The names went on repeating themselves.

There were very few women. One, in the library, startled Anthony with the feeling that he knew her. She wore a flowered gown over a blue petticoat; a mob cap hid her hair. She looked down with just a demure blue glint under dark lashes. It was as if she had looked, and looked away. "Sir Jervis' grandmother," said Lane. "Miss Patience Pleydell she was—done just before her marriage to Mr. Jervis Colstone, Sir

Jervis' grandfather. Begging your pardon, sir, she was Mr. Ambrose's mother—your great grandfather, sir. Mr. James and Mr. Ambrose was her two sons. Mr. James was Sir Jervis' father, and Mr. Ambrose was your great-grandfather—so Sir Jervis said."

Anthony walked over to call on Mrs. Bowyer between six and seven. He stepped round the lavender bush, knocked on the worn front door, and stood for a moment waiting. He heard someone laugh on the other side of the door. And then it opened, and he saw old Mrs. Bowyer sitting by the window in her rocking-chair with a piece of bright carpet under her feet and her hands folded on a clean white pocket-handkerchief. Neither her black silk cap, nor her dress, nor even her shiny alpaca apron were as bright and black as the eyes which looked up at him as he bent his head and stepped across the threshold.

The door shut behind him. He caught a glimpse of a hand and a blue sleeve. And then he was shaking hands with Mrs. Bowyer. Her vigorous clasp astonished him, and her eyes looked him through and through. Then she said,

"A chair, Susan."

Anthony turned, and saw the girl in the blue dress.

"My great-granddaughter," said Mrs. Bowyer.

Anthony put out his hand, but it was not taken. Mrs. Bowyer's granddaughter dropped him a sort of charity bob and made haste to set a chair. She was bare-headed. Her hair was much darker than he expected, and it curled. It seemed to him a very surprising thing that it should curl in that soft way. Her lashes were dark too. She bobbed to him and she kept the lashes down, but there was a glint of blue between them. It was just as if she had looked, and looked away.

He was pricked with a sharp surprise, because he knew now where he had seen Miss Patience Pleydell before. She was his great-great-grandmother. And this village girl had her eyes, and her sweeping lashes, and the secret hidden smile that eluded you when you looked for it and came when you looked away. All the time he was talking to old Mrs. Bowyer he knew very well that Susan was smiling to herself. Yet when he looked up, she was always sitting quite still on a decorous straight chair with some white sewing in her lap, and the face bent over the sewing as grave as if she were in church.

Mrs. Bowyer put him through a most determined catechism.

"And who brought you up now?"

"My mother's aunt, Mrs. Wimborne."

"To think of that now! I don't know what the world's coming to when young folks die and leave their children to be reared by the old uns. I reared twelve, and they're all gone now—and I'm here."

She leaned back, rocked once, and came to her questions again with that vivid flash of interest in her eyes. Anthony found himself telling her about the Wimbornes. She took a passionate interest in the number of acres Uncle Henry had farmed, just what rotation of crops he followed, and what breed of cattle he favoured. She seemed to know all about dairy work.

The visit lasted a long time; and all the time that he talked, Mrs. Bowyer's granddaughter sat sewing and never spoke a word. Suddenly Anthony pushed back his chair a little. He smiled ingratiatingly at old Mrs. Bowyer.

"Isn't it my turn now?" he said.

"And what is the meaning of that?"

"Well, I was thinking that it might be my turn to ask some questions."

She nodded a little.

"And what is it you want to ask, sir?"

It was the first time that she had said "sir."

"I want to ask you about the Coldstone Ring."

Susan's hand, which had been rising and falling as she took her neat, fine stitches, fell now upon her knee and rested there. Anthony knew that just as well as he knew that Mrs. Bowyer was considering what he had just said. She hadn't said "no." She looked him over and considered him. Then she said.

"And what is it you want to know, sir?"

When she said "sir" the second time, Anthony had a flash of insight. She had been weighing him, and he was accepted. He felt an absurd pride.

He leaned towards her and said gravely, "I want to know what you can tell me. No one will talk about the Ring, and that makes it very difficult for me—I'm sure you see that—because Sir Jervis wanted me to promise not to move the Stones—"

Mrs. Bowyer uttered a sharp exclamation:

"Eh—but you'd never do that!"

"Never promise—or never move the stones?"

"Have you promised?"

"No, I haven't. I don't like promising things. And I want to know why. I don't like mysteries either. Why are the Stones not to be moved?"

Mrs. Bowyer rocked.

Anthony got up. Now that he was standing, he could see Susan. She was sitting up straight; the hand with the needle rested on her knee. She had just looked away. He caught the last flicker of blue, the last movement of the falling lashes. He was aware that she was as intent as he. They were waiting together for the answer to his question.

Old Mrs. Bowyer rocked slowly. At last she said,

"What's been told you then?"

"Miss Arabel says—" And then he stopped.

Mrs. Bowyer shook a little. He thought she was laughing, but he wasn't sure.

"Eh? Miss Arabel?" she said. And then, with extraordinary vigour, "Nought's as much as she knows."

He was taken aback for a moment. Then he laughed.

"Well then, I haven't been told anything, and you can begin at the very beginning."

She met his laughing look with a twinkle which was suddenly extinguished. The black eyes remained fixed upon him in a deep brooding look; they gave him the feeling that she was not really looking at him, but past him or through him to something at an immense distance. Then all at once she shook again and said,

"The beginning—that's a long way back—there isn't anyone can tell you as far back as that."

"What can you tell me?" said Anthony.

"Can's one word, and will's another," said Mrs. Bowyer. Her eyes had lost their brooding look, and her voice had an edge.

"What *will* you tell me then?"

"What did Miss Arabel tell you?"

"Nought," said Anthony with a grin.

She rocked herself and shook with that soundless laughter.

"Nought's what all the world knows. Coldstone Ring's been here since the old ancient times—all the world knows that. And the Stones ha' been taken and built into housen and walls—I've one for my doorstep, and another for the hearthstone, there under your heel as you stand now. And the man that laid it there was a William Bowyer, same as my husband and my father. There's allays been a William Bowyer. And William that laid that stone he was my grandfather's grandfather, and he could tell my grandfather of how the Ring used to stand with two rows of great stones and the Coldstone lying in the midst—he could tell my grandfather that, and my grandfather could tell me." She stopped, and her eyes twinkled. "That's nought—all the world knows that."

"Did he tell you the devil came out when the Coldstone was raised?"

She looked at him sharply.

"That's nought too."

"You mean that everyone believes it."

"Maybe."

"Why?"

"Maybe because it's true."

"That the devil came out?"

Mrs. Bowyer pursed up her lips.

"Why don't the grass grow round the Coldstone?" she said.

Anthony felt a strong excitement.

"What happened when they lifted the stone?"

A look slipped over Mrs. Bowyer's face. It came and went so quickly that he could not be sure of it. She might have been afraid, or she might not; he couldn't tell. She said just above her breath,

"Nought." Then, in a much stronger voice, "There's things that all the world knows, and there's things that no one knows, and there's things that didn't ought to be meddled with." She put out her hand. "And thank you kindly for coming to see me, and good evening to you— you'll be kindly welcome whenever you come. Susan—"

The audience was at an end. Mrs. Bowyer terminated it with as much ease as if she had been royalty; her wrinkled hand was very graciously extended.

Susan rose, laid down her needlework, and opened the door for him. On the threshold she bobbed, and he felt an anger that surprised him.

"Why do you do that?"

"Sir?"

He backed away from her a step and pitched his voice for her ear.

"I want to talk to you."

"Sir!" This time the word reproved him.

"Who are you?" said Anthony.

"Please, sir, Gran told you—I'm her great-granddaughter."

"You're like—" He didn't mean to say it, but the words broke from him.

"Sir?"

"You're like one of the pictures at Stonegate."

And at that he saw her colour rise. The blush ran right up to the roots of her hair, and as she felt it, she stepped back. Before he could speak again the door was shut.

Chapter Twelve

SUSAN LEANED AGAINST the inside of the door and shook with laughter.

"Lord ha' mercy! What's come to you?" said Mrs. Bowyer.

"Oh, Gran—has he gone?"

"Out at the gate, cross the road, and in again."

Susan ran forward and dropped on her knees by the rocking-chair.

"Gran, did you hear me say 'sir'?"

"Couldn't hear nought the way you mumbled. What was he saying to make you as red as fire?"

"He said he wanted to talk to me. And I said *'Sir!'* in the most rebuking kind of way—you know, the real 'Unhand me!' touch."

"And let him see he could make you turn colour?"

"No, no—it wasn't for that at all."

Mrs. Bowyer chuckled.

"No maid never blushes along of what a lad says to her or looks at her! 'Tis allays because the sun's too hot, or the wind have caught her, or such like."

Susan put a hand on her arm and shook it.

"Gran, what a low mind you've got!"

"Well, if 'twasn't the sun or the wind, what was it?"

"He said—Gran, he said I was like one of the pictures at Stonegate. *Am* I very red?"

"Middling." Mrs. Bowyer's voice was very dry. She looked at the flushed face and bright eyes and nodded. "Aye—and so you are."

"Red?"

Mrs. Bowyer nodded again.

"Aye—and like the picture, too."

"Oh! Whose picture? Oh, Gran, why didn't you tell me? *Bad* angel—tell me at once!"

"There's names for you! It's easy seen I hadn't the bringing up of you. When you say 'bad angel,' you might as well say 'devil' and have done with it."

"I will if you like. Oh, Gran, tell me who I'm like—angel—*darling!*"

Mrs. Bowyer surveyed her with a curious look of pride.

"You're like Miss Patience Pleydell that was—Mrs. Jervis Colstone, Sir Jervis' grandmother."

"Am I? Am I really?"

"Her very moral."

"What a jest! Why didn't you tell me?"

"Least said, soonest mended."

"You've said that before, Gran."

"And I look to say it again," said Mrs. Bowyer very composedly.

Susan sat back on her heels and laughed.

"I say—I'd better wear my sun-bonnet all the time, and pull it well down over my face, or we shall have the breath of scandal blowing a regular gale in Ford St. Mary. Oh, Gran, I must see the picture!"

"That you can't—not in decency."

Susan began to speak, stopped, and changed to a coaxing tone.

"Gran—tell me about her. Do you remember her?"

"Aye—with white hair."

"What was she like?"

"An old grand lady with brisk ways. 'Old Madam' they called her, and everyone had to do her bidding."

"But she's young in the picture."

" 'Twas done before she married old Mr. Jervis."

"I must see it! What has she got on?"

"A blue petticoat and a flowered dress. You can see them, if you can't see the picture, for Miss Agatha went to a ball dressed up to copy her, and she gave me the dress a long while after when she was turning out her boxes. You can fetch it out if you like—and put it on too if it will fit you. It's in the chest in your room."

Susan lost interest in the dress quite suddenly. She said, "Thank you, Gran," in an abstracted voice. Then she played with the edge of the black alpaca apron, pleating it up and pinching the pleats to make them stay. Then she said,

"Gran, why wouldn't you tell him about the Coldstone?"

"Wouldn't? I'll thank you to leave my apron alone. Wouldn't?"

"Yes—*wouldn't*. You know you could, Gran."

"Ah!" said Mrs. Bowyer. "That's talking. Wouldn't and couldn't are just words."

"Don't you think he's got a right to know?"

Mrs. Bowyer fixed a gaze of bright intensity on the flushing face.

"And what d'you think he's got the right to know?"

"The truth."

Old Mrs. Bowyer chuckled.

"That's a big, brave word. You see here, Susan—when you told the lad your name was Susan, wasn't you telling him the truth? And when I told him you was my great-granddaughter, wasn't I a-telling him the truth then? To be sure I was. And when he's been told the truth by this and that, what does he know? Nought, I tell you—nought."

"What d'you mean, Gran?"

"I mean you can take that for a parable. I'm to tell him the truth about the Coldstone? Well, that's true what he's heard from Miss Arabel—things happened in the old ancient times, and folks believed what they believed. That's true. I'm not saying there's not more things true than everybody knows—I'm not saying that."

"What things?" said Susan in a whisper.

"Things that's hid behind the other things—true things that's hid behind a lot of talk—and maybe other things that's hid behind them again."

"What other things?"

Susan was still kneeling, her face very close to the old wrinkled face. She leaned on the arm of the chair and bent forward and spoke on a low breath:

"What other things—*Gran?*"

"Old ancient things," said Mrs. Bowyer in a hushed voice.

"Won't you tell me?"

"They're not for me to tell, nor for you to hear. Maybe you know that, Susan. Maybe you know more than you let on yourself—eh?"

Susan jumped up.

"Gran!"

"Not telling's a game as two can play." She shook with that silent laughter. "When you've told, you can't take back again—and when you've heard things, you can't go back to where you were before." Her solemn look changed suddenly into one of malicious amusement. "Eh, my dear, there's a lot of fun in finding out!" she said.

Chapter Thirteen

Mrs. Bowyer did not approve of Summer Time, but she regarded it with tolerance. It did not disturb her habits, which were those of an older day. She had always risen and gone to bed with the sun, and she didn't see why other people couldn't do the same without making a lot of fuss about it. In her young days you got up at five in the summer, and you called it five. It was a shiftless modern generation that had to be lured out of bed by calling five six. "Bone-idle when there's work to be done, and strong as oxen when it comes to dancing, or gadding, or trapesing into the town to see they moving pictures. I haven't no patience with them." This was to the address of Mary Ann Smithers, who was being courted by the butcher's lad from Wrane, and who "trapesed" a good deal in consequence.

Susan did not go to bed with the sun. She sat in the garden as long as Gran considered it respectable, or rather longer. It was apparently more than a little scandalous to allow darkness to overtake one in one's own back garden. It was one of the things that weren't done in Ford St. Mary. Still less could one wander abroad in fields made strange and strangely vast by the soft, even darkness.

Susan left the garden reluctantly. The hot, still air was full of the dreams of sleeping flowers. The silent hives were like black hillocks. She wondered if bees could dream, and what their dreams would be. There was a sweetness everywhere—lavender; southernwood; late sweet peas; the cabbage rose and the old-fashioned white, very sweet, with a stray bloom or two; and invisible dark carnations. The flowers of a cottage garden dreaming fragrant dreams.

Susan went upstairs on tiptoe without a light. It was quite dark in the house, with the close indoor darkness which is just a black curtain before the eyes. In her own room there was a little dusky glimmer that came from the uncurtained window. She drew the curtains and lighted a candle. When she lifted it, all the shadows rushed down from the black rafters and hid.

There was a good deal of furniture in the room—a white painted chest of drawers and an old mahogany one; a washstand with a marble top and a double set of china which was the pride of Mrs. Bowyer's heart; a wall-press; and a tall chest that served for a dressing-table. It was made of deal, old soft brown deal, and it was beautifully panelled. The lid was held down by a great iron hasp.

Susan lifted the looking-glass off the lid of the chest, and laid it carefully on the bed. Then she stopped and looked at the chest again, and then she looked at her watch. It wasn't late enough yet. Ghosts don't walk till midnight—a very sensible arrangement for securing privacy. She finished clearing the lid of the chest, removed the clean white cover which converted it into a dressing-table, and slowly lifted the lid.

Anthony Colstone went to bed at eleven, and fell asleep as soon as his head touched the pillow. It was his enviable habit to do this and then to sleep dreamlessly until he was called next morning. He was therefore a good deal surprised at finding himself suddenly awake in the pitch dark. He was not only awake, but very wide awake indeed and sitting up. Such a thing had only happened to him twice before in his life. On the first occasion the Wimbornes' house had been on fire, and on the second an Indian thief, oiled from head to foot, was feeling for his revolver—Anthony got it first. This was the third time.

He was quite wide awake. There didn't seem to be any smoke, and he couldn't hear a sound. Of course, with a really talented thief there wasn't any sound to hear. The oily gentleman had been as silent as a shadow. It wasn't a sound that had waked Anthony then. He didn't think it was a sound that had waked him now. Yet he listened with all his ears. There was no sound at all. A dead still house—a sleeping house; and the sense of someone awake, someone besides himself. It was quite dark, no moon outside, but he could just see the outline of the window.

He put his hand on the matches, then slid out of bed and went to the door. Whatever had waked him wasn't here; there was no sense of another person in the room. He opened the door a chink, then wider, and the darkness and the silence of the house flowed in and rose about him. With the darkness and the silence something else came in—the sense of an alien presence.

He stepped back from the door, went barefoot to the chest of drawers, and felt for the small electric torch which lay there. A candle or a lamp would advertise him to whoever there might be below. He put the torch in the pocket of his pyjama coat and emerged upon the black uneven corridor. By dint of moving very slowly he reached the stair-head with no more than a stubbed toe—a step up, a step down, and another step up. His toe caught the last step, but without making any sound. Then a dozen feet of passage, and the stairs.

Going down the stairs was like going down a black well. He came to the bottom and stood against the newel-post, listening. The square hall was in the middle of the house. He faced the front door, and had on his right the drawing-room, and on his left the dining-room, with the library behind it, and beyond the library a door that led to the kitchens and offices. All this side of the house was very old, but the drawing-room and Sir Jervis' room over it had been built when the glass passage that led to the outer gate had been added.

Anthony stood by the left-hand newel-post. There was a narrow passage between him and the wall. He looked down it, and his heart jumped. For a single instant a thread of light showed where the library door was. It was there, and it was gone again and all the passage was dark. The library must be dark too. But a moment ago there had been a light there. Someone had turned on a light, and a faint silver thread had showed under the crack of the door where the old boards had been worn away.

Anthony began to move towards the place where the light had been. As he moved, his fingers touched the wall and slid without any sound over the smooth panels. The door-post was rougher. His hand slipped downwards, groped for the handle, and closed upon it gently. For a long minute he was turning it. Then when the latch was free, he pushed the door a bare half inch and slowly released the catch again.

There had been a light in the room, but there was no light there now; the half-inch opening was as impenetrable as the door. He made the opening wider, and then wider again, until the door, opening inwards, stood at a right angle with the wall. This brought him into the room. He stood just over the threshold, listening, his hand on the torch in his pocket.

The room was profoundly still and most profoundly dark. It smelt faintly of beeswax and turpentine, and of all the old books which lined its walls. But Anthony had no sooner stepped into it than he was aware of something more than the night, and the silence, and the ghosts of dead books.

He took the torch out of his pocket, and was as sure as he had ever been of anything in his life that there was someone else in the room, someone standing still with caught breath, or moving and breathing with as little sound as he himself had made. He had his finger on the switch of the torch, he had even begun to move it, when he heard a sound. From the moment that he had waked until now everything had passed in dumb show; he had not even heard his own movements; the action had been like the action of a dream. This was the first sound, and it came, not from this room in which he discerned a presence, but from the passage behind him.

In an instant he had stepped sideways, clear of the doorway; and as he did so, he heard the sound again. Someone was moving in the hall. The sound that he had heard was the sound of a cautiously planted foot. Someone was undoubtedly coming down the passage towards the library door. And then, as he stood there straining his ears, there was a faint click on his left and the beam of a torch cut the darkness. A man was standing on the threshold.

Anthony saw three things almost simultaneously. He was standing in the corner of the room about six feet from the door, and at the sound of the click he looked instinctively in the direction from which it came, and he saw three things. First, very dimly, the outline of a man holding out a torch in front of him. Then the long ray, stabbing the darkness as it turned here and there. And lastly the portrait of Miss Patience Pleydell. It hung low on the left-hand wall, where a strip of panelling divided one book-filled space from another. He had noticed only that afternoon how cleverly the painting had been sunk into the panel so as to give the effect of a person standing against the wall. The ray came to rest upon the portrait, and Anthony could have cried out, so lifelike did it seem.

Next moment someone did cry out. The girl in the flowered dress and blue petticoat moved visibly, or seemed to move, as the beam dipped and came to rest on her again. Anthony could have sworn that she moved. And at the same time someone gave a little choking cry, and this cry came from somewhere quite close at hand; he thought from behind the open door.

Miss Patience Pleydell moved her arm, someone cried out, the light went out with a click, and Anthony jumped for the man with the torch—jumped, touched a rough sleeve, made a grab in the dark, dropped his own torch, which he had forgotten, and, to the sound of another little gasping cry, grappled with someone quite extraordinarily hard and lithe. He got hold of a coat-collar, heard something rip, and received a bang on the side of the head from the intruder's torch. At the same time the collar was twisted out of his hand and its owner took to his heels. Anthony slipped and came down sprawling. He scrambled up to sounds of flight. He thought he could hear more than one man running away. A door banged. He had fallen on his torch. By the time that he was up and had switched it on, the passage was empty.

He ran into the hall and found it empty too. The front door was ajar. The door leading from the glass passage into the street was shut, but not locked. Anthony wondered whether Lane had been as slack as all that. He wondered about Nurse Collins, and the keys which Miss Arabel had been so anxious about. But surely there should be bolts to both these doors.

He turned the light on to the outer door, frowning. There were bolts top and bottom. He bent to the bottom one, tried it, and found that it was all he could do to move it at all. He promised himself a few words with Lane in the morning. Somehow he didn't want to wake Lane now.

He went back to the library, wondering about that little gasping cry and about the portrait of Miss Patience Pleydell. He flashed the light here and there, found matches, and lighted the lamp which stood on a table by the fireplace. After the intense dark, its mediocre yellow light seemed quite bright. He held it up and surveyed the room.

Standing by the fireplace, he had the door on his left, and two shuttered windows on his right. The portrait of Miss Patience Pleydell faced him. He shifted the lamp this way and that to see if he could induce that effect of movement. It was the right arm that had moved. Miss Patience stood with her hands lightly clasped before her; her feet were on the bottom step of a dim flight. She appeared to be stepping down into the room, and the portrait was hung so low that the step would have been an easy one.

Anthony moved the lamp up and down, and sideways; but the arm did not move again. He crossed the room and let the light fall on the picture full. In the yellow light the colours did not look so bright as they had seemed by the flash of the torch. The whole effect for that one moment had been startlingly vivid and alive. And he could have sworn that the arm had moved. The arm had moved, and then someone had cried out. The sound hadn't come from the picture at all; it was nearer him, and nearer the door—much nearer the door. He was as certain as he could be that the person who had uttered that gasping cry had been hidden behind the open door.

He crossed over to the spot. There were a couple of armchairs in this corner. If anyone had been hiding, they might have crouched down behind the one that was nearest the door. He moved it, and caught sight at once of something white. It was a scrap of a pocket-handkerchief. Anthony set down the lamp and spread it out—seven or eight inches of fine linen lawn with a border of three wavy lines. It had neither name nor initial. He walked round the room. There was a big sofa, chairs, a writing-table, books—and the portrait; but no conceivable hiding-place. It was all very odd.

He returned to the hall, passed down the glass passage, and drove home two very reluctant bolts. The bolts on the inner door simply wouldn't move at all. He locked it, and then went back for another look at the library. The lamplight seemed to fill it with a steady golden glow.

The handkerchief was gone.

Chapter Fourteen

SUSAN STOOD STILL and held her breath. Her heart was racing with excitement. She did not feel like a ghost at all; she felt most splendidly, radiantly alive. She stood behind the panel which held Miss Patience Pleydell's portrait, and shook with laughter. The rescued handkerchief was crumpled in the hand that had just closed the panel. She pushed it down inside her dress and stopped her laughter to listen. Someone was coming back into the room. She must see who it was; because there had been three people there besides herself.

Another tremor of laughter shook her from head to foot. When a ghost walks at midnight she does not expect to find herself the centre of a family reunion. Yet when she swung the panel back—it swung inwards, portrait and all—and was just going to step down into the room, there were three people waiting for her. It was frightfully funny, but it was also rather puzzling. The person who had dropped the handkerchief was behind the door, scared to death. Susan wasn't worrying about her; she was just glad she had seen the handkerchief, because it might have been traced.

It was the two men who were bothering her. One of them was Anthony Colstone; but she didn't know which one. She didn't know whether it was Anthony who had stood in the doorway and flashed the light on to her in that perfectly terrifying manner, or whether it was Anthony who had sprung out of the dark corner of the room with an even more terrifying suddenness. She wondered if either of the men had seen her move; because she *had* moved when the light struck her.

It was Anthony who had come back into the room and lighted the lamp. There was a little knot-hole on the right beyond where the panelling opened. It had glimmered like a keyhole when he lit the lamp, and when she put her eye close to it she could see him, with his hair standing on end and a puzzled, angry look on his face. She saw him go into the corner of the room, and she saw him come back with the handkerchief in his hand and stand there, turning it over and looking at it. When he put it down and went out of the room, she had her chance, but she had to be very quick. The panel had a catch. She had her hand on it, and the moment Anthony was out of sight, she slipped the catch, pulled the panel inwards, and stepped down into the room with her long full skirt gathered up in her left hand. She snatched the handkerchief, and was back again before she had time to take three breaths. Now she stood and looked through the knot-hole at Anthony.

He was puzzled, and he was angry. She thought he was very angry; and she thought being angry suited him, because his jaw stuck out and his eyes went dark. And then all at once he almost frightened her into crying out, for he picked up the lamp and marched straight up to the picture. She had a dreadful feeling of not being able to move. Her forehead was pressed against the rough inner side of the panelling, and she could neither close her eyes nor move away from the knot-hole. The light seemed to rush towards her, and she remembered having heard that fish will come to a diver's light far down in the dark sea and stay there goggling at it stupidly in a sort of helpless fascination. In her mind she saw herself with bulging eyes and a large open mouth. She said "Cod-fish!" which was about the most withering thing she could think of, and with a jerk—she hoped it was a noiseless jerk—she threw back her head and shut her eyes.

She heard Anthony say "Damn!" on the other side of the portrait, and then after a moment—but it didn't seem like a moment; it seemed like a long time—she heard him set the lamp down, and she opened her eyes and looked through the hole again.

Anthony was standing on the other side of the room. He had put down the lamp, but as she looked, his hand went up and turned it out. The light jumped, and then all the shadows in the room rushed down and smothered it. Anthony went out and shut the door with a bang.

Susan relaxed. She did not know how stiffly she had been holding herself until the door banged like that. She let go, and all at once she wanted to sneeze, and she thought how dreadful it would have been if she had sneezed before. She moved back from the panelling and turned on the torch which she had stowed away in a conveniently large pocket. The light showed a narrow standing-place about three feet square, and beyond it steps going down into the darkness.

Susan moved towards the steps. She ought to go back and be thankful she was so well out of the adventure. It must be getting awfully late, and if Gran woke up.... She didn't want to go back in the least; she wanted to go through the panel and explore.

With her foot on the top step, she halted, whisked round, and switched off her light. The panel swung in, and she stepped down into the library for the third time that night, pulling the panel behind her so that it stayed open about half an inch. First of all she wanted to look at the portrait. That was what she had come here for, and she had only had a glimpse of it, because the minute her light went on, there had come that frightened cry. She turned the light on it now and bobbed a little curtsey to the lady who looked as if she was stepping down to meet her.

"I really am like her," she said to herself—"awfully like." Then she laughed, because she thought of Anthony with his rumpled hair and his blue and white pyjamas, and his puzzled, angry face. She realized suddenly that she was enjoying herself very much, and she hadn't the slightest intention of going back to bed. She switched off her light, went tiptoe to the door, opened it, and stopped to listen. There was something absolutely thrilling about being a ghost. She loved the soft swish of her blue petticoat and the soft feel of the flowered muslin gown.

The skirt swung as she stepped over the threshold and felt her way to the foot of the stairs with the torch in her left hand. She had just touched the newel, when the first sound reached her and stopped her dead. It was the smallest sound that could be heard at all, so little audible that she could not have said that she heard anything; yet all at once she couldn't move and everything in her listened. She listened, and couldn't hear anything at all. There wasn't anything to hear— there hadn't ever been anything. She would count twenty, and then she would go on again. She began slowly, one—two—three—four— five—and just as she said five, someone opened the drawing-room door on the other side of the hall. She heard the handle turn and the latch click faintly, and she heard someone move. She hoped that the someone didn't hear her.

The full skirt swung again as she turned and ran for the library door. Even as she got there, she thought that she would be trapped if they came this way, because she didn't dare show a light, and she couldn't make sure of reaching the panel in the dark. She had got no farther than just inside the door, when a spark of light came dancing past, and as she pressed against the wall, a soft sound followed it.

The light went past the door and down the passage. Susan stood just within the door, pressed close against the wall, and saw it go. Her heart thumped, stood still, and thumped again. The light came from a little lantern held high in a man's hand. There were two men, and they went straight past the open door and pushed the baize door at the end of the passage and went through it. She saw the spot of light move for a moment on the rough baize, making a little green island in a sea of blackness. Then the door swung, the men went through. The door swung back, and the light was gone.

Susan was astonished at her own anger. How dared they? She could feel her cheeks burning with pure rage. She wasn't frightened; she was angry—angry and excited, and quite determined to find out what was happening on the other side of the swing door. She picked up her petticoats and crept down the passage.

The door moved easily. She pushed it an inch or two at a time. Someone was whispering, moving, whispering again. The sound died. She pushed the door quite wide and passed through into the passage beyond. There was a light on ahead. It came through the half open door of a room on the right. Voices came from it too. She came as near as she dared, and stood listening.

There were two voices, both sunk to a whisper. The light was the dim glow from the dark lantern which she had seen in the man's hand. One of the voices said,

"He won't. Why should he?"

The other whisper came—lower, more muffled. She caught only one word, "risk," and heard a smothered laugh.

"His—not ours. He'll get more than the torch this time."

The other voice said, "Ssh!" and then, "Well?"

There was a rustle of paper. Susan crouched down and looked round the edge of the door. She saw a room, very faintly lit. The lantern stood on a table, with the light spreading away from it into the right-hand corner of the room. There was a man with his back to her, and another man leaning forward across the table with a paper in his hand. He was holding the paper to the light. She could not see face or feature, just two black shapes without contour, like flat black shadows; only, when the paper came into the light, she could see the hand that held it—a long, slim hand.

"The second shield—"

She heard the words quite distinctly. The man who held the paper spoke then.

"Where is it?"

"The stone that Merlin blessed—"

"Go on."

"To keep in safety
    The source of evil."

He read, or seemed to read, from the paper in a soft toneless voice that just wasn't a whisper.

The man with his back to Susan broke in:

"You're translating?"

"Yes—it's Latin."

"And it doesn't say where?"

The hand that held the paper sketched a light gesture; the paper rustled. Susan's heart stood still. Her fingers pressed against the jamb, contracted, tried to close, bruised themselves.

The paper rustled. The man who held it said, still in that muffled voice, but with just a hint of laughter in it,

"Under the second shield."

It was as he finished saying it that Susan became aware of the strain on her hand. She had to make a conscious effort to relax. She missed the next words. She felt stiff, and cold, and numb, and she thought that if they came her way, they would find her kneeling here, because all power and will to move had gone out of her at that little familiar gesture. And then the man with his back to her moved. He put his hand on the lantern and began to slew it round; the light slipped in a vague smear over a space of dingy wall. It was coming nearer; in a moment it would strike on the doorpost and shine right into her wide, terrified eyes, and then she would scream—and then she didn't know what would happen. She could see it like a picture in her mind. It was just like being in two places at once; she was in the picture, and she was looking at it. The light was slipping round, and when it touched her she would scream.

Something quite different happened. The baize door behind her burst open and Anthony Colstone charged past her, barefoot in his pyjamas. He ran right into the room, shouting angrily, and the man who was facing the door picked up a chair and hurled it straight at his head. The man with his hand on the lantern dropped it and recoiled. The chair came hurtling across the table, and Anthony went down with a crash. His head struck the floor hard. It was all over in a minute. Susan didn't scream. She got up and stood in the doorway.

Anthony never moved. There was a whispering sound in the room, and the clank of fire-irons. The man who had thrown the chair was stooping by the fireplace. He got up and moved towards Anthony. The other man lifted the lantern. He said,

"What are you going to do?"

The light flickered on Anthony's bare feet. He had fallen sideways with one knee bent; Susan could see him sprawling all in a heap. The man who had held the paper came forward with the poker in his hand.

"I'm going to break his leg—it'll keep him quiet for a bit."

Susan said "No!" in a high, queer voice that wasn't in the least like her own. Her hands came together in front of her. She stood quite still, because it had taken every bit of her strength to say that one word. The lantern swung round, and the light shone right in her face. She didn't move or blink; she stood quite still. She had no idea how pale she was. She gazed at the light with fixed eyes.

The two men stared at the doorway. It framed for them the portrait which not half an hour before they had seen hanging on the library wall. Patience Pleydell stared back at them.

Susan heard one of them cry out—she thought afterwards that it was the one with the lamp. The poker dropped with a crash, the light swung away from her, and both men ran stumbling and bumping into one another for the half open door on the far side of the room. The lantern went swinging through it, and the door banged.

Susan came suddenly alive and tingling. She knew exactly what she was going to do, and she did it with surprising quickness and strength. She took Anthony Colstone under the arms and dragged him through the door into the passage, and along the passage to the baize door. The floor was smooth with the passing of the feet of many generations. She dragged him to the door and through it, and she felt up and down the baize until she found a bolt and drove it home. Then she dragged Anthony into the library and locked the library door. And then she sat down and took his head on her lap and began to tremble very much. Her teeth chattered and she felt cold, and she wanted to cry. She wondered if he were very badly hurt, and she wondered what on earth she was going to do. She ought to call Lane, but somehow she couldn't. Just for a minute she must sit still in the dark and get hold of herself.

Anthony Colstone opened his eyes and wondered where he was. His pillow felt queer, and the bed was very hard. His hand was lying palm downwards on something rough. He moved it a little, and he felt the thick pile of a carpet. He was lying on the floor. But his head wasn't on the floor. It felt stiff. It was supported by something soft, something that moved and shook a little. Odd.... He moved his hand again. Yes—carpet.... Odd—distinctly odd. And then all at once he remembered charging down the passage. He remembered that; but he couldn't remember what happened next. He had gone upstairs and waited, because he wasn't sure that the blighter he had tackled in the library had really got clear away. He might have gone out of the front door and banged it; but then again, he mightn't—it would be quite a good trick to bang the door and hide inside the house. He thought he would lie low and see what happened. And then a light happened, and voices—two of the blighters whispering. And he had charged down the passage, and they had laid him out—Yes, by gum, they had. If his head hadn't been the hardest part of him.... He moved it gingerly, and quite close to him in the dark someone said "Oh!"

Anthony became aware that he was lying with his head in somebody's lap. His other hand touched a soft flowing skirt. Somebody touched his head. Somebody said "Oh!"

Anthony said "Hullo!" and sat up.

Somebody said "Oh!" again, and there was a soft rustle of stuff.

He put out his hand to feel for the flowing skirt, but it had gone.

He said, "I say—" and then, "Where are you?"

The answer came from a little way off:

"You mean 'Where are *you*?' "

"That's what I said."

"*You* are in the library." This was a very faint whisper, and it was going away.

"The library? How did I get here?"

He scrambled up, and felt giddy for a moment. There was no answer.

Then, from the other side of the room, came a little shaky laugh. Somebody said, "Are—you—all right?"

He produced a beautiful groan.

"No, I'm very ill. I say, do come back!"

There was no answer.

He remembered the torch in his pocket, felt for it, switched it on.

The room was empty.

He found matches and lit the lamp. Miss Patience Pleydell gazed sweetly at him from the panel between the bookshelves. There was nobody in the room except himself and her. Somebody had gone. She had pillowed his head. She had trembled. She had laughed her shaky little laugh. And she had vanished into thin air.

And the door was locked on the inside.

Chapter Fifteen

ANTHONY PUT ALL THAT AWAY for a more convenient time. Then he went upstairs and roused Lane, who slept uncommon soundly, and Lane went across the road to rouse Smithers, who slept more soundly still. Then the three of them searched the house; Lane in an overcoat over his nightshirt; Smithers in shirt and trousers, and bristly hair standing straight on end above round drowsy eyes; and Anthony still in his pyjamas. They found no one.

In the room where Anthony had been floored they found the poker in the middle of the room, and a wooden chair upside down. The door on the other side of the room led into a passage out of which opened the kitchen, the butler's pantry, and a heavy door leading to the cellar steps.

"They wouldn't go down there, sir," Lane shivered and held on to the edges of his coat.

Anthony said, "We'll see," and turned the key. "We'll take the other rooms first."

The scullery had a half open window, and Mr. Smithers, who didn't hold with being fetched out of bed in the middle of the night, opined that the thieves had got out that way.

Anthony said "We'll see," again. He had been had once, and he didn't mean to be had again. The window gave upon a flagged yard, and the yard upon the vegetable garden. If Smithers was right, the men could have got away over the garden wall and up through the fields. A fruit tree trained against a wall makes quite a good ladder.

Anthony told Lane to shut and latch the window, and after drawing all the offices blank, returned to the locked cellar door. Opened, it disclosed steps running down into darkness. Lane held up the lamp he was carrying and repeated,

"They wouldn't go down there, sir."

Mr. Smithers didn't hold with cellars—nasty and damp they was, and 'adn't none too good a name—not at night they 'adn't.

"It isn't likely, sir, as hanybody'd go down into 'em as wasn't obliged."

Anthony was half way down the steps. There were about fifteen of them, and they led into a vaulted space out of which a number of cellars opened. Most of the doors were locked. A passage ran out of the far end, low in the roof and damp. It appeared to run back under the house.

Lane entered it with obvious reluctance, and when they reached a door he stopped.

"These old cellars aren't rightly safe, sir—and they're empty. Nobody'd come here, sir—and the door's locked."

"Who has the key?"

"I've got it, sir, along with the other cellar keys."

Anthony looked at the door. It was very old, very black, and heavily barred with iron. A man of his own height would have to stoop low if he didn't want to knock his head. He thought it looked like a dungeon door, and thought how beastly it would be to be locked in on the other side of it, and to hear the retreating footsteps of one's jailer. And then he wondered whether you would hear them. The door looked uncommonly thick. He shook it by the iron latch. It was locked all right. The keyhole was an immense affair—it must take a regular jailer's key to fit it. He pushed a finger into the hole, and heard Smithers' doleful drawl just behind him:

"Nobody wouldn't come down 'ere, sir—not when there ain't nothink to take. Now the dining-room and the droring-room, sir—that's what thieves goes for, sir."

There were no thieves in the drawing-room or the dining-room, or anywhere else. There was nothing missing. They went back to the cellar steps. It was very difficult to get any information out of Lane; he was worried and nervous, and he kept saying that the old cellars weren't safe, and—"Sir Jervis didn't use them, sir."

Anthony kept on asking questions.

"Are there a whole lot of cellars through there then?"

Lane couldn't rightly say how many cellars there were, and Smithers opined that they old cellars wasn't no good for nothing.

Anthony addressed Lane:

"But you've got the key, man?"

Lane didn't seem to be certain. He had all the cellar keys.

"Do you mean to say you've never opened that door?"

Lane looked very worried indeed. He couldn't rightly say when that there door had been opened; to which Smithers added that them old cellars wasn't none too safe.

Anthony could have sworn.

"Have you ever opened that door, or haven't you?"

This time he got an answer:

"Not that I can remember, sir."

"Then you don't really know what cellars there are beyond?"

"No, sir."

They came back along the passage and through the baize door.

"Is there such a thing as a plan of the house? I'd like to see one."

"I don't know, sir."

It would have given Anthony a good deal of pleasure to heave a chair at Lane. He stood there with the lamp in his hand, as mildly obstinate as an elderly sheep.

Anthony gave it up. He sent Smithers home and told Lane to lock up after him. He himself went into the library to put out the lamp he had left burning there. Under the light he looked attentively at his forefinger. It was the finger which he had pushed into the keyhole, and it was smeared with some thick, soft black stuff. He considered it intently. Then he put out the light.

Chapter Sixteen

Susan was up betimes next morning. She borrowed a bicycle from Mary Ann Smithers and went to look for a needle in a bundle of hay—Mr. Garry O'Connell being the needle, and the straggling town of Wrane the hay. She was so boiling with the desire to tell Garry what she thought of him that it wasn't until she actually reached Wrane that it occurred to her that she had probably come on a fool's errand.

Wrane is a junction. There is a local bicycle factory; it is a market town; and it has about twenty thousand inhabitants. If Garry O'Connell was temporarily one of the twenty thousand, it wasn't going to be very easy to disentangle him from the other nineteen thousand nine hundred and ninety-nine. Even the most boiling fury doesn't lead you straight to its object.

Susan rode slower and slower. It was market day. There were pink pigs in the street, cows and cars, sheep, and carts packed with vegetables and eggs. The sheep got under everybody's feet and smelt unutterably. The cows loitered along the footwalk. She began to wish she hadn't come. Why on earth hadn't she made Garry tell her where he was staying? And how on earth was she going to find him now? It went to her heart to waste the things she had got ready to say to him. Her temper flared again at the thought, and she went on threading her way through the live-stock until she got past the market. It occurred to her that the post office might have Garry's address.

Susan's temper continued to rise. The post office stood on its best official manners and quoted regulations to her—They couldn't possibly give her anybody's address—they could forward letters, but they couldn't give an address. In a village they would have given it to her directly. If Wrane had been a village, she would not only have got Garry's address, but also masses of the most helpful gossip about him; if he had received any telegrams, she would have had them repeated to her *verbatim*. Wrane was, unfortunately, no longer a village. The young ladies in the post office only gossiped with each other or with the young gentleman in charge of Old Age Pensions and Savings Bank deposits.

Susan bought a letter-card, addressed it to Garry O'Connell, Esq., and wrote inside:

"I must see you at once.

Susan."

She underlined "at once" three times, and the last underlining broke the post office pen. Then she got on her bicycle and rode back to Ford St. Mary.

It was a lovely day. The blue sky was full of small woolly clouds like clean fluffy lambs. Looking at them made Susan feel a little better. She liked animals, but she didn't like animals going to market. *Sheep* going to market were the limit. The fluffy cloud lambs were refreshingly clean and white. She gazed at them as she coasted down a hill with a fresh breeze blowing in her face. She stopped feeling sorry she had come; but only for a minute, because next moment the back tyre of Mary Ann Smithers' bicycle went off with a bang, and she had to walk the rest of the way.

Susan didn't mind walking, but she resented having to push a flat bicycle that ought to have been carrying her. By the time she reached the top of the hill which ran down to the village, she thought she had earned a rest. She dropped the bicycle on the grass and looked for a place to sit down. There was a wood on either side of the road. On the right a rather sketchy fence defended it. It had uprights here and there, and long rails between them.

Susan climbed up and sat on the topmost rail, which commanded a good view of the road. If she sat here, she couldn't possibly go to sleep; but if she sat down on the grass, she might just find that she was asleep without quite knowing how. She drew a long breath and swung her feet. She felt frightfully sleepy. All her boiling anger had died away. She had been up nearly all night, and she had just walked five miles.

The shadow of the trees was pleasant and green. A bright bar of sunshine lay across the road just where it began to run downhill. Someone was coming up the hill singing in a loud and cheerful voice:

"It was a farmer's daughter, so beautiful, I'm told.
Her parents died and left her five hundred pounds in gold.
She lived with her uncle, the cause of all her woe,
And you soon shall hear this maiden fair did prove his overthrow."

The voice was a not untuneful baritone. It was in fact the voice of Mr. Anthony Colstone. When, to use his own idiom, "up against it," it was his practice to burst into song. He came up the hill at a good pace, skipped some verses which he had forgotten, and sang on:

"A fig for all your squires, your lords and dukes likewise.
My William's hand appears to me like diamonds in my eyes.
Begone, unruly female, you ne'er shall happy be.
For I mean to banish William from the banks of the sweet Dundee."

Susan slipped unobtrusively down from her rail. If it hadn't been for the bicycle, she would have slipped down on the wood side; but with the bicycle lying there looking even more of a wreck than it really was, she abandoned the idea.

"The pressgang came for William when he was all alone.
He boldly fought for liberty, but they was six to one.
The blood did flow in torrents—"

Anthony Colstone stopped dead. He saw a girl picking up a bicycle, and he saw that the girl was Susan. She wore the blue dress and sunbonnet, but the front of the sun-bonnet was turned back so that it did not hide her face any more. She had turned it back as soon as she came into this shady place.

He stopped singing about William and the banks of the sweet Dundee and came towards her. Susan stopped picking up the bicycle and stood up in a hurry. She recognized him at the same moment that he recognized her, and for some extraordinary reason she wanted to run away. There was nowhere to run to. She stood where she was, and, to her extreme dismay, she began to blush.

Anthony stood still and looked at her, and the more he looked at her, the more she blushed. It was the most frightful let down. She couldn't move, and she couldn't look away, and before she knew what was going to happen, Anthony had kissed her. And then they both stepped back, and all the colour went out of Susan's face. She didn't know what she felt. It was so strange. She ought to have been furiously angry. Only a moment before she had been furiously angry with herself for blushing, but it was all gone. When Anthony kissed her, it was just as if they had known each other for a long, long time and had been parted and this was their meeting. It was quite natural, and rather solemn.

She looked at Anthony, and saw that he was pale and serious. He didn't look in the least like a young man who has just snatched a kiss from a village girl. She wondered what he was thinking about, and she said,

"Why did you do it?" Her voice wasn't angry or accusing; it was as serious as Anthony's face.

He said, "I don't know," and his voice was like hers.

He didn't know; he didn't know in the least. It had seemed as natural as breathing. He was rather bewildered.

Susan reminded herself of several things that she ought to be feeling. None of them seemed to mean anything at all. She turned a little paler, and said quite slowly,

"Were you going to beg my pardon?"

"No—" said Anthony thoughtfully. "No—I wasn't—but I will if you want me to."

Susan became suddenly aware that they were under some strange compulsion to speak the actual truth to one another—people very seldom did. She and Anthony Colstone had come by chance into a place where they couldn't help doing it. It was like being enchanted. She said,

"I don't want you to."

Just for a moment she had a stab of fear. If he didn't understand; if he tried to kiss her again... But he only frowned a little and said,

"You didn't mind—did you?"

Susan said, "No."

He bent and picked up the bicycle. A little of the strangeness faded away. Susan put a hand on the saddle. They were quite close together, with the bicycle between them. And then Anthony said quite suddenly,

"Susan—who are you?"

"Mrs. Bowyer's great-granddaughter."

"Really and truly?"

"Really and truly."

"Why did you pretend?"

"Pretend?"

"You know perfectly well what I mean. Why did you pretend to be uneducated?"

A faint sparkle came into her eyes.

"I can read, and write, and add. But I can't do long division or fractions—please, sir."

"Why do you call me sir?" His voice continued to be steady and grave.

Susan's chin went up ever so little. The enchantment was wearing off.

"Because it's the proper thing for Mrs. Bowyer's granddaughter to do. Mary Ann Smithers would do it."

"I don't like it."

The sparkle became more pronounced.

"Nobody axed you, sir!" she said.

He had the bicycle by the handle with his left hand. He put his right on Susan's.

"Susan—"

"Sir?"

"You're not to call me sir."

"What am I to call you?" It might have been said in a variety of ways—innocent, mock-innocent, or coquettish. Susan made it a direct and serious question.

"Anthony," said Anthony Colstone.

Susan stopped being serious.

"That would add immensely to the gaiety of Ford St. Mary!"

"Would it?"

"Of course it would. Mrs. Smithers wouldn't be able to get round fast enough really to do it justice. I think she's the best gossip in the place. But she's so fat that it's a frightful handicap, and sometimes other people get in first with a bit of news—Mrs. Smithers feels it horribly, and the whole Smithers family is plunged in gloom. But of course I might give her exclusive rights. I could go in on my way home—it's her ironing day—and say 'Mr. Colstone has asked me to call him Anthony.' She'd be *thrilled*, and in about an hour I shouldn't have a single shred of character left. I should think it would take her about an hour to tell everybody—but perhaps two hours would be safer, because she'll want to linger over the horrid details and have plenty of time to rub it in that she always thought there was something out of place about the way I went on."

Anthony kept his hand on hers. It was a very nice hand to touch. He looked at her with a grin.

"You talk very good nonsense for a village girl."

Susan laughed, really laughed, with a bubbling mirth that seemed to rise up from some new spring of gaiety. It was a frightfully nice morning, and the wood was green and the sky was blue, and Anthony's hand on hers was the hand of a friend. She laughed, and she said, "Thank you kindly—Anthony!" And she bobbed him a little curtsey.

The most extraordinary thing happened to Anthony. When she bobbed to him like that with her eyes full of wickedness and her mouth suddenly soft and demure, he wanted to kiss her. That wasn't the extraordinary thing; it was the merely obvious thing. The extraordinary thing was that he knew, with a sort of cast-iron certainty, that he couldn't kiss Susan lightly. He had kissed her once without thinking at all, but if he were to kiss her again, he would be kissing his wife. He flushed deeply, and he took his hand away.

There was a breathless pause.

Anthony's mind was quite full of the thing that had happened to him. He said "Susan—" in a shaken voice; and Susan caught her breath and said "Oh!" And then she tried to laugh.

Anthony was looking at her intently.

"You said 'Oh!' "

"Mayn't I?"

"What were you doing last night?" he asked abruptly.

"Why?"

"When you said 'Oh!' like that—"

"Yes?"

"Well I thought I'd heard you say it before."

"It's quite an ordinary thing to say, really."

Anthony felt he had held the bicycle long enough. He let it down on to the grass.

"I want to talk to you," he said.

"We have been talking."

"Not really."

Susan wasn't sure whether she wanted to talk to him or not. One bit of her did, and another bit stood on guard and was rather afraid. If she talked to him, what was she going to say, and how much was she going to say? She looked at the bicycle.

"I ought to go back. I borrowed that wretched thing from Mary Ann Smithers, and it's punctured."

"We might go into the wood," said Anthony.

"And supposing someone comes along and walks off with that wretched broken reed?"

"They won't. Nobody would have it as a gift."

Chapter Seventeen

THEY WENT INTO the wood. Susan couldn't remember when she had felt so undecided in all her life. She couldn't make up her mind what she was going to say. This ought to have worried her. But she didn't feel worried; she felt quite irresponsible, and vague, and pleased with its being such a nice day.

When they had gone a little way into the wood, she stood still.

"What do you want to say to me?"

Anthony wanted to say a good many things, but he thought he had better not say them. One of the consequences of what had happened to him was that it seemed perfectly natural to say anything that came into his head. He wanted to tell Susan that she was going to marry him, but he supposed he had better wait and break it to her by degrees. It wasn't that he felt shy. He could have said it quite easily; in fact he was finding it very difficult not to say it, but he took a good pull on himself.

There was a fallen tree quite close to them. He decided that they had better sit down and talk comfortably. It was quite a nice dry tree, with curly green lichen growing on the bark and ferns poking out from underneath it. He thought it would make a very good seat.

"We'll sit down here and talk."

"What do you want to talk about?" said Susan.

She sat down, folded her hands in her lap, and looked at him expectantly. Anthony sat down too. There was about a yard between them.

"Do you think you could be friends with me?"

Susan nodded.

"I expect so."

"I want to talk to you, but I don't want to talk to you unless we're friends—I mean real friends."

Susan nodded again.

"Go on."

"I asked you where you were last night, because a lot of odd things happened, and I wondered whether you were one of them."

She opened her eyes very wide indeed.

"One of the odd things? What were they?" She thought it would be quite interesting to hear Anthony's version of what had happened last night.

Anthony kept his eyes fixed on her face.

"I woke up in the middle of the night and came down, and as soon as I got into the library I had a sort of feeling that there was someone there."

"How exciting! And was there?"

"Yes, there was—in fact there were several people."

"Quite a house-warming!"

"Er—yes—an awfully jolly one. One of the people gave a sort of frightened squeak—awfully like a rabbit it sounded. And another waltzed in at the door with an electric torch and shone it on to that picture that I told you was like you. I think he had a friend with him, but I'm not sure. Anyhow, when the light shone on the picture it moved."

"The light moved?"

Anthony frowned. She was showing a good deal of duplicity if— On the other hand he wasn't quite sure. He meant to be sure. He said, rather severely,

"No—the picture."

"How could it?" said Susan simply.

"It did—it moved its arm." He paused, and added, "It's awfully like you."

"I do move my arm sometimes," said Susan.

"Yes—I thought you moved it last night. The light flashing on like that must have been a bit of a shock."

"It sounds like an optical delusion," said Susan firmly. "What happened next?"

"I went for the blighter with the torch, and he biffed me on the head with it, and tripped me up and got away, and banged the front door."

"And then?"

"Well, I rather wanted to ask you about that. Was the handkerchief yours?"

Susan looked at him. His face was quite innocent and grave. She felt justly annoyed at having a leaf taken out of her own book.

"The handkerchief?" she said.

"Yes. Did you drop it?"

"What handkerchief?"

"The one that was in the corner of the room behind the chair—I expect you saw me come back and pick it up."

"I suppose you know what you're talking about."

"I suppose so. Don't you?"

Susan raised her eyebrows.

"Perhaps it'll get easier as you go on. *Do* go on!"

"About the handkerchief? But you know all that part. I picked it up and then went to lock up, and when I came back it was gone—so I expect it was yours, because of course you wouldn't steal somebody else's handkerchief."

"I hope it *is* going to get easier," said Susan. "I should like it to, because it sounds as if it might be quite exciting if I only knew what it was all about. *Do* go on."

"Well, I went upstairs, and when I got upstairs I began to wonder whether the front door had been banged to put me off the scent, so I thought I'd lurk for a bit and see—"

"Yes?"

"Well, I lurked, and nothing happened for a bit. And then the library door opened and someone began to come out."

"The man with the torch?"

"N-no," said Anthony. "I think it was a ghost—a family ghost, with a swishing skirt."

"Oh—" It wasn't really a word.

"I expect it was Miss Patience Pleydell's ghost. She began to come out, and she went back again because the burglars, or whatever they were, opened the drawing-room door. I *was* a mug not to search the house."

"Yes, you were—I mean you must have been."

"I was."

"What—what happened next?"

"Don't you know? They went through the baize door, and the family ghost went after them, and I began to come down the stairs as quietly as I could, because I wanted to catch them at whatever they were up to. By the way, what *were* they up to?"

"Didn't you find out?"

" 'M—" said Anthony.

"What does that mean?"

"Oh, any old thing."

There was a pause. Susan said nothing. Anthony said nothing. Susan looked at Anthony, and Anthony looked at Susan. The sun shone, and the breeze moved pleasantly overhead amongst green leaves and little rustling twigs.

Susan looked at Anthony. His face was perfectly grave, but there was just the suspicion of an obstinate twinkle in his eye. She wanted to laugh.

Quite suddenly he grinned and said, "Well?"

"Oh, I do wish you'd go on! Tell me what happened."

"I followed the family ghost—that is to say I followed it as far as the baize door, and then I looked through the chink."

"It was dark," said Susan accusingly. A beautiful bright carnation ran up into her cheeks, and she added hastily, "You said it was dark."

Anthony laughed.

"My mistake! Of course it was dark—only I didn't *say* so. I looked through the chink and saw how dark it was. And then it wasn't quite so dark, because there was a lantern or something in the room on the right, and the door was open and I could just see the family ghost crouching down by the open door. I thought it was a pretty odd thing for a ghost to do. Don't you?"

" 'M—" said Susan. Her eyes were wicked. "I never heard anyone tell a story worse." She put a resigned sound into her voice.

"I'm sorry. There isn't much more to tell. I thought I had better take a hand, so I barged through the door and along the bit of passage and into the room." He stopped.

"Why don't you go on?" said Susan brightly.

"There isn't any more."

"There must be. What happened?"

"I don't know. Someone must have slogged me over the head—I don't remember, but that's what my head felt like when I came to."

"Oh, you did come to?"

Anthony laughed again.

"This *is* a bit like a dream—isn't it? I've thought that once or twice. I've had worse ones. Haven't you?"

"I don't know. Tell me about your coming to."

"It was very romantic," said Anthony. "I was lying on the floor in the dark with my head in the family ghost's lap. She was looking awfully worried."

Susan pressed her lips firmly together. Her eyes said "Liar!" They said it with a good deal of heat.

"Sorry—of course it was dark—you're quite right. I only guessed she was worried by the way she said 'Oh!' And then all of a sudden she vanished into thin air—I expect it was a cock-crow or something of that sort. And when I found the matches and got a light, I was in the library, with the door locked on the inside. And now it's your turn."

Susan gazed at him. There was still a good deal of fire in her eyes.

"What did you say?"

"I said it was your turn. How did I get into the library—and who locked the door?"

"That, I suppose," said Susan, "is what you call a rhetorical question."

"Mary Ann Smithers wouldn't know what a rhetorical question was—so that one counts to me."

"I'm not bothering about Mary Ann Smithers any more," said Susan calmly. Then she frowned a little. Was she going to tell him anything, or wasn't she? And how much could she tell him? She wasn't sure. She jumped up. "That reminds me, I must take her bicycle back and have it mended. She wants it this afternoon."

Anthony got up too.

"You haven't answered my questions."

"No."

"Are you going to?"

"I don't know." Her colour had deepened. She spoke seriously.

Anthony did not speak for a minute. Then he said, in a different voice,

"I don't want you to tell me anything you don't want to."

They came back on to the road and walked in silence until they came to the place where the trees ended and the empty road ran sharply down the hill. Then Susan said,

"Good-bye—I'll take the bicycle now."

"Where am I to go?" inquired Anthony. He held the bicycle by the handle and spoke with deceptive meekness.

"You can finish your walk—and the song about William—you stopped in the middle of his being murdered."

"Not murdered, only carried off by the press gang. Would you like to hear the rest of it?"

"No," said Susan. Then she said "Good-bye" again.

Anthony's manner changed.

"Susan—when am I going to see you again?"

"I don't know."

"I must see you."

"You can always come and call on Gran."

"And have you make that beastly bob, and call me sir, and never take your eyes off your sewing."

"I was brought up to order myself lowly and reverently to my betters—*sir*," said Susan. She put her head a little on one side and looked impudently at him. "Gran loves visitors," she said.

"I might *want* to see you—" he began.

"Gran would say, 'Then want must be your master.' "

"Is that what you say?"

Susan changed again. She said "Anthony," bit her lip, and stopped.

"Susan—"

She flushed, and twisted the bicycle out of his hand with a jerk.

"Susan—I must be able to see you."

She was walking away from him. Just as she came out into the full sunshine, she looked back over her shoulder.

"The family ghost might walk," she said.

Chapter Eighteen

"WHERE HA' YOU BEEN?" said old Mrs. Bowyer. The sun had just gone off the geraniums in her window, and she was watering them out of an old lustre jug.

Susan shut the door and kissed the tips of her fingers to her.

"Don't you ask no questions, and you won't get told no lies, Gran."

"Ho!" said Mrs. Bowyer. She poured the last drop out of the coppery jug with the bright blue band on it; then she turned and fixed her bright black eyes on Susan. "Ho! So that's the way of it? And who is he, my maid?"

"You weren't to ask questions."

"H'm!" said Mrs. Bowyer. She went into the kitchen and hung the jug on its own particular hook on the dresser. Then she came back.

Susan was looking out of the window. She spoke without turning round:

"Why did you think I'd been meeting someone, Gran?"

"By the look in your face," said old Susan Bowyer. She sat down in her rocking-chair. "I been young myself, though 'twas so long ago."

Susan turned round.

"Were you married very young? You were cousins, weren't you? I suppose you'd known him always?"

"No, I hadn't. I hadn't set eyes on him since I was a matter of five years old. You see, 'twas this way. His father and my father was brothers—William and Thomas. My father kept the gardens at Stonegate—a proper gardener my father was. And Thomas, he went off to Fletchley—a matter of thirty miles away, because it stands to reason he couldn't be head gardener at Stonegate, not with my father there, and he wouldn't bend his pride to be second. So he went to Sir John Tuffnell that had a place at Fletchley. And William was brought up at Fletchley and went into the garden under his father. And when I was a matter of seventeen years old, my father broke his leg, and Mr. James Colstone, that was Sir Jervis' father, he said 'You take and send for that nephew of yours—I hear he's a likely lad, and he can do as you tell him and keep things going till you're about again.' So Father he sent for

William, and William he came along—and that was the first I saw of him that I could remember."

"And you fell in love with him at once?"

Mrs. Bowyer tossed her head.

"I never thought nothing about him, though there was others that did. That Cis Dickson fair stared her eyes out of her head at him. I never fancied Dicksons afore nor since, and never thought as any son of mine would ha' looked twice at one, and what Thomas ever saw in the girl is more than I can tell you. But *there*, he never had much sense, Thomas hadn't. Some has sense, and some has looks—and Thomas hadn't neither, and he took up with Cis Dickson's youngest when he was old enough to know better, and I don't never feel that their childern's my flesh and blood. There's only one of them left now."

"Gran!"

"I don't—never did, and never shall."

"But Cis Dickson didn't get William."

"It wasn't for want of trying though. A bold-faced hussy and a runabout, that's what she was."

"But he married you."

"I married him," said Mrs. Bowyer—"after he'd asked me eleven times, without counting the time parson come right into the middle of, nor the time I wouldn't listen to him because I wouldn't demean myself after I seen him talking to Cis."

"How harsh of you!"

"Harsh or no, I got him—and I kep' him," said old Mrs. Bowyer, with a triumphant nod.

Susan turned away and touched a pink geranium petal, stroking it half absently with the tip of her finger.

"You lived a long time together."

Mrs. Bowyer looked back over her hundred years.

"Not so long—fifty years—it's not so long. William died young, my dear."

"But you were happy—" Susan did not look at Mrs. Bowyer, but Mrs. Bowyer looked at her.

"Middling, my dear, middling," she said. The old voice was very sweet.

Susan began to speak, stopped, and began again:

"What makes people happy, Gran? When they're married, I mean."

"Theirselves—just their own selves. There's a lot of foolish talk about making folks happy. They got to make themselves happy—nobody can't do it for them. Nobody can't eat your dinner for you—you've got to eat it yourself. Only you mind this, Susan—don't you go marrying a lad because he's good company, or because there's other girls wants him, or because he's saved a bit. You take the lad that's got a kindness for you—for there's a deal of kindness wanted when you're married."

In at one side of Susan's mind and out of the other there slipped a vivid impression of Anthony Colstone's voice changing when he said, "I don't want you to tell me anything you don't want to." She moved away from the window with a little laugh.

"When anyone has asked me eleven times, I'll bring him along for you to vet!"

She stopped suddenly by the table. A large bible reposed in the midst of it, flanked by a jar of roses and a pot of purple stocks. In front of the bible lay a small crumpled handkerchief. Susan picked it up and turned it this way and that. She felt startled. She had picked up a handkerchief last night; she had left it folded neatly in the top right-hand drawer of the chest of drawers in her bedroom. And here it was, on the table in front of the bible, all crumpled up—plain fine linen with three wavy lines round the edge.

Susan stepped back and held it up.

"Where did this come from, Gran?"

"Miss Arabel dropped it."

Susan turned it over, looking down at it, not looking at Mrs. Bowyer at all.

"When did she drop it?"

"She's been in this morning. She often comes, Miss Arabel does, when there's ought going on." Mrs. Bowyer laughed. "Never knew her equal for seeing into things."

"And she left her handkerchief?"

"Never knew her go away without leaving something. If 'tisn't her handkerchief, 'tis her bag, or maybe 'tis a letter she was meaning to post, and then by-and-by she'll come in all of a fluster and—'Oh, Susan, now did I leave—now I wonder whether—did you notice—I'm afraid I must have left my handkerchief!' 'Tis mostly her handkerchief. She'll be in along of that by-and-by, you'll see."

Susan folded up the handkerchief slowly.

"What do you mean by 'seeing into things?' "

"Why, my dear, just wanting to know the why and the wherefore of everything 'at's going on. There's times when I could have took up my best pot of geraniums and thrown it at her."

"How violent!"

"That sort makes you feel violent." Mrs. Bowyer nodded. "She'll ask questions quicker'n I can shell peas, and I've looked at one of they pots many a time and thought I wouldn't grudge it, not if it was the best plant I'd got."

Susan put the handkerchief back in front of the bible. She laughed a little.

"You'll finish up in prison, Gran! What's Miss Arabel been asking questions about?"

"All sorts," said Mrs. Bowyer in a mysterious voice.

Anthony was just going out after lunch, when he met his Cousin Arabel. She emerged from the gate of the Ladies' House, fluttered across to him, and looked up appealingly.

"I was just coming over to ask—you don't mind, I know—but I needn't keep you—I see you are going out—I can just ask Lane—that is, of course, if you do not object."

He wondered what on earth this was all about. She had quite a bright pink colour in her cheeks. Under the shady black hat her eyes were bright and blue. A little fluff of silver hair stood out becomingly.

"Did you want to see me, Cousin Arabel?"

"Oh, but I needn't trouble you—I couldn't dream of troubling you— if you didn't mind my asking Lane to let me go into the library and see if I dropped a handkerchief there—"

Anthony's attention was arrested. He had picked up a handkerchief in the library last night. Was it Miss Arabel who had cried out in the dark behind the door? How could it have been Miss Arabel?

He said "A handkerchief?" because he simply had to say something.

"Yes," said Miss Arabel eagerly—"in the afternoon! I called to ask Mrs. Hutchins for her recipe for marrow jam—not, of course, that it's time to make it yet, but I happened to think of it—and I also wanted to know whether she had heard from her cousin's daughter, Mary Louisa Berry, who has gone away to service in Salisbury, and I'm afraid she hasn't been writing home as regularly as she might, so we asked Mrs. Hutchins, who has been quite like an aunt to her, though only a cousin really—a second cousin once removed—we asked her to write and point out how *wrong* it was to cause her poor mother so much anxiety—a widow too, and a most respectable and worthy woman, but not very quick with her pen—but then, of course, education is so much better now than it used to be—isn't it?"

"I expect so," said Anthony. He felt a little bewildered.

"And I hope you don't think it was a liberty?"

"How could it be?"

"My coming in to see Mrs. Hutchins when you were out."

"Oh, *please*, Cousin Arabel." There was a genuine embarrassment in his voice.

Miss Arabel fluttered a little.

"Agatha said we ought to be most particular about not running in and out. She said we ought to make it a *rule*."

"I hope you will always come when you want to," said Anthony.

If she had dropped the handkerchief in the afternoon, she couldn't have dropped it in the middle of the night. But he couldn't help wondering why her inquiries about marrow jam and Mary Louisa Berry should have taken her into the library.

Miss Arabel must have had the same thought, for she was already explaining:

"And whilst I was there, I just popped into the library to put back a book which I had inadvertently taken away with me when we moved—I can't think how I came to be so careless. It was—it was the second volume of *The Newcomes*. Thackeray is always so very delightful, don't you think?—and improving too—only I find it takes me rather a long time to read one of his books right through. I hope you *don't* think I took a liberty."

Anthony escorted her back to the library and assisted her to look for the vanished handkerchief.

She explained that she was sure she must have dropped it when she was putting the book back, because she remembered having it in her hand then—"So I'm sure I didn't drop it in the housekeeper's room, where I was talking to Mrs. Hutchins—no, I'm quite sure about that—but it doesn't seem to *be* here—does it? And I mustn't take up any more of your time, I know."

Anthony was polite. He thought afterwards that he had been too polite, because she stayed for at least another twenty minutes. She wanted to know whether he had not enjoyed his friend's visit very much, and whether he did not find the house very lonely now he was all by himself. "But of course you will be filling the house with young people." She put her head on one side and looked at him questioningly.

"Most of my friends are in India."

"But you will make others—people in the neighbourhood will call. I suppose, now, some of them have called already."

"Yes," said Anthony.

"The Pollens—or the Thane-Bromleys—have they called?"

"Mr. Thane-Bromley has."

"He is very much respected," said Miss Arabel. "I suppose Lord Haverton hasn't called?"

"He has asked me to go over to lunch there next week."

Miss Arabel fluttered.

"Oh dear—and I suppose you will go. He had such a—such a regrettable quarrel with dear Papa—but of course he is a very charming man. You haven't met him?"

"He knew my uncle."

"Ah—your uncle. The one who brought you up?"

"Yes."

"How strange! Such a different neighbourhood. It seems very odd. Did they meet abroad? I believe Lord Haverton has been abroad."

"They were college friends."

By the time Miss Arabel had informed herself as to his Uncle James' school and college, together with his age, his tastes, his family connections, and other details, Anthony had begun to wonder whether life was long enough to see very much of his Cousin Arabel. When she had finished with Uncle James, she began about India. Her departure left him rather depleted. Not since he had struggled through his last promotion exam had he had so much information extracted from him.

Chapter Nineteen

A TELEGRAPH BOY bicycled out from Wrane next day and rapped on Mrs. Bowyer's door. Mrs. Smithers, looking out of her window, began to speculate pleasantly as to whose decease he had come to announce.

"There's Jenny—or it might be 'er mother—or one of the 'Merican lot, though that's a norful long way to send a telegram. Someone's gone for certain sure. Always puts me 'eart in me mouth, telegrams do."

Susan took the telegram with calm, but her colour rose as she read it. It was handed in at Vere Street, and it was an answer to the urgent scrawl which she had posted to Garry O'Connell in Wrane the day before. It said: "Should adore to see you not only at once but continuously stop for the moment distance forbids stop business in metropolis stop K stop H stop O stop Garry."

"And please, miss, there's two shillings to pay," said the round-faced telegraph boy.

Susan ran up stairs for the money. Two shillings for this characteristic bit of impudence!

"Any answer, miss?"

She would have loved to send an answer, but it would probably annoy Garry more if she didn't. She said "No," and shut the door. Then she read the telegram again, and boiled with rage. The cryptic letters at the end were particularly infuriating. They stood for "Keep hair on," and she was not in the least mollified by the fact that Garry had condescended to camouflage this impertinence. She tore the telegram into little bits and put it in the kitchen fire.

As she dropped the last bit in, there were three slow taps on the door. Mrs. Smithers stood there, her sleeves hastily pulled down, and an expression of decent gloom on her large white face. Her hair was still in curling pins, which were only partially hidden by an old tweed cap belonging to Mr. Smithers.

"Ah—" she said. It was a voluminous sigh. "And 'ow's she a-taking it, pore soul?"

Susan looked blank.

"How is who taking what, Mrs. Smithers?"

"I see the telegraft boy," said Mrs. Smithers reproachfully. "I see 'im out of the window, and I says to myself, 'Oh, my good gracious me!' I says, 'That's Jane gone for certain sure.' "

Susan lifted her eyebrows. She wasn't terribly fond of Mrs. Smithers. "Who's Jane?" she said.

"Ah—" It was a deeper sigh than before. "Seems so strange me 'aving to tell you about your own relations—and not a thing I should like in me own family—not 'ardly right, it don't seem to me, to 'ave to ask a stranger, 'owever near a neighbour—and Smithers and me we've lived next door to your Granny for twenty-five years, and old Mr. and Mrs. Smithers another forty years afore that. But that's neither 'ere nor there, and it don't seem 'ardly right for you to 'ave to ask, 'Who's Jane?' and for me to 'ave to tell you that she's your Granny's daughter-in-law, 'er son Thomas's widow—Jane Dickson she was afore 'e married 'er, and 'er girl's the very spit and image of 'er, pore thing. And many's the time old Mrs. Smithers 'ave told me 'ow your Granny took on when Thomas married 'er—such a 'andsome man as 'e was, same as all the Bowyers, present company always excepted, and no offence meant I'm sure." Here Mrs. Smithers paused and drew breath.

Susan seized her opportunity.

"It's not Jane," she said.

"Ah!" said Mrs. Smithers with increased interest. "Now who'd 'a thought that Jenny'd go before 'er pore mother?"

Susan wanted to laugh.

"It's not Jane, and it's not Jenny, and it's not anyone. Can't one get a telegram without someone being dead?"

"Not in Ford St. Mary you don't," said Mrs. Smithers. She looked disappointed.

"It was a business telegram," said Susan firmly. Then she went out into the garden and told old Mrs. Bowyer that she would like to go and live on a desert island where people didn't look out of their windows and ask questions every time you breathed.

Mrs. Bowyer was sitting on a wooden bench in the shade of two tall lilacs. The bee-hives stood all along the opposite fence. She sat in the warm shade and watched the bees go busily to and fro.

"Folks is all the same wherever you go," she said placidly.

Susan sat down on the bench too.

"If they were all the same as Mrs. Smithers, I really would go and live on a desert island!"

Mrs. Bowyer laughed noiselessly.

"You wouldn't think to look at her now as she was that thin that her mother went a-whimpering around saying as her Minnie didn't eat enough to keep a sparrow and she was a feared she would lose her in a decline. A poor silly creature she was—one of those as is always telling you something they're afeard of, so as you can contradict 'em."

A peaceful silence settled down upon Susan. It seemed to fall softly from the green of the lilacs. It was very pleasant. She began to wonder why Garry had gone to London—and *when*—and what was keeping him there. And she wondered what she was going to do next. She felt an inward certainty that it mattered very much what she did, and she could not for the life of her make up her mind what to do. She thought about Garry, and she thought about Anthony, and she thought about the handkerchief which lay neatly folded in her drawer upstairs, and she thought about the queer words she had listened to when she crouched at the door of the housekeeper's room in the dark. They said themselves over in her mind, the faint murmur of the bees coming and going amongst them:

"The second shield,
The stone that Merlin blessed,
To keep in safety
The source of evil."

She turned impulsively to Mrs. Bowyer.

"Gran—are there any shields at Stonegate?"

"Shields, my dear?"

Mrs. Bowyer had, perhaps, been just a little drowsy. The air was warm and soft, the bees came and went, the shade was green.

"Yes. I heard someone say a sort of rhyme—no, it wasn't a rhyme—anyhow it said, 'The second shield.' "

Mrs. Bowyer watched the bees, pale honey-coloured bees with the sun on them.

"And why did you think that had to do with Stonegate?"

"I just thought it had. There's more of it—'The stone that Merlin blessed—'"

Mrs. Bowyer woke up.

"And where did you get that?" she said in a sharp, startled voice.

"What does it mean, Gran?"

"Where did you hear tell of it?"

"I can't tell you. I want to know what it means. What is the stone that Merlin blessed? Gran, tell me!"

"What should I tell you for?"

Susan chose her words carefully.

"I think I ought to know, Gran."

"You've a reason for that?"

"Yes."

"And you can't tell me?"

"No, Gran."

"And you want me to tell you? You've a proper bold face on you, Susan, I'll say that."

Susan laughed and blew her a kiss.

"I expect I got it from you!"

"You're a wicked maid, Susan. Tell me true—that piece you said—was it from your father you got it?"

"No, Gran, it wasn't."

There was a pause. The black eyes looked searchingly into the blue ones. Then old Susan Bowyer spoke:

"You're my own flesh and blood—but I've a duty to the Colstones—and I promised Jervis—" Her voice died away.

Susan leaned forward and touched her on the knee.

"Gran, I shouldn't ever do anything—to hurt the Colstones."

"You might, and you mightn't," said Mrs. Bowyer. " 'Tisn't always what we want to do, and 'tisn't always what we think we're doing—it just comes; but when you've spoke a word, there isn't nothing and there isn't nobody can take it back again."

Susan stayed still for a moment, so still that one of the honey-coloured bees dropped down on Mrs. Bowyer's knee and clambered on to the forefinger of Susan's hand. It crawled with sprawling eagerness, helping itself with a fanning of transparent wings. She took her hand back slowly, watching the bee, whilst Mrs. Bowyer watched her. She saw Susan touch the bee very gently with a soft finger-tip, stroking the pale fur on its back. It stayed quite still, the wings just quivering. When she lifted her finger it flew away.

"You've a way with them," said Mrs. Bowyer. Then she laughed. "I'd a deal sooner take a person's character from the bees than from a parson. Whether it's man or maid, bees know what's in 'em, and if 'tisn't sound and sweet, they can't abide 'em, nor mischief-makers, nor quarrel-pickers, nor scolds, nor termerjans—they can't abide none of 'em. Bees won't thrive, 'cept where folks is peaceable. If there isn't love and good-will, they won't thrive—not for anything you can do—'tis honey to 'em, and marrow to their bones, same as 'tis to childern."

Susan put her elbow on her knee, propped her chin in her hand, and looked down into the grass.

"Gran, if I tell you something, will you let me just tell it, and not ask any questions at all—because I can't tell you more than a bit of it."

She did not see the sharp flash of intelligence in Mrs. Bowyer's eyes or the little nod which said, "I thought as much." She was even too much taken up with her own thoughts to observe the dryness of Mrs. Bowyer's voice as she said,

"Say what you like, my dear."

Susan frowned at the grass.

"It's rather difficult to begin. I think I'd better tell you where I heard that bit about the stone that Merlin blessed—but I'm afraid you'll be rather shocked."

"I'm not very easy shocked."

"Well, I went through the passage into Stonegate the night before last and—" She looked sideways, and then quickly down again. She wasn't sure, but she thought Gran was laughing to herself. She felt a little ruffled. Gran ought to have been shocked; she had no business to be amused.

And then all of a sudden she thought how funny it was, and a little bubble of laughter caught in her throat. She went on quickly:

"It was the middle of the night, and there were burglars there."

Mrs. Bowyer's hand fell on her shoulder.

"Sakes alive! What are you talking about?"

This was easier to cope with. Susan felt better.

"Burglars, Gran. That's to say, I suppose people are burglars when they break into a house in the middle of the night and throw chairs at the person it belongs to."

"Chairs?" said Mrs. Bowyer in a loud, vigorous voice.

"Well, it was only one really, but it knocked him flat—'and the subsequent proceedings inter*est*ed him no more.'"

"I don't know what you're talking about."

Susan swung round and took Mrs. Bowyer's hand in both of hers.

"Midnight Meanderings, or The Indiscretions of Susan—a thriller of the first water."

"Burglars?" said Mrs. Bowyer.

"Listen, Gran. It was awfully exciting, and I can't tell you the whole of it, but I'll tell you the bits that I can tell you. I went through the passage, and I was just coming out of the library, when two men with a dark lantern came oozing through the drawing-room door. I was petrified, but I crawled out of sight, and when they went down the passage to the baize door, I went after them."

"Eh?" said Mrs. Bowyer.

"As silently as a *worm*," said Susan. "They were in the housekeeper's room—at least that's what I suppose it was—first on the right through the door. And one of them was reading out that piece I said to you. And Anthony Colstone came along, and they threw a chair at him and knocked him out."

"Lord preserve us!" said Mrs. Bowyer. "What next?"

"They ran away."

"And well they might!"

Susan dimpled.

"It wasn't because well they might—it was because of me appearing suddenly like a ghost in Patience Pleydell's clothes and saying 'No' in a sort of hollow groan when they were going to bash Anthony with the poker."

Mrs. Bowyer pulled her hand away sharply.

"Is this a true tale?"

Susan nodded.

"It's not the whole truth, but it's nothing but the truth."

"The impudent murdering villains! Was the lad hurt?"

"All Colstones' heads are as hard as the Coldstone—you've often told me that yourself."

"No thanks to them," said Mrs. Bowyer. "You're a hard-hearted maid, Susan—but if 'twas day before yesterday, I've seen him since, and he wasn't none the worse." She paused, frowning. "Say that piece to me again."

Susan said it over:

"'The second shield,

The stone that Merlin blessed—'"

She hesitated for a moment, and then went on:

"'To keep in safety

The source of evil.' "

"That's all—and I want to know what it means."

"Ssh!" said Mrs. Bowyer quickly. "'Tisn't a thing to name in an open place where the Lord knows who may be listening. I had ought to have stopped you before. Look over the fence, my dear, both sides, and see that there's no one a-listening."

When Susan came back, Mrs. Bowyer had risen.

"We'd best go where there are doors to shut."

"There's no one in either of the gardens, Gran."

"I'd sooner be in my own kitchen," said Mrs. Bowyer firmly.

Chapter Twenty

THE KITCHEN SEEMED dark and cool. On the tall dresser Mrs. Bowyer's old copper pans gleamed like the sun in a fog; the shadow was dark there, but the copper shone through it. Mrs. Bowyer sat herself down in a heavy oak chair by the hearth.

"Shut the door, and shut the window," she said—"and come you here to me."

Susan latched the window and came. The room seemed cold after that glowing sunshine outside. She knelt on the stone floor, and was aware that Mrs. Bowyer was trembling a little.

"What does it mean, Gran?"

" 'Tis an old, old, ancient tale," said Mrs. Bowyer rather breathlessly. Susan patted her.

"Angel Gran, don't get fussed—it's all right. You'd better get it off your chest—you had really."

"I don't rightly know—"

"You'll feel a whole lot better when you've told me."

A gleam came into the black eyes for a moment.

"That's one for me and two for yourself, my dear."

Susan patted her again, a little harder this time.

"You wicked woman!" Then, coaxingly, "Tell me about the stone that Merlin blessed. Was it the Coldstone?"

"Ssh!" said Mrs. Bowyer.

"But was it?"

There was a pause. The old wall-clock with the white face and the picture of Abraham sacrificing Isaac ticked its slow, heavy tick. Mrs. Bowyer folded her hands in her lap.

"If I tell you, will you swear to me and promise true you'll not tell it again, not to man, nor maid, nor to no living soul, old nor young, rich nor poor, not for nothing that any can do for you, nor for gold, nor for your bare life, 'cept only to one that comes after you of your own flesh and blood, and to Anthony Colstone or to his lawful heirs after him?"

Susan said, "I promise."

"It was my grandfather told it to me, sitting here same as I'm sitting, and me kneeling there same as you're kneeling, and I was a maid fifteen years old, and he five years past his hundred, and he told it me same as he heard it from *his* grandfather that was older still. He told it to me same as it'd been told from one hundred years to another by an old, old, ancient man or an old, old, ancient woman to a young lad or a young maid, and every time it was told there was the promise given not to tell it to none 'cept Colstone and his lawful heirs—and my grandfather he made me put my hand on the Book and swear to it. But I'll take your true promise for just as good. Them that'll break their given word'll break what they've sworn on the Book. So I'll take your true promise."

Susan nodded.

"Go on, Gran."

Mrs. Bowyer dropped her voice to a singular low monotone; she seemed to be talking in to herself and not out to Susan.

"My grandfather sat here, and I come close, and I listened, and I never forgot any word of what he said. 'Tis a very old tale."

"Yes, Gran?"

" 'Tis about the Stones. There was two rows of the Stones in those days—very old, ancient days, before folk began to fetch them away to build with, and long afore Stonegate was built—only there was some sort of a house there, and Colstones was there, but they hadn't the name, not till afterwards."

"Yes, Gran?"

"There was a black Trouble come."

"What was it?"

Mrs. Bowyer looked over her shoulder. Her voice went down to a whisper.

" 'Twas a Trouble. I can't tell you nearer than that. 'Twas a desperate black Trouble, and it come from meddling with the stone that's called the Coldstone."

"Who meddled with it?"

"I don't rightly know, but 'twas meddled with, and *That* came up."

Susan felt a shiver all down her back.

"Gran—what?"

"That," said Mrs. Bowyer. She looked over her other shoulder. The room was winter cold.

"Gran! What on earth do you mean?"

"There's things that's better not said, and there's them that shouldn't be named."

"But, Gran—"

"Fire—and smoke—and brimstone—and *That* in the midst of it. Black smoke—and red flame—and the smell of brimstone—same as Sodom and Gomorrah. And *That* in the midst of it."

"Gran—"

Mrs. Bowyer looked straight in front of her, but she did not see the window-ledge with her best pewter dish standing on it, or the neat latticed panes which were blue against the sky, and green against the lilac bushes. She saw a tilted field under a rolling canopy of smoke. She saw shooting flame and a red and wrathful glare. She smelt the reek of the Pit. Her eyes were fixed and, to the outward world, sightless.

Susan touched her.

"What happened?"

"Folks were like frightened sheep, and the first of the Colstones he were like a shepherd a-standing 'twixt them and the mortal fear that was over them. 'Twas he sent word to Merlin, that was an old, wise, ancient man in those days. And when he come, he laid the Coldstone where it belongs, and he put a charm on it and a blessing to hold That down, and so long as 'tisn't meddled with the blessing 'll stay."

Everything in the room was still except the clock. The stone floor was cold under Susan's knees. She wanted to think clearly, but her thoughts tangled; she felt as if she had been running hard and was out of breath. You can't think when you're running. Something was puzzling her, and she couldn't get it clear. She began to feel for it in the tangle of her thoughts.

"What did he put on the Stone, Gran?"

"A mark—to be a charm," said Mrs. Bowyer.

"What sort of a mark?"

Mrs. Bowyer's finger moved on the shiny black stuff of her apron. It traced a pattern there, and stopped.

" 'Tis a charm against evil," she said in a whispering voice. "And 'tis there on the Stone to this living day. Wind nor weather won't move it, nor running water nor standing water, nor sun nor shine, nor any mortal thing—there 'twill stay unless it be meddled with, until reckoning day comes."

Susan gazed at her with a puzzled frown; her eyes had an asking look. Mrs. Bowyer sat up a little straighter.

" 'Twas meddled with once," she said, and caught her breath.

"Who meddled with it?"

"One that had ought to know better—one of the Colstones, my dear."

"And what happened?"

"No one rightly knows. It was in Mr. Philip Colstone's time—him that was killed fighting the Spanish Armada, and it was the same year and a little before. He'd been a journey out to the Indies, and he come home. He'd been five years gone, and when he come back again his wife was strange to him, and his son that he left a babe in the cradle was a child getting on six years old, and all the whole country was full of rumours of wars along of the Armada coming, and a beacon ready to light on the top of the hill up there, and folks mortal afraid and their hearts failing 'em for fear of the Spaniard a-coming to burn them all, same as in Bloody Mary's time."

"And what happened?"

Mrs. Bowyer moistened her lips.

"They say Mr. Philip went about to raise that that was under the Stone—that's what they say."

"Why?"

"Did you never hear tell of folks that thought they could get good for themselves by that like of black sinfulness?"

"What did he do?"

"That's what no one never knew but himself. There was Bowyers here then same as there is now, and this house was new-built, a matter fifty years maybe, and the old bit of Stonegate a-standing same as 'tis standing now. And the Bowyer that was here he was a William Bowyer, same as my William and same as my father. He was rose up from his bed by the sound of a rushing, roaring noise, and he looked out from the window of the room as you sleep in, and he could see a light in the sky and he could hear the roaring of fire. And he put on his breeches to be decent, and he ran out into the street—and there was every man, woman and child from the whole village thinking no less than that 'twas the King of Spain and all his army that had come to land, and that the beacon had been fired—though I dunno who they thought had fired it, seeing as they were all woke up together and in a maze of fear. And William he runs to the end of the street and he sees the top of the hill all dark, black dark and cold, and everything as quiet as 'tis when one clap of thunder's gone and another to come, and he goes a little further to the turn of the road and he sees a red light low down amidst of the Stones, and a cold fright got hold of him so that he couldn't move—so there he stood and watched."

"What did he see?"

"He saw the light get red and small, and then all of a sudden he saw it shoot up till it was as tall as a tree. And what he saw he wouldn't never rightly say, only he smelt a burning that wasn't like nothing on this lawful earth. And presently 'twas gone again, and he ran back along the way he come and went clattering at the door of Stonegate, because he was in mortal fear. And after a bit a serving man opened and let him in. He come into the house and he asked for the Master, and there wasn't no one could tell him where he was—they were all in a sweat of fear, and some said 'twas the Spaniard, and some said 'twas worse, and there wasn't one of them with as much courage in him as a maid that's scared of a mouse. It was in William's mind that they should go, three or four of them together, up the hill, because it come to him that Mr. Philip was there—but they wouldn't none of them go, so then William went out by himself. He went through the kitchen, and into the yard, and up by the garden way, and it was all as black as coal, and rain beginning to fall. And when he come to where the fields began, his feet were like two cold stones and he couldn't hardly lift them. And he tried to call out, but his voice came back into his throat like as if the wind was blowing it back— only there wasn't any wind. And he stood there and he couldn't move, and it might have been a minute, or it might have been an hour, or it might have been the half of the night—he couldn't tell. He was afraid like death, and 'twas mortal, mortal still, and rain coming down cold as ice. The first sound that he heard was far away, but, so afraid as he'd been before, he was ten times more afraid when he heard it." A shiver went over Mrs. Bowyer and she stopped.

"What was it?" said Susan in a whisper.

Mrs. Bowyer shivered again.

"It wasn't what anyone would have looked for—no, that it wasn't."

"What was it?"

"Someone laughing," said Mrs. Bowyer very low. "And it came nearer, but he couldn't tell where it was coming from. And it came nearer still. William he thought about a many things he'd done as he wished he hadn't, and he tried to say his prayers. There was that voice a-laughing in the dark and the rain—and there was William a-thinking about his sins, and what a pious man he'd be ever after, if he could get another chance. And with that, he could move again. He began to run, but he caught his foot and come down. And then he heard Mr. Philip call, 'William,' and he says, 'How d'you know as it's William?' Mr. Philip said 'twas bound to be Will Bowyer and no one else, because no Bowyer never left any Colstone when there was danger about, and he claps him on the shoulder and he says, 'Were you scared, man?' And William says nothing, because he don't know what to say. Mr. Philip says, 'I've been raising the devil, Will,' and he laughs and asks, 'Did you see him?' And William says, 'Lord forgive you, Mr. Philip! What ha' you been meddling with?' Mr. Philip says, 'The devil's under the Stone again, and there he may stay. There's no one here,' he says, ' 'll want to raise him after to-night. Where the shield's set, the devil's safe. Mind you that, William,' he says. And so they goes down through the garden together. And the smell of burning was on him, plain as plain."

"Gran! How thrilling! What happened after that?"

"No good," said Mrs. Bowyer in a deep voice. "There's no good comes of meddling with things that shouldn't be meddled with. 'Twasn't more than a week later Mr. Philip was called away sudden. And he took William Bowyer with him, and they went on the ship that his cousin was captain of to fight against the Armada. And some come back, but Mr. Philip he never. And that's what come of meddling with the Stones."

"But, Gran, people did take the Stones. You told me so yourself. You said your doorstep came from there, and your hearth-stone."

"They didn't take them no more after that, not till they'd forgot the fear that was on them that night. The most of them had been took already. But no one never laid hands on the Coldstone except for Mr. Philip's meddling, neither before nor since. There isn't anyone in Ford St. Mary, nor never has been, that'd lay hands on the Stone that's got the charm on it."

"What did Philip Colstone *do*?" Susan spoke, in a soft, puzzled voice.

"He did what he shouldn't ha' done, and it lay heavy on him at the last, for when he was hit and William was a-holding him up, he said, wandering in his mind as it were, 'the shield'll keep all safe.' And then he says the piece you said to me, or leastways a bit of it—and I never heard tell that anyone knew more of it than that."

"What did he say? Tell me just what he said!"

"He was wandering in his mind. He said to William, 'Hold me up'; so William held him up. Then he said what I told you, and after that he said 'The stone that Merlin blessed, to keep safe the fount of evil.' "

"That's different," said Susan under her breath.

"Maybe—but 'tis what he said. And then he said, 'Take the book that's in my pocket and give it to my son, and tell him—tell him,' he says, 'what's under the shield is safe.' "

"What did he *mean*?" Susan spoke half to herself.

"It laid heavy on him what he'd done. He meant for his son to know what come of his unlawful meddling, and he meant for him to know as 'twas all safe as long as he let things bide."

"But what's the *shield*?" said Susan quickly.

"Oh, 'tis just the name they give to the charm, my dear. And a shield it is, so long as 'tisn't meddled with."

The silence settled again. The clock ticked. Susan felt as if a great many ravelled ends had been pushed into her hand. She didn't know where they came from, and she didn't know where they would lead her if she followed them. She wanted time to sort them out. Some of the threads were dim, and strange, and rather frightening. She said, "Is that all?" And with the word there came a little tapping on the kitchen door, very faint and hesitating. She turned her head—and the door was ajar. But she had shut it; she had shut it carefully.

Mrs. Bowyer said, "Eh?" very sharply, and then, "Come in!" and Susan got up and ran to the door.

It opened gently before she could reach it, and disclosed Miss Arabel's little black figure. She was smiling in a deprecating manner, and she spoke as if something had startled her:

"Oh, Susan—" It was old Susan Bowyer she spoke to; she looked past young Susan as if she didn't see her at all—"I walked in—I couldn't make anyone hear. I wonder—did I—have you found—did I leave a handkerchief here yesterday?"

Mrs. Bowyer nodded.

"To be sure you did. Susan'll get it for you right away."

Miss Arabel went on looking past Susan even when Susan bobbed to her. She looked past her, but she was aware of a sparkle in Susan's eye that did not seem to be quite in keeping with the respectful bob. When she took the neatly folded handkerchief she allowed her glance to slide aloofly over the blue print of Susan's frock.

" 'Tis my great-granddaughter Susan," said old Mrs. Bowyer in a voice that seemed somehow portentous.

"Yes," said Miss Arabel—"oh yes." She took the handkerchief and for a moment her flustered glance just reached Susan's face. "Yes—yes—Robert's granddaughter—yes—yes." She looked away quickly and met the piercing humour of old Mrs. Bowyer's black eyes. They were so bright and bitter that they fairly put her to flight.

"Up and away like a dandelion clock. Always puts me in mind of one, she does—more especial now her hair's gone white. They aren't things you can't never count upon, and that's Miss Arabel all over. Is she clean gone?"

Susan came back into the kitchen with rather a high colour.

"Oh yes, she's gone."

"Now I wonder how long she'd been at that door, and how much she'd heard," said old Mrs. Bowyer.

Chapter Twenty-One

SUSAN CURTSEYED TO HERSELF in the looking-glass. She thought she looked rather nice. But of course she ought to have had curls, nice fat curls, hanging down on to her shoulders. Here she frowned, because she couldn't for the life of her remember whether Patience Pleydell had long curls or not—she had really only had just one glance at the picture. She arched her foot, pointed it, and frowned again. Her shoes were quite wrong; they ought to have buckles. She dropped the blue petticoat over them, pulled out the panniers of the flowered muslin gown, powdered her nose, and looked at her wrist-watch—a most unblushing anachronism. It was just eleven, and Gran ought to have been asleep for at least two hours. She picked up an electric torch, put out her light, and proceeded very cautiously downstairs in the dark.

She went into the kitchen and shut the door. Since Gran was overhead, it wouldn't do to make the very slightest noise. She crossed to the hearth and switched on her torch. The chimney-place was like a little room. In the old days William Bowyer and his wife—any one of the old Bowyers—would have sat one on either side of it on winter evenings, warm and snug, with the hot brick of the chimney at their backs and the arch of the chimney-piece between them and the room.

Susan moved the chair that Gran had sat in that afternoon. There was no fire; these hot days, Mrs. Bowler used, and grumbled at, an oil stove in the scullery. Behind the chair the bricks of the chimney ran in patterned courses up to an old black beam. She turned her torch here and there, and ran a finger along the bricks counting them, seven courses inwards, and then seven courses down. She put the torch on the chair and pressed with both hands as hard as she could. With a click all the side of the chimney from the blackened beam to the floor turned on an unseen pivot and swung round, showing a dark opening.

Susan picked up the torch, stepped through, and shut the door. It was the third time she had opened the secret way, and each time it gave her the same delightful thrill. The first time was when Gran had showed her the trick of it. The second time was when she had played at family ghosts. This was the third time. She was on the edge of being frightened, but she wasn't frightened; and she was on the edge of laughter, but she came no nearer than the edge. Gran, this old house, and a secret passage leading right back into the Middle Ages were all part of an enchanted, enchanting adventure. She picked up her skirts and moved forward into the midst of the enchantment.

The passage ran straight forward for half a dozen feet, and then came the steps. They went down steeply, ten of them. And then the passage again, slanting off to the right. The air was rather thick, with a cold, damp smell in it.

When Susan had gone a few steps along the passage, she stopped, blotted out the beam of her torch with her hand, and stood listening. She could hear nothing at all. She released the torch and threw the light to the left. A dark opening showed in the wall. She hesitated for a moment, went a few steps along the branch passage, stopped, listened again, and then, turning, came back to where she had started. She was quite sure she knew where the branch went to, but she didn't think she wanted to explore it alone. She went on, keeping always to the right, till she reached another flight of steps, ten of them, and then a narrow passage opening at the end into a sort of T-shaped space. There was only just room for herself at this end, and it was a relief to come out into a place where three people could have stood abreast.

She was now immediately behind the portrait of Patience Pleydell. She had only to pull the wooden knob just in front of her to the right, and the spring that held the panel would be released. She put her hand on the knob and hesitated. Suppose Anthony had gone to bed. It would be most frightfully dull if he had; it was no good being a ghost if there wasn't anyone to see you. She pulled the knob very gently. There was a faint click. If she pulled it towards her now, the panel would open. She switched off her torch and looked for the knot-hole on the right.

It showed like a yellow eye. That meant that there was a light in the library. Her spirits rose, and she began to draw the knob towards her. The panel moved silently. She peeped round the edge of it and saw the left-hand side of the room—two dark shuttered windows; straight brown curtains hanging stiffly; books between the windows; some chairs; a worn brown carpet with a nearly defunct pattern of something that looked rather like green and yellow cabbages—it must have been a nightmare in its prime, but it was now so old, so worn, so dim, that it had slipped imperceptibly into harmony.

Susan opened the panel a little wider. She could see the writing-table now, with the lamp on it and a litter of books. Wider still, and the empty hearth faced her, a shield with worn armorial bearings set above the chimney-piece. She opened the panel to its full width and stepped out. In the far corner by the door a ladder stood against the wall, and on the top of the ladder, with his head in a book, stood Anthony Colstone. Susan's spirits soared. She closed the panel behind her and moved away from it as silently as a shadow. The old carpet was soft and thick. It hushed her footsteps.

She had reached the middle of the room, when Anthony suddenly turned his head and saw her. He dropped his book with a crash, stared for a moment, and jumped down as Susan sank to the floor in a beautiful billowy curtsey.

She came up laughing.

"Did I give you a fright?"

Anthony stood and looked at her. She moved as a tree moves in the wind—effortless grace, and the laughter in her eyes. She took his breath away a little.

He answered her rather stumblingly:

"Not exactly a fright. How—how on earth did you come?"

"That's telling! But perhaps I'll tell you presently. I expect you ought to know, really. There are quite a lot of things you ought to know."

"Yes," said Anthony seriously. Then he said, "I've been trying to find some of them out for myself, but I don't know that I've got very far. I wish—I wish you'd tell me what really happened the other night."

"What do you want to know?" said Susan. She was standing with her back to the writing-table; the lamp shone behind her; her hands rested lightly on the table edge. The laughter had gone out of her face. There was a little line between her eyes.

"There are several points that I'd like to get cleared up."

"I'll tell you anything I can."

"Well then—who was the other person in the room?"

"The other person?"

"Yes. There was the man who flashed the torch on. I think there was another man too—I didn't really see him, but I'd a sort of feeling that there were two of them."

"Yes, there were two."

"And there was you, and there was me—and there was a person who gasped. That's the person I want to know about." Susan was silent. "It was a woman. Did you see her?" She shook her head; the line between her eyes deepened. "Do you know who it was?"

"I think so." She spoke with some reluctance.

"Who was it?"

"She dropped her handkerchief," said Susan.

"Dropped it—or picked it up?"

"Oh, I picked it up. She dropped it."

"No," said Anthony, "you're wrong there. The handkerchief wasn't dropped by the person who gasped. I thought it was at first— but it wasn't."

"Why do you say that?"

"Because it was dropped by my Cousin Arabel. She came to look for it this morning. She'd been in that day in the afternoon to return a book—she must have dropped it then."

Susan looked down at her toes. She was leaning back a little against the table. She looked at the toes of her shoes, and she said,

"She might have dropped it then—or she might have dropped it later."

"What do you mean by that?"

"Why—" She looked up suddenly, defiantly. "You know very well what I mean. I mean that I think it was Miss Arabel who gasped when the light went on, and I mean that she dropped her handkerchief then, and not in the afternoon at all."

Anthony stood opposite her with incredulity in every line of his face.

"Why on earth should you think it was Cousin Arabel?"

"Because it was her handkerchief."

"But if she dropped it in the afternoon?"

"If—" said Susan.

Anthony looked angry.

"You can't say a thing like that for no reason at all."

"Why can't I?" Her eyes sparkled up at him.

"It's absurd. No—look here—I'll tell you what I think. I think it was the nurse. What was her name.... Miss Collins. You don't know about her of course. She seems to have gone off with the house keys. I picked Cousin Arabel up in Wrane a couple of days ago, and she told me all about it. I thought it was pretty fishy then. Well, I went in and saw the nurse and got the keys. She's a glad-eyed sort of female, and she put up a cock-and-bull story about having been away on a case, and the keys being buried in a box. When she gave them back to me there was a little bit of wax sticking in one of the wards—"

"Oh!" said Susan. She looked at her shoes again. Something in her mind said "Garry!"

"So I think it was Miss Collins who was here the other night. That ass, Lane, hadn't bolted the doors—he said they never did bolt them. Miss Collins would have known that. What I want to know is, what was she after?"

"If I tell you something—" She stopped.

"Yes?"

"Well, will you just let me tell you what I can?"

That seemed a queer thing to say. He wondered....

"What do you mean?"

She took a look at him. There was none of Gran's indulgence here. He was puzzled, angry. His jaw stuck out.

"I mean—well, I mean you're not to ask any questions. No, I don't mean that either—but you're not to pester me, and—and—you're not to look at me as if I was in the dock and you were counsel for the prosecution."

Anthony frowned.

"I can't think why women like making mysteries. The sensible thing to do—"

Susan laughed. There was the same sort of sparkle in her laugh as in her eyes.

"My dear, good, blessed *man*—do you expect a ghost to be sensible? Ghosts always drop mysterious hints, and if they're cross-examined, they just *vanish*. You don't know your place a bit. You ought to be in a dithering state of awe—that's a politer word than funk—and you ought to just drink in anything I tell you in a proper spirit of gratitude and— and pious family feeling."

Anthony's chin stuck out some more.

"I see—" he said a little grimly. "All right—I'm waiting. Will you begin?"

"That's better. What do you want to know?"

"Everything. There were two men?"

"Yes."

"Did you see their faces?"

"N-no."

"Sure?"

"How could I, when it was dark?"

"There was a lantern."

"It was a *dark* lantern."

He let that pass.

"You followed them through the baize door. What were they doing?"

"Translating Latin," said Susan. A dimple appeared for an instant; the corners of her mouth quivered almost imperceptibly. Her eyes looked solemnly at Anthony.

"What?"

"Don't speak so loud—you'll wake Lane. By the way, I hope he's gone to bed."

"An hour ago. Did you really mean that?"

"Of course I did."

"Latin?"

"He said so. What would 'the second shield' be in Latin?"

"Was that what he said?"

"He read it off a paper."

"Any more?"

"Lots. 'The stone that Merlin blessed.' What's the Latin for 'blessed'?"

"The stone that *Merlin* blessed?"

"Yes. It's exciting—isn't it? And it ends up:

'To keep in safety
The source of evil!'
That's what they said; but in Gran's version it's 'the fount of evil.'"

"Gran?" said Anthony in a tone of the utmost surprise. "Mrs. Bowyer?"

Susan began to laugh. She took her hands off the edge of the table and caught him by the arm.

"I've got a most frightful lot to tell you—I really have. That's why I came. Come and sit down." She settled herself in the sofa corner and gazed at him with dancing eyes. "I hope you're in a proper frame of mind and that you're not a miserable, scoffing, up-to-date sort of person."

Anthony's eyes laughed back at her. When they laughed they looked blue, and an attractive crinkle showed at the corners.

"How mediæval have I got to be?"

"Oh, frightfully. I don't know when Merlin lived—long before the Middle Ages were ever thought about. That's where it begins, and it's been handed down ever since from an old, old ancient man, or an old, old, ancient woman to a young lad or a young maid. That's what Gran told me. And you oughtn't to be sitting up there at all—you ought to be kneeling, frightfully awestruck and respectful and simply drinking in every word, like I did with Gran, and like she did with her grandfather. He was a hundred and five when he told her, and she was fifteen, and she remembers every word."

Anthony slipped off the sofa and went down on his knees.

"Will this do? And are you my grandmother? I'd just like to know."

"I'm your great-great-grandmother, of course. Patience was your great-great-grandmother—at least I think so." She counted rapidly on her fingers: "Anthony—Ralph—James—Ambrose.... Yes, that's right—Patience Pleydell was Ambrose's mother, and that makes her your great-great."

"Thank you," said Anthony meekly. His eyes were not at all meek. Susan found them rather disturbing.

"It's frightfully serious," she said. "And if I could tell it like Gran did, you'd have creeps all up your spine. You know, she didn't just tell it, she *saw* it. She was looking back hundreds of years and seeing things, and her voice gave me the cold grues—it did really. So you've got to be serious, please."

"All right."

"Gran had to swear a solemn oath she'd never tell what she knew, except to one of her own flesh and blood that was to come after her, and to the Colstones and their lawful heirs. She had to swear it with her hand on the bible, but she said she'd take my true promise, so I gave it to her. I don't know if you have to promise too."

Anthony felt the oddest little thrill of pride. He shook his head.

"No, I wouldn't have to promise. If it's a Colstone secret, you see, it's my secret. I wouldn't have to make any promise about it. Will you tell me the story?"

Chapter Twenty-Two

SUSAN LEANED FORWARD with her elbow on her knee and told the story word for word. She told it as a child tells a story that has been told to it, word for word, with the very inflexions and pauses, making them a part of the tale, as if an altered phrase or a lost word might break the glamour. Where Mrs. Bowyer's voice had dropped into a hardly audible whisper, there Susan's breath failed, and her colour with it. Her eyes looked past Anthony, and she did not seem to know that his never left her face.

He listened, and he looked, and he thought that the story came too soon to an end. He watched the colour come and go on Susan's cheek. Some times it rose to a bright geranium flush that burned for a while and made her eyes look dark and bright; and then quite suddenly it went, and left her pale. That was when her voice shook and she stopped for a moment and drew another breath. When she came to the end, he was watching her still. She turned her eyes to his, and they seemed to be asking him a question.

He said, "Is that all?" and she nodded.

"Yes. It's—it's queer—isn't it? It gives me a shivery feeling."

He was near enough to touch her. He put out his hand, and she moved her own to meet it. His felt warm.

"Don't," said Anthony.

"I'm not." She gave a faint little laugh. "I told you it gave me the shivers." She laughed again and pulled away her hand. "You can get up now, you know."

Anthony got up. Things that he would have liked to say simply tumbled over one another, but he beat them back. He stood for a moment, and then walked slowly to the end of the room and back again, while Susan sat in her corner watching him.

He hadn't said anything. But he hadn't laughed. If he had laughed, she would simply have hated him. His laughter would have broken a fragile indefinable something of which she was just aware. It hadn't any name, but she was aware of it. If Anthony had laughed, she would never have been aware of it again.

He came back and sat down beside her, looking quite serious.

"Look here, Susan—" he said.

Susan looked, and met a glance of frowning intensity.

"Look here—what does it all mean?"

"I don't know."

"I'm going to know. But nothing seems to fit in—it's like a jig-saw puzzle, only I feel as if someone had been monkeying with the pieces. It's like having bits of at least three puzzles mixed up."

"How?"

"I'm not to move the Stones—I'm not to touch the Stones—and there's no end of a mystery. Those are the bits out of Sir Jervis' bag. Then there's your grandmother's very interesting story about the devil being sealed up under the Coldstone—and, by the way, I suppose that's where the name came from—the Cold Stone, because it put the fire out. That's another lot of bits. And then there are the burglars—they're the third lot. And for all I know, there are scattered bits chucked in by Nurse Collins and my Cousin Arabel. It's so jolly easy to put them all together and get a straight picture—isn't it?"

Susan looked a little puzzled.

"Why don't they fit in?" she asked slowly.

Anthony threw out his hands.

"Well, do they? Do you suppose Sir Jervis believed the devil was sitting corked up under the Coldstone, just waiting for someone to come along and move it?"

"I don't know," said Susan—"I didn't know him. People believe all sorts of things. One of our mistresses at school believed the earth was flat—she really did. She was a very clever woman and an awfully good teacher. So you see he might have believed it, especially if he had been brought up on it, so to speak."

Anthony waved Sir Jervis away with an impatient gesture.

"All right—he believed the devil was under the Coldstone, and that's why I wasn't to move it. But what did the burglars believe—and what were they looking for? Can you tell me that?"

"Burglars are generally looking for family plate." Susan wore an air of bright intelligence.

"What? Under the stone that Merlin blessed, and the second shield, and all the rest of it? Do you think they really broke into my house to do a little quiet devil-raising?"

Susan looked at him, and looked away.

"The Coldstone isn't in the house," she said.

"No," said Anthony. He was looking at her, though she wasn't looking at him. He waited a moment, and then he said, "The second shield—" and at once her eyes, dark and startled, were turned to his.

"Why did you say that?"

Anthony did not answer.

"What did you mean?"

"Oh, nothing."

"You did!"

He sat down beside her.

"You've told me your story. Now I want to tell you mine."

"Have you got one?" She relaxed a little, but she was wondering what he had meant.

Anthony nodded.

"It's not such an exciting one as yours, but it's a bit more up to date."

"Oh," said Susan. Then her lashes flickered, and she added, "I hope you'll tell it better than last time."

"I was going to begin where we left off."

She heaved a resigned sigh.

"Very well."

"I'd got to where the ghost vanished."

"Had you?"

"Yes."

"What did you do next? Go to bed?"

"No—I got Lane and Smithers, and we searched the house."

"Smithers would be a *great* help," said Susan. "Smithers the Sleuth!" she added. "Did you—did he—find anything?"

"We found a poker in the middle of the floor in the housekeeper's room. Why?"

"Couldn't Smithers explain it?"

"I thought perhaps you could."

Susan shook her head. Her eyes were round and innocent, but she was a little pale. ("I'm going to break his leg. It'll keep him quiet for a bit. No!" Why did it come back like that? She didn't want to remember it. She didn't want to think about it.) She grew paler still.

Anthony said, "Susan—" but as he leaned forward, she leaned back.

"Why don't you go on?" she said.

"I thought perhaps you could tell me that part of the story."

"I'm not a sleuth," said Susan firmly.

"Well," said Anthony, "we didn't find the burglars—they had departed by way of the scullery window. But we searched the cellars."

"Did you find anything?"

"Yes, we found a locked door."

"Did you unlock it?"

"No—there didn't seem to be any key."

"What door was it?"

Anthony hesitated.

"Lane and Smithers both seemed to think it led into some very old cellars that were not safe. Lane's been here forty years. He's never seen the door opened. Smithers was full of bright thoughts about the roof falling in. Lane supposed the key would be with all the other cellar keys, but it isn't—I've been through them all, and there isn't anything that goes near fitting. It's an awfully old lock, and the key must be immense. I could very nearly put two fingers into the keyhole." He stopped, leaned right forward, and said, "I did put my finger in, and it came out covered with lamp-black."

"*Lamp-black?*"

"I won't swear to the composition. It was something soft and black."
He broke off again. "That doesn't convey anything to you?"

"No, it doesn't."

"You haven't moved in burgling circles. It's one way of taking an impression when you want to forge a key, so I don't think we've seen the last of those burglars yet."

"You think they'd been down there?"

"The stuff was quite fresh," said Anthony.

There was a silence. A room that is full of books can be still with a peculiar stillness of its own; it can be still with a deep, remembering stillness. Susan felt this silence rise around her like the waters of a deep, invisible sea. Under its tide there were secrets. Each generation had added to them. The deep waters of silence kept all these secrets hidden.

Anthony broke the silence. He said abruptly.

"Oh yes, they'll come back—I'm prepared to swear they'll come back. What I want to know is—Why? What's their game? What are they looking for? What do they want?"

"I don't know," said Susan,

"Really?"

"Really, Anthony."

He looked at her for a moment more, and then got up.

"Quite definitely, the burglars and whatever they're looking for won't, don't, and can't fit into the same picture as Philip Colstone and raising the devil, or Merlin laying him. And the burglars—the burglars, Susan—*were* they looking for the stone that Merlin blessed?"

Susan sat forward.

"That was the Coldstone," she said quickly.

"Then why weren't they up the hill instead of in my cellars? If they were looking for the Coldstone, they were going a queer way about it. It's not as if it was a thing they could possibly miss."

"No—" Susan's tone was thoughtful.

Anthony walked over to the writing-table.

"I've been looking for anything that might throw a light on it all."

Susan got up.

"Did you find *anything*?"

"I don't know. I was really looking for a plan of the house." He hesitated for a moment. "I asked Lane about one when I first came down. He seemed—bothered. Then I asked my cousins. They didn't like my asking. I want to know why—and I want to open that door in the cellar. I'm getting a key made."

"Did you find anything?" said Susan. She came a little nearer.

"Not what I was looking for."

"Did you find anything?"

He hesitated again.

"I found—I don't know if it fits in or not—I don't suppose it does—I don't suppose it's got anything to do with it, but—well, I found that Sir Jervis refused what was evidently a very good offer for the place—" He broke off.

Warmth leaped into Susan's voice.

"Of course he did."

He frowned.

"I don't mean that. It was the way it was put. What I found was a letter from Leveridge's father—I suppose it *was* his father. It's dated March, 1879, and he says—" He picked up a thick, crackling sheet, turned it over, and read from it:

We must apologise for again bringing the matter under your notice, but the sum offered is so much in excess of the estimated market value of the property that we feel that we cannot refuse to place the offer before you. We have, however, informed Messrs. Stent Rogerson and Twyford, the firm who have approached us, that we have no reason to believe that this offer will be any more acceptable than previous offers from the same source—

He stopped and turned to Susan with the letter in his hand.

"Well?" he said.

"I suppose he refused."

"Damned them into heaps, I should say. He has scribbled all over the letter—had to get it off his chest—just snappy bits of abuse. But at the end, where there's a blank space there's a queer thing—at least I wondered whether it wasn't a queer thing."

"What was it?"

"It's one of the things that doesn't fit in. Perhaps it doesn't mean anything, but he had scribbled across the bottom of the letter: 'J. E. W.? Can't believe it. No.' "

A look of apprehension had been succeeded on Susan's face by one of blank surprise. She said,

"J—E—W?"

"Yes—initials, you know."

"They're quite plain?"

"Printed. Why?"

"Oh, I don't know. Who is J. E. W.?"

"I haven't an idea. But it looks as if the old boy knew of someone who might have some ulterior motive for offering a fancy price for Stonegate."

"Yes—it looks like that." Her voice sounded tired. Old Mr. O'Connell and his delusion about the Mutiny treasure.... Was it possible that it could have taken him the length of making extravagant offers for the estate on which he believed it to be concealed? It sounded perfectly mad. But then she had always thought he was mad on the subject of the treasure; and if he was mad, he might have been mad enough for that.

Anthony's voice broke in on her thoughts.

"I wonder if it does fit in," he said. "I wonder if J. E. W. wanted the same thing that the burglars wanted the other night."

A sudden nervousness assailed Susan. Old Mr. O'Connell—the Lahore treasure—Garry—all swam together in her thoughts. She felt giddy and frightened.

"What's the matter?" said Anthony.

Susan put up her hand.

"Did you hear anything?" Her voice shook a little.

"What sort of thing?"

"A—a footstep."

"No."

"On the stair. Please, *please* see!"

"I don't hear anything. All right—don't look like that. I'll go and prospect."

"Yes," said Susan. "Yes!"

As he turned, she had her skirt in her hand, her eyes not on him but upon Miss Patience Pleydell's portrait.

Anthony looked out into the hall. A lamp burned serenely. The house was silent, as a midnight house should be. He stepped across the threshold, listened, stepped back.

"There's no one there," he said, and stopped dead.

There wasn't anyone here either. Susan was gone.

Chapter Twenty-Three

ANTHONY WENT UP to town next day. He drove himself into Wrane and caught the one decent up train. It was after he had given up his ticket, and whilst he was making his way down the incline which led to the tube station that he caught sight of Susan. Afterwards he wondered how it was that he recognized her with such absolute certainty. She had her back to him; the close hat hid not only her hair but the shape of her head; she was dressed quite differently. He had seen her in blue print and a sun-bonnet, and he had seen her in a quilted petticoat, flowered gown, and fichu. She wore now a thin navy-blue frock that only just reached her knee, and a little navy hat, very plain, severe, and smart. Nothing could have looked less like Ford St. Mary or Mrs. Bowyer's granddaughter. Yet he never had the slightest doubt.

She took her ticket, and he took his. They went down in the same lift, she on one side of it and he on the other, but she never turned her head. He caught one glimpse of her profile. It was unsmiling and intent.

When she got into the train, he chose a different carriage. She hadn't seen him, and he wasn't sure that he wanted her to see him. Yet presently when she left the train, he left it too. It seemed impossible to throw away such a frightfully good opportunity. He would be a mug if he didn't ask her to lunch with him. And then he thought it would be rather a lark to see how far he could get without her tumbling to it that he was travelling with her. He was boy enough to throw himself into the game. It would really make quite a good game, he thought—so many points for the lift, so many for getting in and out of the train without being seen, and top score for travelling on the same bus. He would certainly have the laugh on her for that. She very nearly saw him too, because she reached her seat inside and turned just before he got his foot on the stair. He got the outside front seat on the left, and wondered if she had seen him.

It was a warm cloudy day, quite still and rather airless. The houses and the pavements seemed to give out a faint stuffy smell of dust. Anthony wondered why anyone lived in London who wasn't obliged to.

Every time the bus stopped he kept a look-out for Susan. When she did get off, he had to take the risk of her turning round or looking back. She did neither. She walked straight up the steps of the Victoria and Albert Museum and disappeared.

Anthony found himself at the bottom of the steps. He wasn't quite sure what he was going to do next. He ought to have caught her up— he would have caught her up if everyone on the top of the bus hadn't wanted to get off at just the same moment as Susan did. Perhaps he oughtn't to have followed her. On the other hand, the Victoria and Albert Museum was a perfectly public place, and he had just as much right to be there as she had.

He walked up the steps, had his stick taken from him, and discovered that he had now lost Susan. Of course as soon as you have lost a thing you become possessed with a dogged determination to find it. Anthony pursued Susan in this spirit. He pursued her, or the elusive hope of finding her, amongst walnut cabinets, and Stuart day-beds, and ancient panelling, and other antique objects which diffused an atmosphere of historic interest and furniture polish. He then began to pursue her amongst ceramics, which were colder and altogether less hopeful. He climbed a great many steps. And the more he didn't find Susan, the more persevering and determined he became.

And then he found her.

He had entered the room in which coins and medals are displayed in show-cases like tables whose tops slope down on either side from a central ridge. Tall sets of shelves, glass-fronted, form partitions on either side of the long room. Anthony came round a partition and saw Susan standing with her back to him at one of the show-cases. She was not alone. Across the case a man was facing her, his head and shoulders darkly relieved against a bright background of window.

Anthony received a most curious impression. Just at the first glance he did not see the man's features at all. What he saw was an attitude, a silhouette, a particular poise of the head, a particular forward stoop of the shoulders as the man leaned upon the show-case. He had both hands on the case, and he leaned on them.

With a quick movement that was purely instinctive Anthony drew back behind the shelves. He was amazed, excited, horrified; because this pose, this attitude, this silhouette, fitted line for line over the black, deeply etched impression which had remained with him from the encounter in the housekeeper's room. He hadn't seen features then, only a man stooping forward with his hands on the table, the yellow beam from the dark lantern sliding farther and farther away from him, the whole thing a study in shadows. He had only to shut his eyes to see it again. To shut them? He could see it with his eyes open if he moved six inches to the left.

He moved the six inches cautiously. Susan had moved a little; he could see her profile. And as his eyes shifted to the man, the silhouette effect seemed to dissolve. He saw long black hair tossed back from rather a high forehead, eyes that looked black in a pale oval face. He drew back again. He was watching the man whom he had twice seen watching him—from the hedge that overlooked the Coldstone Ring; from the window of Nurse Collins' sitting-room. He was also watching the man who had pitched a chair at his head on the night that Stonegate had been broken into. And this man was here, talking familiarly to Susan. The last thing Anthony saw as he drew back was the worst— Susan stretching out an impulsive hand which was taken and held. And the brute looked at her in a way that made his blood boil—a careless, fond, possessive look.

With a furious effort Anthony turned and walked away. He had seen enough. He wasn't going to spy on Susan. He had seen more than enough. He went down the steps and out of the building.

Chapter Twenty-Four

ABOUT HALF AN HOUR LATER Susan bade Mr. Garry O'Connell a firm farewell, caught another bus, and proceeded to a block of flats in Chelsea. She was about to visit her stepmother, and she would have liked to have been feeling a little more settled in her mind. A visit to Camilla always left her with the impression that she had been taking part in one of those cinematograph performances in which everything and everyone is moving or being moved at about six times the natural speed. Camilla herself emerged unruffled, but other people were apt to feel battered. In the days when Susan had to live with Camilla this battered feeling never really went away.

She climbed forty-five steps, and arrived. Officially, Camilla shared this landing with three other people. At this minute, however, most of her furniture obstructed their ingress or egress. There was a piano across the door of No. 17, whilst the dining-table, with a sofa poised on top of it, blocked the approach to the next flight of stairs. Camilla occupied No. 16, the door of which stood wide open.

Susan squeezed herself past a book-case, stepped over some mounds of books, and entered the tiny hall, which was quite full of chairs balanced upon one another and of a raucous smell of paint. Four doors opened out of the hall. Two were open, and two were shut. The open doors were those of the dining-room and drawing-room. Susan knocked down three chairs and squeezed her way into the drawing-room. She looked about her, and said "Golly!" under her breath.

Camilla was descending from a ladder on the far side of the room. It creaked alarmingly under her weight. Her enormous, shapeless figure was draped in an orange jibbah. She wore thick cream-coloured stockings and sandals. An unbelievable amount of short grey hair waved, clustered, and stood on end all over her head. A paint-brush dripping with bright blue paint was stuck negligently behind her right ear. Her hands, her face, her jibbah, the ladder, and the whole floor were also spattered with blue. She had just finished painting the ceiling and the upper part of the walls in the brightest shade of cobalt obtainable. Her broad, flushed face beamed. The eyes, under strong grey brows, radiated a triumphant welcome. The left side of her nose was entirely covered with blue paint.

"Golly!" said Susan again. "What an orgy! No, darling, I *won't* kiss you. I'm a sordid slave of convention—I blench at going home in a bus all covered with woad."

"Woad was *quite* a different colour," said Camilla. "How well you're looking—but what dark clothes! At your age you should diffuse joy and light and colour—in fact at any age. I'm bringing that out very strongly indeed in my next Talk at the Central Institute."

Susan giggled. Camilla always made her feel a little weak; she was so kind, so expansive, so unremitting; and she had so many irons in the fire that one or other always seemed to be clanking.

"What *are* you doing?"

"I'm going to have a jungle drawing-room," said Camilla in rapt tones. "I thought it all out in the bus on my way back from my last Talk on Thursday. I just snatched a cup of tea and rushed out and got the paint and began at once. I've been working day and night to get done, but of course I positively had to take half an hour here and there to keep up with the articles I'm doing for *The Magnet*—'Early Italian Painters.'"

"I didn't know that was one of your subjects."

"My dear, it isn't. It wouldn't have been any trouble if it were—or is it 'had been'? No—'were'—decidedly 'were.'"

Susan began to laugh.

"I'd really give anything in the world to have your nerve!" she said.

Camilla looked pleased.

"Everyone ought to be able to do anything. I've never painted a room before—and look at it!"

"Is—is that the sky?"

"I think it's original—not the sky part, of course, but the scheme, the jungle. You see the idea of course. A tropic sky, intense with heat. Then palms." She drew the paint-brush from behind her ear and waved it with a sweeping gesture at the vague outlines described upon the walls. "You see the idea?"

Susan murmured, "I get you, Steve."

"Rather bold and free, I think. Palms in three shades of green, and the distance blocked in in sapphire and violet. Below the palms a decorative frieze of tiger lilies slightly conventionalized."

"T-tiger lilies?"

Camilla went on firmly:

"*Slightly conventionalized.* And I wanted to have gold paint all over the floor—a glorious Oriental sunshine effect—but it was too expensive. Gold is a simply wicked price. So I'm just going to paint the boards brown, with a perfectly matt surface, and have splashes of gold here and there—sunshine *glinting* through the palms."

"Won't it be rather cold to the feet?" said Susan.

Camilla went on beaming and expanding.

"How materialistic! But it won't, because I shall have green rugs—*moss* green—and a tiger skin."

"Darling Camilla! Why not a tiger?"

There was a momentary gleam in Camilla's bright, restless eyes. Then she shook her head regretfully.

"There wouldn't be room. But I've sometimes thought a panther, or an ounce—yes, an ounce. They are excessively friendly to man and make affectionate and intelligent pets."

"A Persian cat would be more to scale," said Susan hastily. It would be perfectly awful if she had to go back to Ford St. Mary with a conscience weighed down by the thought that she had flung Camilla into the arms of a panther. Fortunately the idea of a cat being to scale seemed to have its appeal.

"Jenny Carruthers has a striped tawny kitten," murmured Camilla. "She wanted me to have it a week ago, but I was thinking of turning the dining-room into an aviary then, and a cat is always such an anxiety with birds, though of course they can be *taught* and become most friendly. My very first Talk was about animal families. The instance of the snake and the chickens is really too wonderful—yes, really, Susan—a perfect foster mother, and perfectly well authenticated. Where was I?"

"I haven't the slightest idea," said Susan. She took hold of Camilla by a more or less paintless portion of her arm. "I gather you've abandoned the aviary. What are you turning the dining-room into now? A lion's den?"

Camilla thrilled with pride.

"Come and see!"

They squeezed out of one door and in at the other.

"There!" said Camilla.

The dining-room was rather startling. The ceiling was bright green, the walls and floor black. There was no furniture at all.

"Are you going to sit on the floor?"

"I'd love to—with cushions, you know—scarlet, purple, orange, green, and gold—but I've *got* the dining-table and chairs. Cushions mount up *terribly*. It's a mahogany table, and the chairs have horsehair seats—you remember them—so I thought I'd just give them all two coats of gold paint, and do the sideboard sealing-wax red with a little gold worked into it."

"And your sofa and chairs for the drawing-room?"

Camilla looked worried.

"I don't know—I can't *see* them yet. Perhaps green would be best—green and brown—banks, you know, and cushions in bright colours to suggest flowers. What do you think?"

"I think it would be unique," said Susan truthfully. "And now—I really did want to talk to you."

Camilla rumpled her hair.

"But you're staying of course?"

"Darling—*where?*"

"I could put the sofa into the dining-room—I think the floor's dry enough."

Susan patted her.

"Angel! You'd take me in if there were ten of me and you hadn't a roof over you at all—wouldn't you? But I can't stay. I want to ask you about something, and then I've got to get back to Gran."

"But you'll have lunch? I'm trying a receipt Sophy Karelin gave me—Oh!" She uttered a sharp exclamation of horror, stuck the paint brush back in her hair, and made for the nearer of the two closed doors. "I forgot I left it on! I do hope—"

As she opened the door, an intensive smell of fish and burning leapt into the hall and grappled with the smell of paint. Susan followed her into the kitchen, wondering whether fish flavoured with paint would be better or worse than paint flavoured with fish. She hadn't any doubt when she got into the kitchen—the fish had it every time. A sort of blueish haze hung in the air. Camilla stirred vigorously at something in a saucepan. There was an undertone of cheese and onions.

Susan said, "Good Lord, Camilla!" Then she opened the window.

"I don't think the draught's good for it," Camilla protested.

"Then it'll just have to be bad for it—unless you've got a gas-mask you can lend me. What on earth *is* it?"

Camilla stirred with happy enthusiasm.

"I think I was just in time. What a mercy I remembered! It's salt fish soaked in olive oil overnight and stewed with burnt sugar, and you serve it with little forcemeat balls made of cheese and chopped onions, with a touch, just the merest touch, of garlic. The Finns adore it—or is it the Letts? It's a national dish. I can't remember whether it's Finns or Letts—

or Kurds." She began to look worried. "Dear me, it's most unlike me not to remember, but she gave me several receipts at the same time, and I can't remember which is which. There! Do you suppose this is done?"

"Yes," said Susan with her head out of the window. "Done—and overdone. And if you don't come out of this like a streak of lightning, I shall be done too—I really shall. Come back into the jungle and talk to me."

She shut the kitchen door and the drawing-room door, and inhaled the paint-laden air with relief.

"Now!" she said. "I really do want to talk to you."

Camilla's eyes roved to her paint pots.

"Can't you talk whilst I get on with the palm trees?"

"No, darling, I can't."

Camilla looked disappointed.

"I ought to be getting on—I'm having a house-warming to-morrow night. You *must* stay for it."

"I can't—I can only stay five minutes. Be an angel and clear your mind of jungles, and house-warmings, and Talks, and national dishes, just for five little minutes."

"What is it?" said Camilla quickly.

Susan observed with horror that a flood of kindly solicitude was about to be unloosed upon her.

"Nothing—nothing. I only just want to ask you something. It's about the Colstones."

Camilla looked a little disappointed. She wouldn't have wished Susan to be in need of sympathy, but she did love sympathizing.

"What is it?"

"Only a little thing, but I thought it was just possible you might know."

"But I've never known anything about the Colstones."

"I thought my father might have known about this, and if he knew, he might have told you."

"What is it?"

"It's about Philip Colstone, who was killed at sea at the time of the Armada."

Camilla's bright, restless eyes fixed themselves upon Susan's face.

"What about him?"

"Gran was telling me about it. When he was wounded he told William Bowyer, who was with him, to take a book out of his pocket and give it to his son, who was a child only six years old."

"Well?" said Camilla. Her eyes had remained like bright fixed points.

"Well, I want to know what the book was."

"What the book was?"

"Yes. I thought there might have been a tradition—I thought it was just possible my father might have told you something about it."

Camilla ran both hands through her hair.

"It had a needlework cover," she said. "Yes, needlework—awfully dirty and faded, but, I think, a pattern of roses."

"Camilla! What on earth are you talking about?"

"Yes, roses—red—only the red had gone brown. And I can't remember whether the Museum wanted it on account of the cover, or because.... How stupid of me! But I shall remember in a minute."

Susan seized her by the arm. This time she did not look to see whether she was covering herself with paint or not.

"Camilla—you don't mean to say you've seen it!"

"Of course I've seen it. How could I tell you about it if I hadn't seen it? I always told your father it was a mistake to let the Museum have it. Museums are *most* dishonest."

Susan shook her.

"Do you mean to say my father *had* that book?"

"Yes, darling, of course he had it."

"And he gave it away to a museum? What museum?"

"Not gave—only lent. But, as I said to him at the time, it comes to the same thing unless you're terribly persevering."

"What museum?"

"That's what I'm trying to remember. It was either the British Museum or the Victoria and Albert—unless it was a private loan collection—but I don't think it was, though I do remember his sending something to a most interesting loan collection about the same time—but I think that was a water-colour which he was quite sure was a Turner. My dearest child, you really are pinching me most dreadfully!"

"Sorry," said Susan. "Don't ramble, darling. Let's get back to the book. What was it?"

"I'm trying to remember, but I only seem to be able to visualize the outside. The needlework cover was made by Philip Colstone's wife, and it's got his initials and hers intertwined in the middle—a P. and an E. and a C.—but I can't remember her name."

"It doesn't matter about her name. It's the name of the book and the name of the Museum that I want."

"And I'm sure I've got the receipt somewhere. Your father was so terribly unbusinesslike that he would never have asked for one, but I simply insisted on having a receipt. And if I insisted on having that, it's not to be supposed that I wouldn't have put the receipt away carefully—now, is it?"

"I don't know—you might."

"I'm most businesslike," said Camilla. "It was your father who didn't seem to know what the word meant. I often told him so. Now let me see... where would I have put the receipt? It's sixteen years ago, and I think Edwina was storing a lot of my things about then. And then she went abroad, and I had to store until Connie had a house—but she could only take about half, so the Fenwicks and Ursula divided the rest. And I know there were three despatch-boxes, but I turned one out ten years ago and gave it to Connie's boy when he was going to Australia—and it wasn't in that, so it must have been in one of the other two."

Susan said "Golly!" under her breath.

Camilla laid a blue forefinger against her forehead.

"Just let me see.... The Fenwicks had their house burnt down... but my things were saved and Sarah O'Connell took them in.... I know there was a despatch-box there.... I'll have to write to Sarah.... I can't remember any more than that."

Susan went away with her brain whirling. She had never hoped that the book was still in existence. She was so thrilled that she wanted to stop total strangers in the street and tell them about Philip Colstone's book. When she was half way down the flight of stairs she heard Camilla's voice calling her:

"Susan! Susan!"

She stopped, turned, and began climbing again. Camilla's voice came floating down to her, eerie and echoey:

"Don't come up. It's only the name of the book—it came to me suddenly."

Susan's heart thumped.

"What is it?"

"The Shepheard's Kalendar."

Chapter Twenty-Five

THE SHEPHEARD'S KALENDAR was by Spenser—Susan did know that; but she had never seen a copy or heard a word of it quoted. She thought over Camilla's vague statement, and, putting the private loan collection on one side, she decided that a book would be more likely to have been lent to the British Museum than to the Victoria and Albert—unless it had been lent, not as a book but on account of its cover, as a piece of Elizabethan needlework.

A sensible person would wait until Camilla found the receipt. A sensible person would reflect that, after three hundred and fifty years or so, a few more days, weeks, or months were neither here nor there. Susan wasn't a sensible person. When she thought about doing a thing, she wanted to do it at once, not to-morrow, or next week, or in a year or two. She wanted to find Philip Colstone's book now. She produced a sixpence and tossed up. Heads the Victoria and Albert; tails the British Museum. It was heads. Susan was a very feminine person; any decision that was made for her would always send her off at a tangent. She put her sixpence away, shook her head, and set off for the British Museum.

Finding the book was the slowest thing that had ever happened. People kept going away and fetching other people, and then going away again. She bore up, because quite early in the proceedings it transpired that they had a copy of *The Shepheard's Kalendar* in a needlework cover. Susan smiled at all the people who came and spoke to her, and the cumulative effect of a great many smiles was the appearance of a most charming old gentleman who actually produced the book.

Camilla had been right about the finely worked cover. The faint dead roses wrought upon it by the fingers of Philip Colstone's wife had once been red. Susan wondered whether they had been worked before she grew strange to him.

The charming old gentleman opened the book.

"You see, it's got his name and the date—'Philip Coldstone, 1582.' And now here is what makes it really valuable, in fact unique—Spenser's autograph."

Susan looked at the discoloured page. The ink was brown on Philip Colstone's name—a pale, wan brown, as if it had been written with the water of some stream long choked with rotting leaves. Below, in a different hand but even paler, were the words: "The gifte of his frende Colin Clout."

She looked so puzzled that the old gentleman condescended to explain.

"That is Spenser's own name for himself in this poem, and also, as you will doubtless remember, in the later poem dedicated to Sir Walter Raleigh—'The Right Worthy and Noble Knight Sir Walter Raleigh'—*Colin Clout's Come Home Again.*" He touched the signature with the tip of a long, careful finger. "It's unique—quite unique."

Susan took the book in her hand and turned a leaf or two. There was a long title, a dedication to "the noble and vertuous gentleman, most worthie of all titles both of learning and chivalry, Maister Philip Sidney"; an introduction, and a "generall argument"; and then, "Januarie. Aegloga Prima."

She went on turning over the leaves, the old gentleman, polite but in a fidget, at her elbow. And then all at once there were words scrawled on the margin, very faint, some of them crossing the lines of print. She turned the book. They were dreadfully faint.

She made out a word here and there. *Scutum*—that was a shield... *Merlino*... and two words together, *fons malorum.*

The old gentleman came to her aid.

"Yes, that's curious—some spell or conjuration, I should say. It is a coincidence that you should have noticed it, because only about a week ago someone else was so much interested that he asked if he might make a copy. It is very faint, as you see, but I think we made it out. It is rather surprising really that the young man should have been so much interested, for his Latin was so rusty that I had to translate for him."

"Will you translate it for me? What does it mean?"

The old gentleman adjusted his glasses, turned the book to get a better light, and traced the fading words with that long, thin finger.

"It's of no importance, you know. Here—yes—this is what it says: 'The second shield...*lapis*'—h'm—I think that's what we made it out to be—very faint indeed... 'the stone consecrated, or blessed'—h'm—'by Merlin... to keep safe... the fount... of evils.' It is, as I said, some spell or charm against malefic influence." His voice flowed on. "Merlin... an invention of Geoffrey of Monmouth, who got the idea from Nennius... Welsh vernacular literature... Joseph of Arimathea... Robert de Borron... Taliessin...."

Susan wasn't really listening. It was frightfully dry, and she wanted to go on turning over the pages. Suddenly she asked a question:

"What month was the Armada?"

The old gentleman stopped short, pushed up his glasses, and looked at Susan with an air of courteous surprise. From Welsh folk-lore to the Armada was a longish flight.

"The Armada? Oh July—July—*July* 1588."

Susan turned the pages again and found: "Iuly. Aegloga Septima." A curious thought had come into her mind. If Philip Colstone had written some special message for his son, might he not have chosen this seventh month, the month in which he had gone up to fight the Armada? She was at once disappointed. The page was a good deal discoloured—speckled here and there. There was no writing on it. She flicked over the leaf. The next page was the same.

The old gentleman was looking at a large old-fashioned watch.

"I am afraid"— He was still the soul of politeness, if a little chilled by a lack of interest in Nennius, Taliessin and Robert de Borron—"I am very much afraid that I have an appointment to keep."

Susan's smile made amends to him, if not to Nennius.

"Oh, of course." She went on smiling. "May I take the book with me?"

He was so much shocked that she felt as if she had committed some frightful breach of good manners.

"But it *belongs* to me," she said. "It was my father's—he only lent it." And then she knew how silly it was to talk like that when she hadn't got the receipt.

The old gentleman took the book out of her hands. He was still polite, but he was also firm. He said, "Allow me," and he took the book away from her very firmly. Then he looked at his watch again and said "Tut, tut!" and wished her good day and went away in a hurry.

Susan missed her train by ten minutes. It was very late before she got back to Ford St. Mary.

Chapter Twenty-Six

Anthony went to tea with the Miss Colstones next day. He found himself in the middle of a tea-party—the Pullens, middle-aged ladies about a decade younger than Miss Agatha and Miss Arabel; the Thane-Bromleys, he small, wiry, precise, and she the largest, heartiest creature, with a jolly laugh and a nursery empty for the first time for nearly twenty years.

"My eldest boy's in India—I wonder if you came across him—and my eldest girl's married and has a baby of her own. And *my* baby is going away to school next term—he's only eight—and my old nurse and I won't know what to do with ourselves. All the in-between ones are out in the world, or at school and college, so we shall be too dreadfully dull and empty as soon as the holidays are over. Perhaps you'll come over and play tennis with the horde whilst they are still here—some of them are quite good."

The elder Miss Pullen was an enthusiastic gardener. She attacked Anthony on the subject of neglected borders, and was so vehement that he was afraid for Miss Agatha's susceptibilities, and relieved when Miss Maria turned her attention elsewhere.

Miss Amy Pullen, a dried-up, brown-faced little lady, then tackled him on the subject of bee-keeping. It had been a marvellous honey season, "the biggest yield for years." She turned and addressed Miss Agatha: "Do you know how much Susan Bowyer has taken, Agatha?"

Anthony hoped that he did not start. Susan Bowyer meant *Susan* to him—Susan, and not old Mrs. Bowyer. But he recovered himself at once. It was "Gran" they were talking about, not Susan.

Miss Agatha made an impatient gesture with the tea-pot.

"Susan always has more than anyone else. She'll never say how much—I believe she thinks it's unlucky."

Miss Maria Pullen stopped telling Miss Arabel that she was going to manure her roses in spring, and how stupid she thought it of Agatha to stick to the old-fashioned autumn manuring. She stopped in the very middle of a sentence to cast a bomb.

"Who in the world has Susan Bowyer got staying with her?"

Agatha took up the sugar-tongs.

"Maria, I forgot your second lump."

Miss Pullen shook her head.

"All the better for my figure. Who's staying with Susan Bowyer? I saw an uncommonly pretty girl at the window as I came past."

"Her granddaughter—that is, her son Robert's granddaughter. Helen—another cup?" Miss Agatha addressed Mrs. Thane-Bromley, who said "Thanks, dear—so refreshing."

"We pride ourselves on our tea," said Miss Agatha. "I always say it is a gift." Her colour had risen, and her voice was a little louder than usual.

"Robert's granddaughter?" said Miss Pullen. "*Robert's* granddaughter? Why, I always understood that all the Robert Bowyers were in America."

Miss Agatha turned to Mrs. Thane-Bromley.

"You're eating nothing. Some ginger cake? A lettuce sandwich?"

"I always understood that Robert Bowyer went to America, and that all his family had remained there."

Miss Amy Pullen looked a little nervous. "Perhaps this girl has come over on a visit, Maria," she said.

"She didn't look in the least American," asserted Miss Maria.

"Some Americans don't," said Miss Amy.

Miss Agatha said nothing.

Miss Pullen frowned.

"I remember Robert. He was one of the younger ones, wasn't he?"

Miss Agatha's colour deepened unbecomingly.

"Really, Maria—what nonsense! You can't possibly rememb-er Robert."

"Oh yes, I do. He'd be about your age, and I remember very well having tea with Susan Bowyer when I was ten years old, and she was all upset because Robert was just going off to America." She nodded triumphantly. "I remember him perfectly well. He hadn't the looks of the others. The girl I saw doesn't take after him—I thought she was an uncommonly pretty girl. I shall go and see Susan on my way home and find out whether the granddaughter has really come over from America. I thought her a most uncommonly pretty girl."

Anthony felt a boiling rage spring up in him. It infuriated him to have all these people discussing Susan. What did it matter who her grandfather was? Anyhow he would rather have old Mrs. Bowyer for a relation than Miss Pullen. He felt that he loathed Miss Pullen.

She began to tell Mr. Thane-Bromley that he kept his greenhouses too hot.

Anthony took the vacant place beside Miss Arabel, and in a minute she was asking him innumerable questions about India. Was it really so very hot? Had he ever ridden on a camel? Did he know Lahore? Papa was once there, in the Fort. It was a very old fort, was it not? Did the natives ever speak about the Mutiny? Papa was in the Mutiny. Papa never spoke about it. Had he ever been to Tibet? Had he ever travelled in other countries? Wouldn't he like to go to China? China was not so hot as India, she believed. Japan must be very beautiful. Did he not wish that he had had an opportunity of visiting Japan? Of course India was very interesting, very interesting indeed; but some of the things one heard—it was really so very difficult to know whether to believe them or not. Now the rope-trick—had he ever seen the rope-trick?

It became a little wearing after a time. The china-blue eyes never left his face. His answers were received as if each were the final word on that particular subject. In the end she drew a soft sighing breath.

"I have hardly ever been out of Ford St. Mary. Papa thought girls ought to stay at home."

"You would have liked to travel?" It sounded awfully stupid, but he found himself saying it. And then he wished he hadn't.

Miss Arabel looked away. But just before she looked away he saw something. It was like looking for a moment through a window and seeing something which you weren't meant to see. He wasn't sure what it was. It looked like—hunger. Yes, that was what it was—something that was starving with hunger. He wished he hadn't seen it.

Mrs. Thane-Bromley got up to go. Mr. Thane-Bromley's eye had been upon her for some time, and though she was one of the best-natured women in the world, she didn't think she could bear much longer with old Maria Pullen telling her how she ought to have brought her children up. She said good-bye, listened with a twinkle to a deeply bored but always polite husband thanking his hostesses for such a pleasant afternoon, pressed Anthony to come and see them soon, and departed, leaving the room colder.

Miss Arabel followed her into the hall, and Miss Pullen took a chair by the tea-table.

"If you're thinking of making any bramble jelly this year, I can give you my receipt, Agatha."

Miss Agatha had a receipt of her own. She said so, and cut Maria's next remark short by leading the way into the garden, where Miss Amy and Miss Arabel paired off and after a few minutes Anthony took his leave.

Miss Arabel came into the house with him. In the white-panelled drawing-room she seemed disposed to linger. She showed him the portrait over the mantelpiece as if he had not seen it before, and narrated the entire history of the Lady Arabella Stuart. In the middle of it she stopped and asked him if his friend would not be coming to visit him again.

Anthony looked surprised.

"West? Oh no—he's on a walking tour in Wales. I had a card from him a couple of days ago. I don't expect to see him again. He suggested coming to look me up, but we're not such great pals."

Miss Arabel said "Oh—" Then she went on telling him about Arabella Stuart.

Anthony was not very much interested. She had a way of catching herself up and making small corrections as she went along, and she was very diffuse. His attention wandered, and presently became fixed upon a large square object just inside the glass-fronted cupboard on the left side of the fireplace. It was a book with a worn leather cover. It looked like a bible. If it was a bible, it was an old one. He thought it would be very interesting to have a look at an old family bible. He had a vague idea that a family bible would be likely to contain a family tree.

As soon as Miss Arabel drew breath he stepped forward, and with his hand on the cupboard door, asked if he might look at the book.

Miss Arabel became much agitated.

"Of course, my dear Anthony—of course. And I hope—you see, we had for so long been accustomed—not, of course, that that is any excuse, but I am sure that Agatha fully *intended*, and that she meant to take the first opportunity of a *private* explanation—"

Anthony turned with his hand on the open cupboard door. He felt rather as if he had upset some delicate vase full of flowers. Miss Arabel's agitation—her flow of words—the confusion of her speech—he hadn't an idea what it was all about. He bridled a feeling of exasperation and said, as gently as he could.

"I'm afraid I don't understand."

Miss Arabel fluttered.

"I am quite sure that Agatha would have taken the earliest opportunity. You will understand, I am sure, that she could not—neither of us could—just give it back to Lane—and an opportunity for a private explanation—"

Anthony began to understand that he had been tactless. The bible was apparently his property, and the old ladies had removed it. He couldn't help wondering whether the opportunity for that private explanation would ever have occurred. He reproached himself for the thought, and asked if he might look at the book.

Miss Arabel's distress deepened. He gathered that the bible was undoubtedly his.

"And I hope you won't for one moment think—"

"Of course I won't. But I'd like to look at it. Is it very old?"

"The first edition of the King James version," said Miss Arabel.

He took the book in his hand and turned the pages. He was looking for a register of names. He thought it would be between the two testaments.

Miss Arabel watched him. Her little twittering explanations and apologies went on.

Anthony found what he was looking for. A long column of entries in many hands, from the first crooked "Ambrose," through a string of Ralph, James, Jervis, and Ambrose again. His eye was caught by Patience Pleydell's name—"Jervis, married Patience Pleydell, March 1789." Below, their children, James and Ambrose. Ambrose was his great-grandfather. "James, married Anne Langholm, and had issue, Jervis, born 1828." That was old Sir Jervis, Miss Arabel's father. Under

Jervis' name, a name blacked out. Then, "Jervis married Agatha Yorke, had issue, Agatha and Arabel."

Anthony looked at the blacked out name.

"What's this?" he said, and turned the book for Miss Arabel to see.

Miss Arabel looked everywhere else.

Anthony touched the black smear.

"Had Sir Jervis a brother or a sister?" he asked. "What's this?"

"The Colstones have never had large families," said Miss Arabel. Her voice was small and cold.

Anthony persevered. His question had been an idle one. Now he meant to have an answer to it.

"Was this a brother or a sister?"

"A brother," said Miss Arabel. Then she added, "He's dead."

Anthony supposed so.

"Why is his name blacked out? By the way, what was his name?"

"Philip—" It was just an impatient breath. Then, louder, "He quarrelled with his father and with Papa."

"What did he do? It seems a bit drastic to blot him right out like this."

Miss Arabel drew back a little.

"He—they—they quarrelled," she said. Then she put out her hand. "I'm afraid I must go back to the others. Pray take the bible with you, Anthony. Good-bye—you will excuse me—perhaps you would not mind letting yourself out."

Anthony got as far as the door. There had come into his mind, for no rhyme or reason, the matter of old Mr. Leveridge's letter to Sir Jervis and the note at the foot of it. J. E. W. were the initials—yes, J. E. W. He wondered if Miss Arabel knew anything about the letter. She might. And she might know who J. E. W. was. It seemed a very good opportunity of asking.

He turned back with the bible in his hand.

"Cousin Arabel—"

Miss Arabel turned too. She stood framed by the open doorway, a little black silhouette against the green and gold of the sunny garden.

"Yes?"

"If you could spare a minute. I came across a letter the other day—a business letter—and I wondered whether you could throw any light on it."

"Oh, certainly—but I am afraid—poor Papa never talked to us about business—he did not think that ladies—"

"It was an offer for the estate from a firm called Stent and Rogerson. They had, apparently, made more than one offer."

"Oh!" Miss Arabel sounded most dreadfully shocked. "Papa would never have sold Stonegate!"

"No—he was evidently refusing. But he had made rather a curious note on the letter. Do you happen to know who J. E. W. was?"

Miss Arabel turned, took a step towards the garden, tripped, and fell quite gracefully. Anthony's absurd impression of flight vanished in extreme concern. He picked her up, carried her in, arranged her upon the sofa, and inquired anxiously whether she was hurt.

"No—no—oh no. I slipped. So very foolish. No indeed—I am not at all hurt—not in the least. And—and—you were asking me something?"

"It doesn't matter—I can ask Cousin Agatha."

A bright little flush came into Miss Arabel's face.

"Oh no! It's—I'm sure it's very interesting. What did you say the name was?"

"There wasn't any name—only initials—J. E. W."

Miss Arabel leaned back against the cushion which he had put behind her.

"What did it say about him?"

Anthony made a mental note that J. E. W. was of the male sex. He had not meant to hesitate. He received a shock when Miss Arabel said, with a little gasp,

"Why don't you tell me what he said?"

"Oh, it was nothing. But who is J. E. W.?"

"What did it say about him?"

He tried to recall the exact words.

"There were the initials, with a question mark after them; and then, 'I can't believe it.'"

"Is that all?"

"Yes, that's all."

She drew a long breath. It was absurd to fancy that it was a breath of relief. Then, before he could speak, she was rising, thanking him for his kindness, and once more bidding him good-bye. It was gracefully and competently done—her other guests claimed her—she looked forward to seeing dear Anthony again soon. She gave him her hand.

This time he went.

Chapter Twenty-Seven

SUSAN CAME THROUGH the panel and found the library empty. The lamp burned on the writing-table, and the book-ladder stood against the wall just behind it. She closed the panel and advanced warily. It was most frightfully annoying of Anthony not to be here. It was only half-past ten and the lamp was burning, so he hadn't gone to bed. On the other hand, Lane probably wouldn't have gone to bed either, and if he came along to put the lamp out, she would be very nicely caught, unless he were really and truly to believe she was a ghost. He might; but then again he mightn't. And if he didn't, what fun for Ford St. Mary. She murmured "Poor darling Gran!" and advanced to the writing-table. Spread out upon it was an open book with a magnifying glass laid across the page.

Susan came round the table and stood looking down at the names in the Colstone bible. They interested her very much. Her colour rose, her foot tapped the carpet. All of a sudden she picked up her skirt, ran over to the panel, opened it, and disappeared, closing it behind her with a perceptible bang. The portrait of Miss Patience Pleydell gazed placidly at the empty lamp-lit room. Her colour did not come and go. Her little foot remained poised for the step which she never took. The yellow lamp-light gave her an air detached, serene. The clock, in its tall inlaid case, ticked out a slow three minutes.

Then the panel opened, and Susan, in her blue petticoat and flowered gown, stepped down into the room. She held in her hand a worn brown book in a leather cover. She breathed a little more quickly. Her colour was still high. She took up Anthony's bible, closed it, and substituted the one she had fetched. She wondered whether he would remember that he had left the book open, and she wondered where he was and why he didn't come. And then, whilst the thought was still in her mind, the door opened and he came in.

Anthony shut the door. He had wondered whether she would come, and if she came, how he should meet her. Since the moment when he had seen her in the museum he had thought about her differently; the moment had changed something. Whenever he thought about Susan—and he could not help thinking about her—he saw beyond her the man who had come secretly into his house in the night, and he saw this man meeting Susan, talking to her, touching her with an accustomed familiarity that was as damning as a kiss. And he remembered that Susan had slipped away from his questions about what had really happened on the night that the house was broken into. He didn't know what had happened after they floored him. He didn't know. But Susan knew—Susan knew, and Susan wouldn't say, and she wouldn't describe the men. Why?

The answer came pat enough, but not in words. The answer was a picture in his mind. Susan and the man who had watched him from the hedge. Susan and the man who had looked down on him from Nurse Collins' window, Susan and the man who had been bending over the table in the housekeeper's room, a black shadow in a dark room. But the shape of the shadow—the forward stoop, the movement—he was as sure as he had ever been of anything in all his life that the man in the housekeeper's room was the man who had watched him from the hedge and from the window, and that Susan had met this man in the museum. Susan had met him. Susan had gone to London to meet him. Susan and he were on such terms that she did not draw back from an intimate, possessive touch.

Anthony had been thinking all this, sometimes with anger, sometimes with hot resentment, sometimes with a kind of sick disappointment; but now, when he came into the library and saw Susan standing beside his writing-table, he did not feel any of these things; he just felt most frightfully glad to see her.

Susan dropped him a curtsey.

"I thought you were Lane."

"Do I look like Lane?"

"Not very."

And then all of a sudden his anger came over him again.

"I'm so glad you weren't Lane," Susan's voice sounded pleased and eager. "I've got a most frightful lot to tell you."

Was she going to tell him about that meeting—and what was she going to tell? He said this out loud:

"What are you going to tell me?"

Susan took him by the arm.

"Come and sit down. There's heaps and heaps of it. I've found the book!"

"What book?"

"Philip Colstone's book—the one William Bowyer took back to his son after Philip was killed. And it's in the British Museum, and it's got the thing in it that I heard the men saying—the—the burglars, you know—only it's in Latin. And a darling old woolly lamb at the museum translated it for me, but he wouldn't let me bring the book away."

Anthony was hardly attending; his mind was set on the thing which she did not tell. He frowned and said,

"What museum?"

"I told you—the British Museum."

"But you were at the Victoria and Albert," said Anthony with a long, hard look.

Her colour rose.

"What do you mean?"

"You were at the Victoria and Albert—I saw you there."

Susan's head came up.

"Why shouldn't you see me there? Good gracious, Anthony, if there is a proper place in this world—" She broke off with a little clear laugh. "Do you know that you're looking at me exactly as if you had tracked me to some particularly low haunt of vice? Mayn't I go to the Victoria and Albert Museum without asking your leave first?"

Anthony hit straight and hard.

"I saw you meet the man who burgled this house," he said.

Susan's hands came together in her lap. If he had been looking at them, he would have seen the knuckles whiten; but he was looking into her eyes, which were bright and angry.

"What do you mean by that?"

"It was the way he was standing—it absolutely hit me. And of course I recognized him. It was the blighter who was watching me from the hedge the first time I went to look at the Coldstone. I suppose you knew that all the time?"

Susan did not answer. She leaned back in the sofa corner, and she kept her eyes on Anthony's face.

"Who is he?" said Anthony.

Susan looked at him steadily. After a minute she said,

"Are you—insulting me?"

"I'm asking you a question."

"I'm afraid I can't answer it."

Anthony leaned forward.

"Who is he?"

"I can't tell you."

"Susan—is he your brother?" The thought had come to him suddenly. If she had a brother, she would be bound to screen him.

"No, he isn't."

"Is he—in love with you?"

Susan smiled at him. There was a burning anger behind the smile. It made her eyes look as bright as sea-water with the sun on it.

"It's possible," she said. "Have you any objection?"

Anthony turned very pale.

"Are you—in love with him?"

"That's possible too," said Susan.

"Is it true?" said Anthony.

She felt his hands come down hard on hers; they were cold and very strong. She was furious because something in her shook. Her voice shook too as she said,

"Is it your business?"

"Yes," said Anthony.

"Why?"

"You know why." Then, as she was silent, "You know very well—you know very well that I love you."

All at once Susan did know it. The anger went out of her. Anthony's love put it out. You can't really be angry with love—not with real love. She heard him say "Susan," and she pulled her hands away.

"It's my business because I love you. If you—care for him—Susan, do you?"

"Oh!" said Susan. It was a sound of muffled protest because he had caught her hands again and was holding them so tight that it was no use trying to free them. She stopped trying. She took a long breath and said "Anthony—" Her voice was steady and gentle.

Anthony said, "Yes?"

"Please let go of my hands. I want to talk to you."

"Does it prevent your talking?"

"Yes, it does. Please let go."

He let go of her, but remained leaning forward.

"What do you want to say to me?"

"I want to ask you something."

"Yes?"

"It's not very easy. I want to say things. Perhaps you won't believe me. If you don't, it's all finished."

He looked at her steadily.

"Why do you say that? I'll believe you all right."

"I wonder," said Susan with rather a shaky laugh.

"Go on."

She was sitting up quite straight with her hands in her lap. Sometimes she looked down at her hands, and sometimes she looked at Anthony. There was a little frown between her eyes. She said, speaking quick and low,

"I can't tell you anything—about him—I just can't. I can't tell you why. You see, there were things I knew in confidence, so I can't tell you about them. It's very difficult."

Anthony frowned too.

"You mean he told you things in confidence before you came down here?"

"I can't answer that," said Susan. "I can't answer anything, and I can't tell you anything. It's just like that. Only I wanted to tell you that anything you told me was quite safe."

"I see." Then, very suddenly, "Susan, he's not—your *husband*?"

Susan began to laugh.

"I haven't got a husband. What a horrible imagination you've got!"

"Susan—do you care for him?"

"Would you mind if I did?"

"You know I would. You know I care—you *must* know it."

Susan's smile came out sweetly, but he thought there was mockery in it.

"What happens when the squire falls in love with the village maiden?"

"Susan! Won't you be serious?"

"Oh, sir, it's a vastly serious situation—especially for the maiden. In most of the stories, you know, she's left lamenting. It's not a fate that attracts me."

Anthony gave her a very straight look.

"You know very well that I'm asking you to marry me."

The colour flew into her cheeks.

"Nobody axed you, sir," she said.

"Susan, will you marry me?"

"I don't know. Do you want me to?"

"Yes," said Anthony.

Susan bit her lip. It threatened to tremble, and she simply wouldn't have it. Lips are the hardest things to keep in order. She bit hers fiercely.

"Squires don't marry village maidens—they only trifle with them."

Anthony got up and pulled her on to her feet.

"Anthony, you're hurting me!"

"You deserve a good shaking. Will you marry me?"

"I'm Susan Bowyer's granddaughter."

"I wish you wouldn't talk such utter piffle! You're no more a village girl than—than—well, you're *not*."

"Your fingers are digging into me!"

"Let them dig! Will you marry me?"

"What will Ford St. Mary say?"

"Why should either of us care a damn what it says?"

Susan looked at him gravely, but behind the gravity he thought he still discerned a mocking gleam.

"You wouldn't mind?"

"Why should I?"

"And what would your cousins say?"

Anthony laughed. She hadn't said "No." She was teasing him, but she hadn't said "No." An immense exhilaration flooded him. He put both arms round her.

"Let 'em say anything they like! What do you say?"

"Don't!" said Susan. "Oh, Anthony—*please!* I want you to let me go—*Anthony!*"

His arms dropped. She stood away from him, very pale.

"Wait!" She was a little breathless.

Anthony waited. He had thought she was playing with him, but now she was really pale, really shaken. If he had been rough, if he had hurt her—

She drew two or three troubled breaths, then turned and went to the writing-table. The book which he had brought from the Ladies' House lay where she had left it. She opened it at the place between the two testaments and laid her finger on the blacked out name.

"When I came in here I saw this. Do you know whose name it is?"

Anthony stood beside her. He too touched the blotted name.

"It was Philip," he said. "Cousin Arabel said it was Philip."

"Yes. Do you know why his name was blotted out?"

"No. Do you?"

"Yes, I know. When I saw this my blood boiled. I went back and I got Gran's bible to show you. Look! They're twin books. Yours has all the Colstones in it, and Gran's has all the Bowyers." She opened the second book. "Look! It's William—Thomas—William—William—" Her finger travelled down the page. "Here is Gran's father. He was William. Her husband was William too. They were first cousins. Here's his father, Thomas. And here are all Gran's children—William—Thomas—Robert—Susan. Look, Anthony!" She moved her hand. He read, "Susan, born May 1860, married June 1878 Philip Colstone."

"*Philip,*" said Susan with her finger on the name. "*Philip.* That's why they blotted out his name. He ran away with Gran's daughter, Susie, when she was just eighteen and he was twenty-eight. She was awfully pretty—I'll show you her miniature. And she had been brought up with Agatha and Arabel—you know Gran was Sir Jervis' foster sister. But it didn't make any difference—they just blotted him out, and no one ever mentioned him again."

Anthony put his arm round Susan as they leaned together over the book.

"What happened to them?" he asked.

"Philip took Susie down into Kent. He had a little property there which came to him from his mother. They were very happy. Gran used to go and see them. They died young. Their son Ralph sold the property and went abroad to study art."

"Where do you come in?" said Anthony.

"How clever you are!" said Susan in a shaky voice. "How *did* you guess?"

Anthony drew his arm closer.

"Where do you come in?"

"I'm Ralph's daughter. I'm Susan Colstone, *Cousin* Anthony."

Chapter Twenty-Eight

COUSIN. THE WORD had a teasing sweetness. The look she turned on him teased him too. But the sweetness was over all; it seemed to flow from her with a gay and delicate breath. It was like the colour and the light of a spring day. He saw the sparkle of tears on the blue of her eyes, and a tremendous emotion filled his heart and took away his breath. He dropped his head on her shoulder and stood there, holding her close, feeling how the beating of his heart shook them both.

Susan was lifted into a dazzling calm. "It's like going up in an aeroplane," she thought. And then she stopped thinking, because she felt Anthony's tears run hot through the thin stuff of her fichu. She slipped her arm about his neck, touched his cheek, and said in a soft whispering way,

"Have you been—so lonely—poor boy?"

Until this moment he had not known that he was lonely. He only knew it now because there had come to him the sudden lover's thought of what life would be like without Susan. It was like looking over a precipice and seeing beneath one the terrible endless void. He raised his head with a jerk and kissed her until she pushed him away.

"Anthony!" This wasn't the creature she had comforted; this was a lover of a very disturbing sort. She pushed him away, blushing. *"Anthony!"* Her voice trembled and reproved.

"I'm sorry. No, I'm not. You don't want me to be sorry, do you? Susan, we're engaged! Isn't it topping? We *are* engaged—aren't we?"

"I don't know." Susan spoke with a slow gravity. She was holding him away. Now she stepped back and dropped her hands. "No—*please*—I want you to listen."

"What am I to listen to? I give you fair warning—" He was flushed and eager.

Susan smiled at him.

"Yes, I know. But please listen. There are a great many things I can't tell you. I may be able to tell you about them some day, but perhaps not—perhaps never."

"What does that matter?"

"When you live with people," said Susan, "it does matter. It makes things difficult. You'd have to trust me."

"You can't tell me?"

"No."

"All right." There was finality in his tone. He seemed to toss the whole thing away.

"Don't let's waste any more time. Susan, I do love you. You haven't said—you haven't said anything about loving me."

What do lovers talk about? It can't be set down in black and white, because it needs the laughing inflection, the glance that meets another glance, the shining rainbow light that sets every word, every look trembling with all the colours of joy, hope, love. The words are nothing; it is the coloured light that charms.

Susan and Anthony went hand in hand into the enchanted place where all the sand is gold and all the trees are green, where the bud and the flower and the fruit hang thick on the self-same bough, and the sun and the moon shine together in a sky which has all the freshness of the dawn and all the beauty of the day. In Merlin's day the name of that place was called Avalon. No man may stay there, but some keep the key of it all their lives long.

Susan and Anthony came back slowly to the sound of the tall clock striking twelve. Susan sighed and pulled her hand away.

"I must go back. If Gran is awake, she'll think I've eloped."

"I want to tell your grandmother—I want to tell everyone—I'd like to bang the big drum in the street and wake everybody up to tell them. Wouldn't you?"

"No, I wouldn't." She laughed a little. "What will Miss Arabel and Miss Agatha say?"

"Oh, they're old dears really. But—Susan—do they know who you are? They don't—do they?"

"Of course they do."

He frowned.

"They don't. They were talking about you this afternoon—at least someone was. They had a grim tea-party, and I was there, and an old lady said she'd seen you, and who were you? And Cousin Agatha looked fearfully repressive and said you were Mrs. Bowyer's son Robert's granddaughter."

Susan crinkled her nose.

"That is the official explanation." She laughed softly. "You see I fell on them like a bomb, poor old dears, because—Anthony, you're to listen, because you don't really know anything about me."

"I am listening."

"You can't listen properly whilst you're kissing my hand. You see, my mother died when I was a baby, and I don't really remember my father, because I was only six when he went too—only fortunately for me he had married Camilla first."

"Who is Camilla?"

"She's my stepmother, and a heart of gold, but she has to be seen to be believed. And she brought me up and made me have a profession, thank goodness."

"What do you profess?"

Susan drew herself up.

"I'm secretary to a Member of Parliament—a perfect old lamb. Well, you see, I never knew anything at all about the romantic history of Susie and Philip until about six months ago when Camilla turned me over a boxful of old family letters; and then I thought next time I had a holiday I'd come and have a look at the ancestral village. So when Easter came I ran down here, and it was simply too thrilling to discover Gran. I'm having my proper holiday now. And of course I simply had to be explained, so Miss Arabel came to Gran and said of *course* I was Robert's granddaughter, and Gran"—Susan gurgled—"*Gran* said she didn't mind other people telling lies so long as she wasn't asked to tell them herself. So, officially, I'm Robert's granddaughter, but of course

every single solitary soul in Ford St. Mary knows who I really am."
She sighed and got up. "I must go, my dear. And I don't think we'll tell
anyone just yet, except Gran. I must tell Gran. Come along and I'll show
you the secret passage. The catch is awfully well hidden."

Anthony went into the passage with her. When they came to the
place where it forked, he said,

"Where does that go?"

"Where do you think?"

"To the Ladies' House?"

"Yes—but I don't know where it comes out. Somewhere in the
drawing-room, Gran says. I've never had the nerve to go and see. Ours
comes out in the kitchen, which is much more suitable to our station
in life."

She was kissed for that. After which they climbed the steps and she
released the catch of the secret door. The section of the chimney wall
with its stout oak backing swung round. A steady yellow light came
through. Susan clutched Anthony and drew a shaky, laughing breath.

A voice came from the lighted kitchen:

"Susan—"

Susan let go of Anthony and stepped out into the ingle. Mrs. Bowyer
was sitting in her solid oak chair by the hearth with her patchwork
quilt across her knees. She had about her shoulders the white woolly
shawl which Susan had brought her as a present, and over her head a
little grey cross-over with a faint pink border, all done in shell-pattern
crochet which she had made herself. The light came from the wall-lamp
on her right.

She looked at Susan, sniffed slightly, and said, "Where ha'
you been?"

Anthony came through the opening.

Mrs. Bowyer sniffed again.

"And what's the meaning of this?"

Susan broke into a laugh, and the black eyes under the grey cross-
over fairly flared.

"Eh—you may laugh, my maid—laugh first and cry after!"

"Gran!"

The eyes turned on Anthony.

"What's your purpose with my maid, Anthony Colstone? Is it marriage?"

"Gran!"

"Mrs. Bowyer, we're engaged."

Mrs. Bowyer lifted her head.

"Then let me tell you that I think very little of you for letting my maid risk her good name this way. What do you think folks 'ud say if they knew that she slipped down in the dark and went the old secret way to Stonegate?"

Susan pulled her hand away with a jerk.

"Gran! What an *abominable* thing to say!"

"No," said Anthony quickly—"she's right. I'm sorry. You mustn't come again."

"Folks'll say worse than I've said," said old Mrs. Bowyer, nodding. She looked kindly at Anthony, and found him a proper young man. She thought the better of him for blushing.

Susan was pale and angry. Old Susan Bowyer felt a malicious satisfaction as she noted it.

"Folks'll say a sight worse than that," she repeated.

"They won't know," said Susan coldly.

"Eh?" said Mrs. Bowyer. "Folks know everything. I've lived near on a hundred years, and 'tis astonishing what they'll know. And what they don't know they'll make a pretty fair guess at—and it don't lose in the overturn neither." Her voice dropped and sobered. "Come here, Anthony Colstone, and give me your hand. Has she told you she's a Colstone too? True born Bowyer and Colstone—and that's the best gentry's blood and the best yeoman's blood of any in England. Right away back they go, both of 'em—true born and true bred, and whether 'twas Colstone or Bowyer, never a light woman as I heard tell about. That's what I said to my Susie when Mr. Philip began to look her way. I said it to Philip too, right out to his face." She stopped and looked straight in front of her with a strange, silent look. "Eh dear! They'd been married a month when I spoke, though I didn't know it till long after. And folks talked light of Susie, but they'd no call to, for I saw her lines myself. There's never anyone had any call to talk light about any of the Bowyer women." She paused and tossed her head a little. "And so I told Sir Jervis when we had words about it."

"About Susie?" said Susan. She had relaxed a little. She came nearer and took one of her grandmother's hands, whilst Anthony took the other.

Mrs. Bowyer nodded.

"Bitter words we had, and I told him to his face that he could look to his own daughter. That was Miss Arabel, my dears—a year younger than Susie and as pretty as a picture, and Sir Jervis' friend that we called the Jew courting her behind Sir Jervis' back."

"Oh, Gran, tell me! What happened?"

"He got sent about his business."

"Did she mind? Why wouldn't Sir Jervis allow it?"

"She must have been awfully pretty," said Anthony.

"Pretty as a picture, and mad about him—and mad to go off into foreign countries with him. That set on travelling Miss Arabel was, and after all she's had to live out her life in the place where she was born."

"Wouldn't they let her marry him because he was a Jew?"

Mrs. Bowyer went off into her soundless laughter.

"Mercy me, he wasn't a Jew! If he'd been a proper Jew, he might have had some money. He was just some kind of an engineer, making his living in foreign parts out of telling folks about mines and such like." She laughed again. "The Jew was just the name the young folks called him—Philip and Agatha and Arabel—because of his initials reading that way."

Anthony's hand tightened on hers. Jew.... J-E-W.... He saw the initials, in Sir Jervis' writing—J. E. W.

"What was his name?" he said quickly.

"Why, it's getting on for fifty years since I heard it," said Mrs. Bowyer. Her voice fell slow. "John—yes, 'twould be John for sure— John—Edwin—" She stopped, looking up at Anthony. "That's a kind of a soft name, and I can't abide a lad with a soft name. I never rightly took to him myself. John—Edwin.... Now what in the world was the rest of it? Something to do with the sky, for it puts me in mind of the red sky at night that oftener means a wet day than a fine one."

"What could it be, Gran? It's got to begin with a W."

"North—south—east—*west*—" said Mrs. Bowyer. "Red sky at night in the west. That's it! Bowyers never forget nothing. John Edwin West was his name, but the young folks called him Jew. And Miss Arabel broke her heart for him." She looked up straight at Anthony. "You'll not break my maid's heart, Anthony Colstone?"

"She's much more likely to break mine," said Anthony. And then he laughed, not very steadily, because he was remembering what it had felt like to see Susan leaning across the glass-topped medal case in deep, intimate talk with the man who had broken into his house. And she couldn't explain it; she wasn't ever going to be able to explain it. There was a secret running between them like a dark crack—

Old Susan Bowyer's face crinkled into hundreds of tiny lines, every one of them the shadow of a laugh.

"Colstone's hearts are none so easy broke," she said. Then her eyes went black and solemn. "Do you love her true?"

"Yes, Gran," said Anthony.

She nodded.

"Eh—there's queer things in life! I had a Colstone to my son, and now I have another to my great-grandson, and Susie's granddaughter at Stonegate. Who'd ha' thought it?" She lifted her chin at him with a jerk. "You'll bring her to Stonegate?"

"Yes, of course."

Mrs. Bowyer turned to Susan.

"And you, my maid—"

"What, Gran?"

"Is he your man?"

"He seems to think so," said Susan.

"Is he your man?" said Mrs. Bowyer. "There's none but you can say for sure."

Susan flushed scarlet. She wanted to pull away her hand, but Gran had it fast; she felt it drawn nearer to Anthony's. Something in her fluttered. It was like being in church; it was like being married. The kitchen with its one oil lamp, and Gran in her white woolly shawl, had suddenly become part of a mystery. When Anthony took her hand and Mrs. Bowyer laid both of hers over the joined clasp, Susan felt as if something irrevocable had happened.

The old lips moved without any sound of words. Then she released them and leaned back.

"Kiss me first, and Susan after," she said to Anthony.

Chapter Twenty-Nine

"I MUST SEE YOU," said Anthony. He stood with his back to the geraniums in Mrs. Bowyer's front window. The morning sunshine poured down outside.

"You are seeing me," said Susan.

Anthony groaned.

"Gran will be back in a minute—you know she will."

Susan's eyelashes flickered.

"She's very *fond* of you," she said. "She says you can call every day and see her. She says you're like my grandfather Philip—and she simply loved Philip." She burst out laughing at his face of dismay. "No—what she really says is that we've got to give it out."

"I said so too."

Susan made a face.

"It's so stupid and public. But of course I do see that it's going to be frightfully difficult for us to see each other unless we're engaged. Gran's the most frightful dragon really, but I've got her to promise not to do anything for a day or two, and I thought if I went for a walk across the river and you came along in the car and picked me up, we *might* go out for the day."

They went out for the day. The sun shone—everything shone. Life had become a joyful adventure. They left the car presently and climbed a little hill. The country below them was all gold and green, with here and there a patch of woodland, and here and there the gleam of water. There was a beechwood at their backs, and in front of them the ground fell away sharply. There was no sting in the sun, only a mellow warmth.

"Now we can talk," said Anthony.

"You've never stopped."

"Oh, that was about us. This is business."

"What sort of business?"

"Well, I'd a letter this morning that made me sit up and think."

"What sort of letter?"

"From old Leveridge, Sir Jervis' solicitor. You remember that letter I found, from his father to Sir Jervis about an offer for the property?"

Susan was leaning on her elbow picking at a little tuft of thyme. She looked up under her hat and saw Anthony's face, puzzled and intent.

"Yes, I know—the one with the note about J. E. W."

"Yes. Well, my letter—" He broke off. "Susan, it's odd. Leveridge says he's had an offer for Stonegate. He wrote to ask if I would consider it. It's from the same people his father wrote about—Stent Rogerson and Twyford."

Susan sat up. Her fingers crushed the thyme, and the sweet herby scent filled the sunny air between them.

"How extraordinary!"

"Too extraordinary," said Anthony. "One odd thing's nothing, but a whole lot of odd things must mean something. There's something— *something* behind all these odd things, and we've got to find out what it is."

Susan dropped the little crushed pieces of thyme. She put her hands in her lap and looked at a yellow cornfield that was shining like gold in the sun.

"What do you think it is?"

"I don't know. But there's something. Look here—you heard what Mrs. Bowyer said last night about my cousin Arabel and the man they called Jew?"

Susan nodded.

"Well, of course I thought at once about that letter and Sir Jervis' note—you remember: 'J. E. W.? Can't believe it. No—' And after I got Leveridge's letter this morning I thought a lot more. J. E. W. was a friend of Sir Jervis. He was an engineer—a mining engineer. He came down to stay, and he made love to my Cousin Arabel and got sent about his business. And afterwards Sir Jervis was repeatedly offered a price for Stonegate which old Leveridge described as so much in excess of the estimated market value that he didn't feel justified in accepting previous refusals as final. And at the bottom of the letter Sir Jervis himself connects the offer with J. E. W. Do you see what it looks like?"

Susan nodded again.

"Gran doesn't know any more. I asked her. She said Sir Jervis was mad with rage about Arabel. Fathers had awfully unrestrained tempers in those days—hadn't they? I gather he simply foamed, and Arabel wilted and didn't dare say 'Bo' to him. And she was ill for a long time, and then she just settled down into being an old maid. At nineteen, Anthony! Doesn't it make you boil?" She paused, frowning. "Talking about odd things—Sir Jervis said one frightfully odd thing to Gran."

"What was it?" said Anthony.

"Well, I thought it was odd when Gran told me; but you know how it is when you say a thing again—the oddness seems to evaporate."

"What is it?"

"Gran was standing up to him about Arabel, and he was in a fearful temper, and all of a sudden he banged with his fist on the table. It was in her front room. And he said, 'I'd sooner he ruined my daughter than my land, but as long as I live he won't lay a finger on either.' And Gran said he wasn't a swearing man, but he swore so fearfully that she was afraid. And she said it was the only time in their lives that she'd ever been afraid of him. What do you suppose he meant?"

Anthony was whistling some shred of an air between his teeth. He pursued it for a bar or two. Then he turned over on the short grass, leaning on his elbows with his chin in his cupped hands.

"J. E. W. was John Edwin West, and he was a mining engineer. And Sir Jervis raises Cain about his spoiling his land, and feels suspicious when he gets an offer for it. Does that suggest anything to you?"

Susan laughed.

"Yes, of course it does. It suggests that John Edwin—Golly! What a name! I say, Anthony, it has just struck me all of a heap. If he'd *married* Miss Arabel, he'd have been our cousin John Edwin, and there might have been little Edwins and Edwinas."

Anthony grinned and frowned.

"They'd have been middle-aged. Anyhow you're not sticking to the point.

"It was such a frightful thought," said Susan. "All right, I'm coming to the point. John Edwin found out something that Sir Jervis didn't like. I don't know what he found; but he was a mining engineer, and Sir Jervis said he wouldn't have his land ruined, and the price of Stonegate went right up. I wonder what he did find. But of course any sort of mine makes a nasty mess of things. I wonder if it was coal."

Anthony shook his head.

"Coal's a bit of a wash-out now. Whatever he found, it's something with a present-day value." He paused, biting his lip. "And anyhow, what were those two after in the cellars, and where does Philip Colstone's piece about Merlin's stone come in? I can't make it all fit in."

Susan looked away across the open country. The distant fields were like squares on a chessboard—gold, and brown, and green, and dun. She stared at the fields, but she was seeing a yellow, blotted page in an old book—seeing it as if it were being held up before her eyes. All of a sudden she pressed her fingers against her eyelids.

"What's the matter?" said Anthony.

"I don't know—I had an idea. I don't want to tell you about it, because it's just a—a sort of impression." She opened her eyes again. "Don't talk about it now, there's an angel. It's so vague that if I try and put it into words, I shall just lose it."

"What shall we talk about? I'm most awfully intrigued about those cellars—I've an idea that we shall find something when we get the door open. I'm having a key made, you know."

"Anthony, you won't open the door without me! I simply *couldn't* bear it. I don't care what Gran says, and I don't care how shocked anyone might be if they knew, but I've simply got to be there when you open that door."

Anthony said "All right." Then he laughed. "Perhaps other people will want to be there too."

"What do you mean?"

"Hasn't it struck you," he said, "that I may be having another midnight visit?"

"From me?" She looked at him between her lashes.

"No"—rather drily—"not from you."

"You mean you think *they*'ll come back?"

"Why did they take an impression of the lock if they didn't mean to come back?"

"Oh!" said Susan. She was leaning a little over on one hand. Anthony saw the knuckles turn white. He said nothing. "But you can stop them," she said.

"We bolt the doors now, so their keys won't be much good to them. Still, I've got a sort of feeling that they'll have a shot at it."

Susan turned quickly.

"Anthony—you'll be careful—"

"What have I got to be careful of?"

She did not say anything. She looked down and saw a spider with thin legs and a round white body run under and over the scattered heads of thyme she had thrown away. It ran aimlessly, moving quickly and getting nowhere. As she watched it, there came up in her inner mind the clear picture of Garry's face, pale and smiling, as she had seen it for an instant by lantern light in the dark housekeeper's room. She was afraid of Garry when he smiled. He had the poker in his hand, and he smiled. But the room was dark; the light from the lantern missed his face. She hadn't really seen him smile, but somehow she knew just how he had looked as he straightened himself with the poker in his hand. She heard again her own horrified cry. She said, in a very low voice,

"They might be—dangerous."

One of Anthony's hands came out and caught her wrist. The warm, strong clasp frightened her. It was so difficult not to tell him things—and she mustn't.

"What—the poker?" he said. "Were they going to hit me over the head with it? You might as well tell me."

Susan made up her mind. She tried to free herself, but she couldn't.

"They were going to break your leg."

"Good Lord! Why?"

"To keep you quiet for a bit."

She did not look at him, but she felt his clasp tighten.

"What? In cold blood?"

She nodded. Her eyes stung. She felt suddenly, dreadfully, afraid. With a wrench she freed her hand and dashed away two scalding tears.

Chapter Thirty

WHEN SHE LOOKED ROUND again, Anthony was sitting up with his hands clasped about his knees. He was looking at her with a serious expression; but when he spoke he said the last thing on earth that she had expected him to say; his direct look and his quiet voice gave her no warning.

"When are we going to get married?"

Susan said, "Married?" She looked a little bewildered. Her eyes were still wet.

"Yes—married. It's what happens after you get engaged, you know. I think being engaged is a wash-out as far as we are concerned because of the relations, and the village, and things like that. And I was thinking that we'd better get married at once, because then we could really get down to exploring without bothering about whether our characters were being taken away."

"What do you mean by 'at once'?"

"Well, I think a licence takes about three days—but that's only if you bustle them most frightfully, and we're miles from our native parson, so I'm afraid it's too late to do anything to-day, but to-day week would give everybody plenty of time."

Susan laughed, partly because she was nervous, and partly because Anthony looked so determined. She liked him when he looked like that. She wondered if he were really like her grandfather Philip. Gran said he was. He had the Colstone height and breadth, the bright brown hair and the ruddy brown skin. His chin was rather square, mouth large and well cut under a small moustache, nose rather blunted from the family type. She remembered how Gran had asked her what colour his eyes were. They were blue as he looked at her now, with just a hint of a teasing sparkle breaking through.

"It's a Thursday," said Anthony. "I should think it would be an awfully good day to get married."

Susan laughed again.

"My dear child, one doesn't get married like that."

"Why?"

"It isn't done."

"But it's so frightfully respectable to get married."

She shook her head.

"Not all in a hurry like that. Besides—" Her voice became quite serious. "Anthony, we don't really know each other—do we? Not well enough to get married, I mean."

"How are we going to get to know each other if we can't meet without all our relations to chaperone us?"

"I expect Gran would let us go for walks occasionally."

Anthony edged towards her and put his arm round her waist.

"Thursday's a ripping day to get married."

"Gran would say, 'Marry in haste and repent at leisure,' You see, you only know the nice side of me, and I only know the nice side of you. People ought to know each other's faults before they get married."

"All right," said Anthony, "you shall tell me yours, and I will tell you mine. Just in case you're too horrified to go on being engaged after you've heard the worst you'd better give me a sort of farewell kiss."

There was more than one kiss.

Then Susan said, "I've got a temper."

"I knew that."

"You don't know the sort of temper it is. I can go on being angry a long time, in a sort of cold, hateful way, and there are some things I don't think I could ever forgive."

"What sort of things?"

"Oh, I don't know—mean things—things that people do behind one's back—and—and being cruel to an animal or a child—or when people are rude to someone they don't think it matters about because they're poor, or old, or stupid. I—I hate that. And I'm fond of clothes—and if I've got any money I spend it—and I simply can't keep accounts. And once I stole something."

"What did you steal?"

Susan did not look very guilty.

"It was a puppy belonging to the woman next door—when I lived with Camilla. The people used to go away for days and leave it without anything to eat. And at last I couldn't bear it, so I burgled their back yard at midnight. I was about twelve. And first Camilla scolded me like mad, and then she became an enthusiastic accessory after the fact, and we went out hand in hand with the puppy in a basket, and walked about four miles in the middle of the night, and knocked up some friends of hers who were all fast asleep in bed and made them accessories too. They were just moving into the country, so they were frightfully pleased, because they were meaning to get a dog, but they couldn't really afford to buy one."

"After that," said Anthony, "of course the whole thing's off. My heart is broken"—he clutched it—"but I can never, never, *never* marry a puppy-snatcher."

"If you're not going to marry me, you oughtn't to kiss me," said Susan. "Now tell me about your vices."

"I haven't got any."

"None?"

"No, no—not one."

Susan held up her left hand and touched the forefinger.

"I can tell you three right away. Untruthfulness"—she moved to the next finger—"conceit—hypocrisy"—she arrived at her little finger—"brazenness. That's thrown in as an extra."

"You've got rather pretty hands," said Anthony.

"Yes, I know I have."

"Go on telling me about my vices—there's something very soothing about it. But I'm just wondering whether we can't get married before Thursday, because if you go on finding me out at this rate, I shall be such a monster of iniquity in a week's time that Gran will interfere and forbid the banns."

He rubbed his cheek against hers. Susan's voice became soft.

"Gran said to marry a lad who had a kindness for you."

"Have I a kindness for you?"

"You know."

"Don't *you*?" said Anthony very low.

Susan did not answer for a moment. Then she said,

"After we were engaged Gran talked to me a lot. She said kindness was what mattered most when you were married. She said that was what lasted—"

Her voice stopped, because she was hearing old Susan Bowyer's voice: "There's folks as goes through life same as a cat goes through a dairy—they'll take the cream and spoil the pan, and off to the next one. There's men like it, and women too—when the cream's gone they've no use for the skim. But proper married folk have got to take things like they come, and with the Lord's blessing they'll find enough cream to make 'em relish the skim."

Anthony put his head down on her shoulder.

"Please God we'll be kind to each other."

Chapter Thirty-One

ANTHONY MADE SURE of the bolts before he went to bed that night. When he was come to his room he stood for a long time at the window looking up the hill with the room dark behind him. It was after eleven o'clock and there was no moon. He had put out his candle, and for a time he saw the shape of the flame wherever he turned his eyes. Then it was gone, and the shape of the hill began to emerge from the general blackness. The haze which had clung about the skyline all day had risen until it hid the stars. Very little light came through it, but when he had been looking out for some minutes the arch of the sky showed faintly luminous. Beneath it the tilted fields lay dark, and the hedges black. He could not really see the Stones, but he fancied that he could make out the two tall monoliths.

As he stood there, he went over in his mind all that he knew about the Stones. It was like handling half a dozen pieces from a puzzle which perhaps contained a hundred; none of his bits would fit, because he lacked the pieces to fit them to. He went on thinking, until at last he turned away from the window and lit his candle.

After he was in bed he tried to put the whole matter from his mind. He thought about Susan. They could be married quite soon; there was nothing for them to wait for. He began to make plans and build castles, and he began to get drowsy.

He was slipping down into sleep, and as he slipped, something he had kept at a distance began to push its way among his thoughts and to come so near that he could not help seeing and hearing what he had not meant to hear and see. He saw Susan leaning towards the man who had watched him. "He was going to break my leg with the poker." And he heard Susan say, "I can't ever tell you." And she said, "He isn't my brother," and she said, "Perhaps he is."—"Is he in love with you?"— "Perhaps he is." And he saw Susan put up her hand and dash away two bright shining drops. And then she had put her face in her hands and he had had hard work to comfort her. He could feel her trembling now—trembling up against him—dumb. "I can't tell you—I can't ever tell you."

All at once he was awake and the room was dark. He had been seeing the grassy slope with the sun on it. Susan was there, crying. Now all at once he was awake in the dark, remembering the other time that he had waked like this. He got up at once and went down, carrying a torch ready to switch on. When he came to where the stair ran down into the hall, he stood and listened for a while. There was no sound at all.

After a while he switched on his torch and turned the beam here and there. When it crossed the hall door, his hand tightened and his arm went rigid. The light touched the bolt at the top of the door, touched it and dropped with his sudden movement. He brought it back to the bolt and kept it there, staring incredulously at what it showed. The clock in the library was beginning to strike twelve. It was not an hour since he had looked to the bolts and gone up to bed. The beam fell now on a bolt drawn back.

Anthony came down the stair at a run. Both bolts were drawn, and as he turned the handle, the door opened easily, noiselessly. Whoever had drawn the bolts had also turned the key. Beyond the door the glazed passage lay empty. The bolts of the door into the street had been drawn back too. The key had been taken from the lock and lay on a little ledge to the right. The door was locked.

He shot the bolts and replaced the key. It was perfectly clear that the bolts had been drawn back for the convenience of somebody who had a key—the inner door had been unlocked to make things as easy as possible.

As Anthony pushed home the bolts of the inner door, he asked himself insistently whose concern it was to make things easy for a midnight visitor. Someone inside the house had come down to slip back the bolts and turn the key. Lane? Mrs. Hutchins? One of the maids? Lane had been here forty years, and Mrs. Hutchins thirty. The housemaid was the sexton's daughter, a worthy middle-aged woman. The between-maid, the youngest Smithers, Ellen by name, a fat rosy child with a giggle and a blush and an outrageous capacity for breaking china, honest stupidity stamped on every feature. Which of these four people was the least unlikely to have come down in the dark to admit a burglar?

As Anthony stood there without any answer to this question, he heard from behind him on his left the faintest sound which it is possible to hear at all. The silence of the sleeping house was just touched and no more. The sound that touched it came from the library.

In a moment Anthony was running down the passage, and as he flung open the library door and threw up his hand with the lighted torch in it, he heard footsteps and the rustle of a dress, and a moment later, as the beam of the torch came to rest, he saw the panel which carried Patience Pleydell's portrait swing round and slam. There was no one in the library. Whoever had been there had gone again. The panel was shut between them. A door had shut. Some doors can never be opened again.

Anthony stood stock still, and saw the light of his torch shake like a Jack o' Lanthorn. A full minute passed before he realized that it was shaking because the hand that held it—his own hand—was shaking. He steadied it with an effort, went forward to the panel, and opened it. If it was Susan who had come by the secret way, it was in his mind to ask her why she had come. Impossible that Susan could have come to draw back the bolts. Only this afternoon they had sat on a hill in the sunlight and he had told her that the doors were bolted at night. Quite, quite impossible that Susan should have come to draw back the bolts.

He hadn't seen her; he had seen the closing panel and a flutter of blue; the light had caught the blue before the panel shut. His fingers shook on the catch. Close, close to him here in the picture, his great-great-grandmother wore that bright, deep blue for a petticoat. The panel opened. It was only a minute really since he had seen it shut on the glimpse of blue. He sent the torchlight ahead of him and ran down the steps.

As he came to where the passage forked, he stood still, listening and throwing the beam to the right. If it wasn't Susan who had come down the passage, then it was someone who had come from the Ladies' House. He heard no sound and could see no sign. He thought he would follow the left-hand passage to the end. He felt a longing to be near Susan, to see her. The temptation to pass through the secret door into the kitchen and by some means have sight and speech of her was overwhelming. He would at any rate go as far as the door. Perhaps he would open it. Perhaps Susan would know how much he wanted to see her and come down. Only that afternoon, when they had been sitting silent for a while, he had put out his hand on a sudden impulse, and her hand had met his as if the one impulse had moved them both. Perhaps it would be like that now—she would know that he was there and come down.

His foot struck the bottom step with a little grating sound. The light was focussed low to show where the ascent began. With one foot on the step he checked, and heard above him the sound of a closing door. After a moment he flashed the light ahead. There was no one there. The door had shut upon someone passing out of the passage, and not upon someone entering it.

For a moment Anthony felt sick. All the thoughts which he had refused to entertain rushed in upon him. Susan saying "I can't tell you." Susan with a knowledge of men whom she confessed to be desperate and dangerous—"I can't tell you. I can't ever tell you." Susan in her blue petticoat playing at family ghosts. A scurry of frightened feet and a dazzle of light on a fold of blue as the panel slammed. Bolts drawn back as soon as he had gone to bed. And Susan knew that he shot the bolts at night. And Susan knew who it was who had come that way before. And when he had come before, she had been there. "I can't tell you. I can't ever tell you, Anthony." He felt sick.

He did not know how long it was before the sickness passed; but all at once it did pass, and with it his acceptance of these thronging thoughts. It didn't really matter what things looked like. There were things that were possible, and there were things that were so starkly impossible that all the evidence in the world could not make them real enough to believe.

He walked slowly back along the passage. His mind, empty of thought, had become unusually sensitive to surface impressions. He found himself noting, as by instinct, the number of steps leading down into the passage, its height—an inch or two over six feet except in the middle, where the floor dipped and gave some extra inches. The width he put at four feet, but the passage that led to the Ladies' House was less, and both passages were lined with brick. That accounted for their being so dry.

He climbed the steps on the Stonegate side and came to the space behind the picture. Here the passage widened out, leaving room to stand on either side of the panel. He turned his light here and there, looking for the catch. He had his hand on it, when one of those surface impressions returned so vividly that it startled him. On the right the brick wall ran right up to the wooden panelling; but on the left the last foot of the wall was not brick but panelled wood.

Anthony turned the light to the left. There was a foot-wide panel just like the picture in his mind, but it did not go quite up to the top nor reach to within a foot of the floor. It seemed impossible that it should be there without any reason, and as he shifted the light and came nearer, the reason disclosed itself. The panel was the front of a cupboard sunk in the wall. It formed a door, and this door stood ajar.

As he pulled it open, a book which had been insecurely held in place by the door slid forward and fell at his feet. He picked it up, and experienced some disappointment. What he held was no relic of a remote past, but a perfectly modern exercise book about half an inch thick.

The cupboard was a shallow one with three shelves. The exercise book had fallen off the top one. On the second shelf lay a long envelope. For the rest, the cupboard was empty.

Anthony took the envelope and the exercise book into the library and lit the lamp. In spite of the modern appearance of his finds, he was conscious of a good deal of excitement. As he turned up the wick, the light fell full upon the envelope. It was of a yellowish colour, rather faded, and a thick layer of dust covered it except where his handling had brushed it clean. He shook off the rest of the dust against the table and read, in Sir Jervis' writing: "J. E. W.'s report." The flap was unstuck. He turned it back eagerly and said "Damn!" The envelope was empty.

He stared at it, asking questions which had no answers. What had happened to the report? Had Sir Jervis destroyed it? Or had it been stolen? If so, who had stolen it? To this question he thought he had an answer. He thought it a good enough answer to suppose that it had been stolen by the person who had come through the passage to unbolt his doors and had afterwards run away from him in such a hurry. He thought the person must have been in rather a hurry altogether, since she had been careless enough to leave the cupboard door ajar.

He turned to the exercise book, and discovered this also to have been Sir Jervis' property. It appeared, in fact, to be some sort of a diary, and the first page bore the date 1860. There was no month given. The first entry read:

> The house requires more in the way of repair than my pocket will stand. Leveridge tells me that my father had considerable losses over a venture which he undertook to oblige a friend.

There followed entries of a brief character with regard to the granting of leases; and then, under the heading June 14th:

> Another letter from poor O'Connell, full of abuse like the last. It sounds to me as if he should be under some restraint. He accuses me in set terms of making away with his share of a treasure which, so far as I can make out, he supposes himself to have discovered during the time that we were quartered in the old Fort at Lahore. As I left him in a high delirium when I received my orders to proceed to England, I can only imagine that this strange accusation had its origin in some feverish dream, and that it has most unfortunately persisted as a fixed delusion. I wish to set down here my assurance that this delusion rests upon no foundation of fact. It was common talk among the officers stationed in the Fort that a good deal of treasure was supposed to have been buried there. It was said that Grayson had come upon some of it. He certainly made haste to leave the Company's service, and I have heard that he has bought himself a fine landed property, a fact which gives colour to this supposition. But as far as I am concerned, I most solemnly asseverate that I neither found any treasure nor knew for a certainty of anyone else having done so, and that so far as Major O'Connell's assertion concerns me it is utterly baseless and chimerical. N.B.—I make this statement in case there should prove to be anything in my grandfather's belief regarding Philip Colstone. I have some recollection of having touched upon the story to O'Connell. I think he had been talking about treasure trove, and I recall that he showed a good deal of interest and excitement and would have had me pull Stonegate down to get at the truth of the matter.

Anthony read this passage through several times. He had never heard of Major O'Connell, and did not therefore take any interest in the passages relating to him. It was the last paragraph which arrested his attention. If it meant anything at all, it meant that there was some family tradition which connected one Philip Colstone with some buried treasure, and that Sir Jervis had been apprehensive lest, if this treasure came to light, it should seem to lend colour to Major O'Connell's wild accusation.

He read on eagerly; but the next entries dealt with drainage, crops, and the erection of a conservatory.

Anthony turned the pages slowly. Sir Jervis wrote a clear hand and did not waste words. Sums disbursed in repairs were set down. Family events were noted briefly; as, the death of his wife in 1863: "March 1st. My wife died to-day. Funeral Thursday;" and, two years later under date of August 3rd: "Heard to-day from Leveridge that James, my Uncle Ambrose Colstone's son, is dead. He leaves a son in infancy. The child's name is Ralph." After that the entries were very sparse, one or two a year, and then a gap of four or five years. Somewhere about '75 they began again.

The first entry bore no date, but the ink being of the same colour as the next one, which was plainly headed "January 29th, '75," it was presumably not very far removed in point of time. The entry ran:

Old cellars to be looked to. William Bowyer reports them unsafe.

The entry under January 29th may, or may not, have had any connection:

January 29th. Asked Leveridge to recommend good man. He says young West is extremely competent, and that he would undertake to make a survey on reasonable terms. As he will be leaving the country in a month's time to take up an appointment in Brazil, I should prefer him to someone resident in England. I have asked Leveridge to exact a pledge of professional secrecy.

A week later he wrote:

J. E. W. arrived. He looks young, but has had experience abroad. Very good credentials, but a talker. I impressed upon him the necessity of regarding the affair as strictly confidential.

There were no more entries for ten days. Then:

February 15th. J. E. W.'s report. It is in the safe place. It is useless to regret, but I feel that I have put it in his power to do us what I should consider an irreparable injury. He seemed surprised that I should take it in this way—spoke to me in his inflated style of the wealth which would now be at my command. And when I informed him that I had no intention of butchering my estate and ruining my property, which had come down to me through more generations than I could count, he had the impertinence to smile in my face and observe that I should probably change my mind. He leaves next week. I am sorry that he was asked to stay so long.

On February 17th there was another entry:

J. E. W. left.

And on the 20th:

I have destroyed J. E. W.'s report.

Well, that disposed of that anyhow. Anthony felt relieved. The report at any rate had not been stolen. Sir Jervis had destroyed it. He read on, but the diary had relapsed into a dry record of business transactions. There was no mention anywhere of Miss Arabel who had broken her heart for the young man who was a great talker. Perhaps the fact that he had been abroad had appealed to her if, as Susan Bowyer said, she had always wanted to travel. Perhaps he had won her heart with tales of adventure delivered in the inflated style of which Sir Jervis disapproved. The diary ignored the whole affair, as it had ignored Philip Colstone's elopement.

On March 30th Sir Jervis wrote:

J. E. W. sailed yesterday for Brazil.

There were only three more entries, and they concerned payments made in respect of fencing a field, repairs to stables, and the purchase of a lawn-mower. The rest of the book was blank.

Chapter Thirty-Two

ANTHONY TOOK SIR JERVIS' DIARY up to his own room and locked it away in the dispatch-box at the foot of his bed. It was obvious that the secret cupboard was no longer the "safe place" which Sir Jervis had called it. He thought he would find it impossible to sleep, but in the midst of a resolve to show Susan the diary next day and to persuade her by some means or another to marry him at once he slipped into dreamless slumber and did not awake until the sun was up. He decided that he would go and see Susan at nine o'clock, to which end he breakfasted at half-past eight, a good deal to Lane's surprise.

He found Mrs. Bowyer dusting the china from the corner-cupboard in her living-room. She turned to greet him with an old silk handkerchief in one hand and a spotted cow in the other.

"Eh, my dear, she's gone to London."

"To London?" Anthony felt as if he had stubbed his toe against something hard and unexpected.

"London," said Mrs. Bowyer, nodding. She put down the cow very carefully on the table beside the bible with the record of Philip and Susie's marriage and took up a white greyhound spotted with black. A hare dangled from its jaws. Its expression was mild and fatuous. "Bright and early," continued Mrs. Bowyer—"and got a lift into Wrane with Enoch Adams. She came into my room as soon as the post was in and she says, 'Gran, I've got to go to London.' And I says, 'And how are you going to get to Wrane, my dear?' And she says, 'I'm sure I don't know, Gran.' And then I remembered Enoch, and I says 'You run down to Adamses and you'll just about catch Enoch.' And so she did."

Anthony frowned.

"Is she coming back to-day?"

Mrs. Bowyer rubbed at a mark on the greyhound's back.

"I don't know, my dear—and what's more, it's my belief she didn't know herself. And she went off all in a hurry, but she caught Enoch, for I looked out of her window and saw 'em go by."

"I suppose she had a letter calling her up to town."

"I suppose she did," said Mrs. Bowyer placidly.

Anthony went away with all last night's whispers ringing loud in his ears. Someone had come through the passage and drawn back the bolts—someone wearing Susan's blue petticoat—someone who had run away—someone who had gone through the secret door into Mrs. Bowyer's kitchen. And Susan had gone away to London by the early train and left no word for him.

He was at the door, when Mrs. Bowyer called him back.

"You haven't asked if she left you a message."

"Did she?"

Mrs. Bowyer nodded.

"Just to tell you she'd gone, and to say it was about *The Shepheard's Kalendar*."

Anthony bounded across the street, got out the old Daimler, and made a sporting effort to catch the nine-thirty at Wrane. He missed it by no more than a couple of minutes.

To sit down for hours and do nothing was a most appalling prospect. To see Susan was a necessity, because the moment he saw her, those horrible whisperings would depart once and for all. It wouldn't be possible to look at Susan and believe…. He didn't believe the whispers; he hadn't ever believed them—no, not for a single second. It was like having stones and rotten eggs chucked at you—beastly. And the fact that you didn't want them didn't make it less beastly, but a good deal more so. He decided to push on to London and chance the old bus falling to bits on the road.

Susan had gone to town because the early post brought her a letter from Camilla. In a characteristically illegible hand Camilla wrote:

Jungle now complete with tiger rugs. Elaine Herbertson positively pressed two gorgeous skins into my hands. One of them nearly ate Bobby, so she hates it—and the other is its mate, so she said a pity to part them. Anyhow she says cannot carpet entire house with tigers. Bobby has shot forty-one, and his sisters now turn up their noses. (They always did—hideous family!)

Am taking up aviation. Hope to get certificate soon. Am planning Articles on Cloud Effects, The Flat Earth, Above the Rainbow. Poetic side of flying has been hopelessly neglected. Lois Tarnowski just back from (name totally illegible). She assures me that the rumours about (another dense tangle of letters) are undoubtedly true—Sensational disclosures at any moment. But don't breathe a *word* to a *soul*, as it was told me in the *strictest* confidence.

Take about a dozen large snails. Sprinkle lightly with brown sugar and leave overnight. In the morning snails will be found to have dissolved. Strain off liquid. Take one large cabbage, three onions raw, a clove of garlic, and any fresh shell-fish—

This was lightly stroked out. The letter continued:

Didn't notice I had begun to copy Lois' receipt for *Tarsch*—the most marvellous dish, but takes a little getting used to. You shall try it next time you come and stay. By the way, that receipt *you* asked me for—British Museum, not cookery—after writing to Sarah I found it in your father's old pocket-book. Garry happened to come in, and offered to cope with the Museum authorities and get the book back. He says it is a man's job. *Do* thank him nicely. He doesn't put himself out for people as a rule, but of course *you* are different. I always feel that what he needs is a *woman's* influence.

Your devoted,

Camilla.

P.S.—I thought he was looking pale. His hand quite trembled when I spoke of you—I noticed it because I was giving him the receipt.

Susan fairly ground her teeth over this letter. She looked at her watch, decided that she might with luck catch the early train, rushed into civilized clothes, and ran all the way to the Adams', where she was just in time to ask for a lift into Wrane. It was market day. Enoch had eggs, honey and vegetables in his cart, but he made room for Susan, and Mrs. Enoch produced a cushion for her to sit on.

All the time that Susan was thanking them and engaging in agreeable conversation with Enoch, who was a great talker, she was calling Camilla the most frightful names in her own mind. This ought to have been a relief, but it wasn't. The situation was now so desperate that a whole commination service would have been inadequate. Susan simply felt that she didn't know enough words to deal with it. She went on feeling this all the way up in the train. Garry had the receipt. By this time Garry probably had the book too. That is to say Garry had the book, and the Museum had the receipt.

She looked at Camilla's letter again. Naturally, it was not dated. Camilla never dated letters. Sometimes she scrawled across the top of one. "Thursday morning," or "Sunday afternoon." This one was simply headed eleven o'clock. It had been posted at four, but it might have been written at eleven o'clock at night, or eleven o'clock in the morning, on any day since Susan's last visit to town. Garry might have three days' start, or two, or only one. If the Museum had dug in its toes and made difficulties about giving up *The Shepheard's Kalendar*—Susan seemed to recollect having heard that Museums were rather given that way—then perhaps Garry hadn't succeeded in getting any start at all.

When she thought about Garry her anger fairly shook her. She had been angry with him so often that she might have got used to it; but this time the quick rush of feeling had a freshness and an intensity which fairly startled her. She recognized that an element of fear was mingled with her anger. Lately Garry had frightened her more than once. But the things that had frightened her were foolish little things. A sort of stab of fear went through her. She was afraid without reason, and because she could find no reason for her fear it became a hundred times more terrifying.

The thing that frightened her most came back again and again; as a picture; as words spoken by Garry, spoken by herself, when she had met him only a few days ago at the Victoria and Albert Museum. She could see the medal case with its sloping glass top and the light shining in through the window on her right, and Garry leaning towards her across the case with something hard and strange in his eyes. She could hear herself say, "What do you want at Stonegate? What on *earth* are you looking for?" And then Garry, in his light, smooth voice, "Why, my grandfather's treasure to be sure. What else?"

And that had frightened her; without the least, faintest shadow of a reason it had frightened her. Something in his voice, something in his look, something in the way he had leaned a little nearer and laid a light caressing touch upon her shoulder—She broke off in her thoughts, and a cold shiver ran down her back. It is much, much worse to be frightened of nothing than it is to be afraid of anything that you can see, or touch.

Garry's "What else?"... That was just it—what else? What was Garry looking for that he needed a key for the old Colstone cellars? What was Garry looking for that he needed the book which Philip Colstone had sent to his little son when he lay dying? What was Garry looking for? If the answer was anywhere, it was in Philip Colstone's book. Ever since she had turned over the discoloured pages Susan had been haunted by a strange impression. She kept seeing, as it were by flashlight, the pages of the July eclogue. They were faded and spotted. She could see them, and lose them again in the space of an instant—come, go—come, go—come, go. But every flashing glimpse deepened an impression of purpose in the blots. The pages were stained, the letters blotted; not every letter, but here and there, and so on from line to line, one here and one there, a faint round blot below it or above—

Susan had found herself wondering, guessing, jumping to a wild conclusion. She could not verify it unless she had the book in her hand; but if she had it, it would not take more than a minute to put it to the test. If the blotted letters made words, then her wild guess would have hit its mark, and the *Septima Aegloga*—the July eclogue, the eclogue of the month in which the English fleet met the Armada—would prove to contain Philip Colstone's message to his son; a message so important that he would not write it down plainly, so secret that he had neither trusted it to his wife nor to William Bowyer. And Camilla had given Garry the receipt. When? That was the all-important question.

At the terminus she went straight to a telephone box and rang up Camilla. It seemed ages before she heard a rather breathless "Hullo!" Thank goodness Camilla was at home. It would have been so exactly like her to be flying to Australia.

Susan drew a breath of relief and said, "Susan speaking."

"How nice, my dear! Are you in town? Because if you are, you *must* come and have lunch with me and meet Lois and—"

"Camilla—listen! I got your letter this morning. *When* did you give that receipt to Garry?"

"When? Oh, my dear, weren't you touched at his offering, actually *offering*, to see the whole thing through for you?"

"Camilla, do *listen*! When did you give him the receipt?"

"I think," pursued Camilla in a warm, pleased voice, "I think it really does show that he is becoming more altruistic."

"Look here, Camilla, I have *not* come up here to discuss Garry's character. I've come up about that receipt, and I want to know when you gave it to him."

"I found it," said Camilla, "the very day you came up, after I'd had all the trouble of writing to Sarah—you know I told you I thought she'd got a dispatch-box of mine. Well, it was after that. And Garry came in next morning—no, afternoon—or was it next day? Yes, yesterday, because I know Lois wasn't there, and she was the day before, so it must have been yesterday."

"You gave him the receipt yesterday?"

"Yes, darling—that's what I keep telling you—yesterday afternoon. And then I wrote and told you about it. But I couldn't stop my letter to Sarah, because Stella posted it after she came to tea the day before—no, it was the day you were up, because I was still painting the drawing-room."

"Where—is—Garry?" said Susan in her loudest and firmest tones.

"Darling child, I haven't the least idea. He may be anywhere—positively anywhere."

Susan strove for patience.

"I mean is he in his old rooms?"

"Oh, so far as I know."

Susan rang off. If Camilla had really only given Garry the receipt yesterday afternoon, *The Shepheard's Kalendar* might still be in the Museum. Susan had a sort of feeling that the woolly old gentleman would not give up Spenser's autograph without a struggle. She began to consider what would happen if she went straight to the Museum and said, "Look here, the book belongs to me." That might stop them giving it up to Garry; but on the other hand it would probably result in their hanging on to it indefinitely on the plea that the ownership was in dispute. All the same—

Susan came out of the telephone box and looked at her watch. It was eleven o'clock. Quite suddenly she made up her mind to go first to Garry's rooms. If he was there, he was going to hear some plain home truths, and if he wasn't there, she would just have a look around. She had a feeling that it might be quite interesting to spend half an hour in Garry's rooms.

She took a bus, and then walked. It had been sunny in the country, but the London sky was blurred and grey. There was no breeze, and the air had a sort of chill stuffiness.

Susan rang the bell of a tall, narrow house standing in a row of other tall, narrow houses, and was told that Mr. O'Connell was out.

"When will he be in?" she said.

The slatternly woman who had opened the door fingered her pale chin with limp, smudged fingers.

"Well now, that's more than I can say."

"Can I come in and wait?"

The woman looked sideways. Her voice sounded sulky.

"Not in the morning, with all the work of the house to be done."

"Will he be in in the afternoon?"

"He might be."

"Then I'll come back."

She made her way to the Museum. She was a fool not to have gone there first. She had wasted time and accomplished nothing.

She did not accomplish very much at the Museum. After some delay there appeared, not the woolly old gentleman, but a much younger man. No, he said, he was afraid he couldn't help her at all. Yes, he believed someone had been making inquiries about the book—Mr. Wrexham had mentioned it. No, Mr. Wrexham wasn't here this morning. No, he couldn't say whether he would be here this afternoon. No, he was afraid he couldn't show her the book, as he believed Mr. Wrexham had locked it up in his private room. He was very sorry not to be able to assist her.

Susan thanked him and came away. Over a cup of coffee and a bun she wondered whether she ought to have said that the book belonged to her and was on no account to be given to anyone else. She began to feel depressed and inefficient. And then all at once she thought that what she ought to have done was to stay at the Museum and make sure that Garry didn't get away with *The Shepheard's Kalendar*. Only you can't stay in a Museum for ever, and even if she went back there now, Mr. Wrexham might have returned, and Garry might have come and gone again.

She went back to Garry's rooms, and this time the woman let her in. She had not exactly washed her face, but this morning's black smudges had, as it were, been merged into a general dingy grey. She had removed her dirty apron and wore a sack-like collarless garment of magenta repp, pinned crooked at the neck with a large cheap paste brooch.

"You can go up, but I'm not saying when he'll be back, though he did say something about coming back to pack his bag, and if you're his young lady, he'll be put out above a bit if he misses you. Recognized you at once, I did, from the photo in his room—though I always say there's some of these photos is dodged up so as their own mothers wouldn't know them. But there—it stands to reason a young lady wants to look her best when she has her photo took—specially if it's to give to her young gentleman. Go right up, and it's the first door on the top—and a nice light room too, if the roof does slope a bit."

Susan found her way up a stair that grew steeper with every flight. Only the bottom flight was carpeted; the others were covered with a cheap cracked linoleum. There were three doors on the top landing. The first on the right opened into Mr. Garry O'Connell's sitting-room, which was furnished chiefly with a round old-fashioned mahogany table and a large shapeless armchair. The table had a battered top and an air of having come down in the world. On one side of it was an inkstand, a dirty blotter, and a huddle of papers; on the other, relics of Mr. O'Connell's last meal, such as a pot of marmalade, a few lumps of sugar in a cracked basin, and a litter of toast crumbs. Against the opposite wall there was a cheap gimcrack cupboard, and, partly on the floor and partly in piles on a bamboo bookcase, there were a good many books. The window looked down into the street, and on the other side of the room a narrow door led into the bedroom.

Susan took a good look out of the window and then started to hunt for *The Shepheard's Kalendar*. If Garry had got it yesterday it might be here, and that would save a great deal of trouble. After ten minutes she decided that it wasn't there, unless it was locked up in the dispatch-box under Garry's bed. Of course it might be. But Garry's dispatch-box was always full to bursting, and there was no sign of a wad of papers having been thrown out to make room for something more important.

Susan sat down in the lumpy armchair and wondered what Anthony was doing. She felt all of a sudden as if she wanted Anthony very much. She also wanted to cry.

Chapter Thirty-Three

ANTHONY WAS ENGAGED in looking for a needle in a bundle of hay. He was so set on getting to London that it was only when he had garaged his car and attended to a little matter of business that it occurred to him that he really hadn't the slightest idea how he was going to find Susan. He thought himself rather clever when the idea of looking for Camilla in the telephone directory occurred to him. Since Camilla was Susan's stepmother, her name was bound to be Colstone. He looked for a likely Mrs. Colstone, and when he found a Mrs. Ralph Colstone he rang her up.

There was no reply from Mrs. Ralph Colstone. He tried twice more, and then gave it up. Then the idea of the British Museum came into his mind and stuck there. Susan had come up to town about *The Shepheard's Kalendar.* She'd be bound to go to the Museum—only she had a couple of hours' start, worse luck. He jumped into a taxi.

It was just as the taxi stopped that he caught sight of a face which he recognized instantly. Coming towards him, with a parcel under his arm and a soft hat on his head, was the man whom he had seen glaring at him from the hedge by the Coldstone Ring and looking down from Nurse Collins' window. He was also quite sure that it was the man who had leaned on the table in the dark housekeeper's room, and the man who had talked to Susan in the medal room at the Victoria and Albert Museum.

Anthony was leaning forward, his hand on the half-open door, his foot already moving towards the step, when he stopped, jerked the door to, and flung himself back out of sight. The man with the book under his arm passed so close that if Anthony had stayed where he was, he could have touched him. He waited a moment. Then he put his head out of the window and told the driver to follow the man with the parcel.

Susan got very tired of waiting. Sometimes she wondered what she was waiting for. If Garry came back with the book, what was she going to do about it? She couldn't take it away from him by force, and if he suspected what she suspected, he certainly wouldn't give it up for the asking—and he must suspect *something*, or he wouldn't have got the receipt out of Camilla. Garry being unselfish and obliging was an insubstantial and unconvincing figment of Camilla's imagination.

If Garry came back with the book—somehow Susan had a feeling that he would come back with it—well, what about it—what was she going to do? That was it. What was she going to do? All at once she knew, and her spirits rose with a bound. It might not come off, but it was worth trying. Anyhow she would be doing something. It was so frightfully depressing just to sit still and feel limp and inefficient whilst other people stole your hereditary secrets. Now at least she would be doing something.

The first thing she did was to pick out from the jumble of Garry's books the nearest in size to *The Shepheard's Kalendar* in its needlework cover. Then she routed about and found some brown paper in Garry's trunk and an odd bit of string in the sitting-room cupboard. She wondered how museums tied a book up, and then she wondered whether they would tie it up at all. The needlework cover reassured her—and one book tied up in brown paper looks very much like another. Anyhow it was a chance. It was more than a chance, it was a good chance; because if Garry had the book, he wouldn't want her to see it, so he would try and put it down somewhere out of sight—he'd be bound to.

She put the brown paper down on the table and laid the book upon it. The edge of the paper caught the jumble of letters there and pushed some of them off on to the floor. Susan stooped to pick them up. There was an envelope, two letters, and a newspaper cutting.

One does not read other people's letters; but newspaper cuttings are a different matter. Susan's eye was first caught, and then held. Right at the top of the cutting was the sign which was cut upon the Coldstone, the sign of the two interlaced triangles. Over this sign ran the heading, "The Shield of David."

She read the whole paragraph with a beating heart and burning cheeks; and then, just as she came to the last line, she heard a door bang somewhere below. She pushed the cutting down inside her bag and finished her parcel in a rush. Then she tucked it under her coat, high up where she could hold it against her side by the pressure of her left arm. She was thankful she had come up in a coat and skirt, and not in a thin muslin dress. She felt as hot as fire. She ran to the window and once more looked down into the street. There was a black cloud darkening all the sky above the houses opposite—one of those inky clouds which promise rain and an early falling dark. There were hours of daylight still, but the light seemed to be failing every moment. She looked up and down the street for any sign of Garry. Three children were playing in the gutter on the right. A girl in a bright pink cotton dress and a bright green hat was wheeling a perambulator down the left-hand pavement and looking back over her shoulder at a young man who was staring after her. On the opposite pavement someone was standing looking up at the house she was in. She leaned right out of the window, and only just stopped herself from crying out, because the man was Anthony.

And Anthony, staring at the house into which the man he had been following had just disappeared, lifted his eyes to the top storey and in a sort of agony of amazement recognized Susan.

In the same moment Susan flashed round and faced the opening door. Mr. Garry O'Connell came in with a parcel under his arm. For an instant Susan thought the beating of her heart would have choked her. Then, as she bit the corner of her lip and told herself just what a fool she was, it dawned upon her that Garry was at least as discomposed as she was herself. Never had he seemed less pleased to see her. Then all of a sudden he threw his parcel on to a chair, tossed his hat down upon it, and came towards her with outstretched hands.

"My darling child—if this isn't a pleasant surprise!"

Susan got away from the window. If Garry was going to kiss her, it was just as well that the embrace should not take place where Anthony could hardly help seeing it.

"It's a surprise—but you didn't look as if it was a pleasant one."

She avoided the kiss by about half an inch, and felt dreadfully self-conscious about the book, which she hoped her coat really did conceal.

If Garry put his arm round her, he would feel it. She put the table between them.

"Do you keep your kisses for him?" said Garry shortly.

Susan put her chin in the air.

"I don't keep them for you, Garry," she said. Her voice shook a little with excitement.

"Do you keep them for him?"

"I haven't the least idea what you're talking about."

"Liar!" said Garry. He spoke smoothly and pleasantly and his lips smiled, but his eyes had the fierce smouldering look of a dog who is going to bite.

Susan was never afraid of Garry when they were face to face, but afterwards she would be afraid when she remembered that look. She put out her hand as if she were pushing him away.

"My good Garry!" Then, with a laugh, "No—honestly—I have not got time to quarrel—not this afternoon. Any other day I'd simply love to, but now—No, really, Garry—I've got to catch a train. And oh, do be an angel and tell me whether there's anything between the four-forty and the seven-eleven."

Garry didn't move.

"Why did you come?" he said. One of his hands rested on the table. She saw it twitch.

"Well, I came because Camilla told me you were going to get back some book my father lent to the British Museum. She said she'd given you the receipt. I suppose it'll take simply ages. But I really mustn't stay to talk about it now. I wouldn't have stayed if I'd thought you'd be so long."

If Garry had *The Shepheard's Kalendar* in that parcel under his hat, he'd want to get rid of her now, just as quickly as ever he could; he'd want to look her up a train and push her off to catch it in the biggest possible hurry. And the time-table was in the next room.

She took a single hurried breath, and saw his face change.

"Oh yes, there'll be delays. I'm on the spot, so you'd better let me push it through. Of course the book mayn't be worth much when you get it. What train did you want to catch?"

"The four-forty, if I can."

"To Wrane?"

"Yes, Wrane."

Garry flung away from the table.

"Are you going to stay there for ever?" he said angrily. Then, as he passed her, he just touched her on the shoulder, said "Susan" rather as if the word hurt him, and passed quickly through the open door into the bedroom.

Almost before he was out of sight Susan reached the chair where the parcel lay. She put her own parcel under the hat, and was back in her place by the table, her left arm tingling as she pressed it down upon what she felt certain was *The Shepheard's Kalendar.*

Garry O'Connell, coming back with the time-table, looked at her, and felt a sudden rush of admiration. According to his lights, he had loved Susan for years—loved her when she looked pretty, and when she looked plain, and when she looked tired, and when her nose was shiny. She was always Susan. But at this moment she touched beauty. He stood in the doorway wondering. Her eyes were bright and startled, her colour was like a wind-blown flame. She filled the bare, ugly little room with colour and emotion.

Garry, his hands clenched on the time-table, stood there and took the colour and the emotion to himself for just one moment. The next carried him to Susan's side. Before she knew what was going to happen he had his arms about her and she could feel the thudding of his heart. There was a moment in which they saw each other. What Susan saw she hated; and what Garry saw was this hatred looking out of Susan's eyes. In a whirl of rage she twisted herself free and reached the door.

"Are you mad?" And then, in the middle of being angry, something pricked her heart. He had turned so white. She said "Garry!" and he passed his hand across his face, breathing hard. She said "Garry!" again, this time with a note of appeal in her voice.

He swallowed, let the time-table fall on the floor, and then stooped to pick it up again.

"Why—did you—look at me like that?" he said.

Susan dropped her eyes. She could not very well say "Because I've been stealing your—no, *my* book, and I was all worked up." She said quickly,

"I must fly. Have you looked up the trains?" Then, as he shook his head, "I can't wait. I'll chance the four-forty. Don't come down. Bye-bye!"

Garry went on looking at the place where she had been. He hardly saw her go. He heard the sound of her feet running down the stairs in the same sort of way that a man in a dream hears some sound from the waking world. It meant nothing to him; it was just a sound. Every conscious thought and feeling was given up to a cold, bitter anger which blotted out everything except itself.

Susan ran down the stairs at a break-neck speed. When she was a little girl she used to dream that she was being chased by wolves. The terror of this dream came upon her now. The last dozen steps were just a scramble, and she burst out of the front door into the street with such extreme suddenness that she at once attracted Anthony's attention, riveted though it was to the top window at which he had last seen her. He heard the bang of the door, saw Susan fly down the steps, and met her in the middle of the road, only to be gripped hold of and pinched very hard.

"Run!" said Susan with all that remained of her voice.

"Why?" said Anthony. "Here—steady on! What's happened?"

Susan had no more voice, so she didn't answer in words; but she took his arm and pulled him towards the nearer pavement, and having got him there, she began to run. Anthony ran too.

"What on earth's the matter? Why are we running away?"

Susan didn't say anything. She pulled her hand out of his arm, snatched a parcel from under her coat, and holding it to her chest with both hands, she went on running as fast as she could. When they turned the corner, she stopped dead and clutched at him. She was panting as if they had run two miles instead of two hundred yards.

"What on earth?"

"Taxi!" said Susan. "Taxi!"

Chapter Thirty-Four

IN THE TAXI Susan did not speak. She sat and held the brown paper parcel. Arrived at the garage where Anthony had left his car, she followed him into its dark recesses, still without speaking. Anthony, after asking her whether she was all right and getting a nod, had also relapsed into silence.

The garage was very dark. It smelt strongly of petrol and iodoform. With one part of her mind Susan dealt with the problem of why a garage should smell of iodoform; the rest of her mind was quite full of a queer, thick terror which she did not attempt to explain at all. Presently she would be able to think, and then she would reason herself out of it; just now she could only feel. She felt as if she had had an electric shock, as if she had been in contact with something violent, and violently destructive. At the time she had been shocked into anger, but now everything in her shuddered. She kept seeing Garry's face, very white, and his eyes. She kept seeing them.

She put her parcel down on the folded hood of the car, rested her arms upon it, and bent her head upon them. The garage floor seemed to be tilting with her. She leaned against the car with her eyes shut, and saw showers of little sparks go up in the dark. Then Anthony's arm round her shoulders.

"Susan—what is it? *Susan*—"

Susan lifted her head slowly. She said slowly and stiffly,

"I'm all right."

"Look here, don't you want some tea or something?"

"I'm all right."

"I don't believe you've had anything to eat."

"Yes."

"I knew you hadn't!" There was triumph in his tone.

Susan let go of the car and leaned against him.

"I did—have something, so—you're wrong." Then speech came back with a rush. "Oh, do let's get away! I'm perfectly all right, but I want to get away—I don't want to stop in London another minute—I—I—" She began to laugh in a weak, unsteady sort of way. "Oh, I've stolen *The Shepheard's Kalendar.* Do—do—*do* take me away before anyone comes!"

"You've burgled the Museum?"

She shook her head, still laughing.

"No—no! Oh, do take me away!"

Anthony's hand came down hard upon her shoulder.

"You're not to go on like that! You're to pull yourself together! If you have hysterics or do a faint, there's only petrol to pour over you—so drop it! In you get!"

Out in the open air and on the move, Susan really did pull herself together. The black cloud she had seen from the window still hung overhead. The air was heavy, and a little chill. As they began to move faster, she took a long breath and shivered.

"Cold?" said Anthony.

"No. Anthony—"

"We'll talk presently. Let's get out of the traffic first."

When they were on a straight road bordered by cabbage fields he stopped the car.

"*Now.* What's all this about? What have you been doing?" His tone was grim.

Half an hour ago Susan might have been meek; she might even have cried and told him things which she didn't really mean to tell him. Now, comfortably conscious of having left Garry miles away and with his mind firmly directed towards the train service, she was in no mood for meekness.

"Anthony—I've got *The Shepheard's Kalendar*—at least I'm sure— oh, I *must* look! *There*—it *is*! Look! I knew it was! Now say I'm clever!" The book, in its needlework cover, lay half on her lap and half on the seat between them. She faced him, glowing with excitement. "Look at it! You're not looking."

Anthony was looking at her very directly.

"How did you get it? You haven't told me that yet."

"I've got it—that's all that matters."

"No, it isn't." His voice was quite level, but it held an obstinate note. "I want to know how you got it."

"I can't tell you. It doesn't matter a bit."

He took the book in his hand without looking at it. He did not look at Susan either.

"I came up to town to look for you. I went to the British Museum, because you told Gran you were going up about *The Shepheard's Kalendar*. When I got there, I saw—" He paused, and then said, without emphasis, "him."

Susan said, "Oh!"

Anthony balanced the book on his hand.

"It would really be a great deal more convenient if I had a name to call him by." He paused again. "He keeps cropping up so."

Susan said nothing at all. She looked at the faded initials on the needlework cover.

"Would you like to tell me his name?"

She shook her head.

"I can't—I told you I couldn't." She was aware of Anthony frowning.

"He had a parcel under his arm. I suppose it was this." Then, irrelevantly, "I saw you up at the top window, and I very nearly bashed in the front door."

Susan lifted sparkling eyes.

"That *would* have been helpful!" She caught him by the arm and shook it. "Anthony, don't let's waste time. We can quarrel *any* day, but to-day there are much more exciting things to do. Do stop glowering and poking out your chin, and listen! I believe there's some sort of cipher here." She laid her hand over his on the cover of the book. "I'm sure Philip Colstone sent a message to his son. And we can't look for it in an open cabbage field, and I want some tea most frightfully, so what we've got to do is to stop at the first tea place that isn't crowded and see whether I'm right."

The writing-room of the George and Crown certainly fulfilled the condition of not being crowded: it would, in fact, have been difficult to find any place better adapted for their purpose. The inn itself dated back to a period before a George had ever worn the English crown, but the writing-room was most strictly and definitely mid-Victorian. It had a large spotted mirror over the mantelpiece, blue plush curtains tied up with sashes, massive dingy furniture, and a floor space overrun with tables of all sizes and shapes, from the solid rosewood centrepiece down to a three-legged atrocity that had once been enamelled pale blue and now displayed a wreath of grimy roses on a dark grey ground.

Susan laid *The Shepheard's Kalendar* on a walnut table with an oval top beautifully inlaid in coloured woods. She opened the book and turned the pages with fingers that shook a little from excitement, until she found the Seventh Eclogue with its heading, "Iuly."

"Look!" she said. "I believe it's here. I shall scream with rage if it isn't. You know, when I saw it in the Museum I was only thinking about the 'stone that Merlin blessed,' and all that. And I thought the page was badly spotted—but I never thought about the cipher—not till afterwards—and afterwards I kept seeing the page—and when I thought about the spots there was something odd about them—and there is. Look!" The words came tumbling over each other.

When Susan said "Look!" she pinched him very hard and gave an excited little laugh.

"Look! Look! *Look!*"

Anthony looked, and saw a page badly speckled with damp. There were large brown stains and little round spots here, there, and everywhere. He didn't think much of Susan's discovery.

Susan went on talking:

"Take a pencil and paper and write down the letters as I read them. Are you ready? T—O—M—Y—S—O—N—" She pinched him so that he cried out. "It is—it is! It really is! Oh, I knew it was! Don't you see? Read it out! Read the letters together!"

Anthony read slowly: "To—my—son—" Then he looked from his paper to the book and protested, "That's what I've written down, but I'm hanged if I know how you get it. This says:

'THOM. Is not thilke same a gotehearde prowde,
           That sittes on yonder bancke,
           Whose straying heard them selfe doth shrowde
           Emong the bushes rancke?'"

Susan snatched away his pencil and pointed.

"The 't' in 'gotehearde' has got one of those little dark brown specks right on top of it, and so has the 'o' in 'prowde'"—the pencil moved to the third line—"and the 'm' in 'them'—and the 'y' in 'iolly." That's how it's done!"

"Of course you can make any words you like out of anything if you can just pick and choose what letters you want as you go along."

"How unbelieving you are! That's just what Philip Colstone did—he took what letters he wanted, and he made up a message to his son. And oh, do go on quickly and write it down!"

She pushed the pencil into his hand again.

"You must play fair and give me the spotted letters just as they come."

"Of course I'll play fair. Oh, do let's go on! The next letter's an N— and then E—T—H—O—"

"That doesn't make sense. What's 'Netho'? You're off on a wild goose chase."

Susan looked over him.

"It's not 'Netho.' Look! The 'ne' belongs to 'sonne.' You've got to allow for the old spelling. It's 'To my sonne.' 'Tho' belongs to the next word. Now we've got to find out what it is." She went on reading out letters, whilst he wrote them down. "Don't let's put the letters into words till the very end. Just write them down and make your mind a blank. I don't think I can bear to find out a secret one letter at a time. Oh, Anthony, do be quick!" Her voice thrilled and trembled with excitement, and the dull room was full of the scarlet and emerald and blue of high adventure.

A fat red-haired girl brought in tea on a black japanned tray in the middle of the eclogue. She seemed to expect them to move *The Shepheard's Kalendar* to make room for it.

"E—" said Susan in palpitating tones.

The red-haired girl flounced. Her lips shaped the word "balmy." She set down the tray with a clatter on a funereal side table of very highly polished ebony, demanded three shillings, and withdrew. The tray with its load of cold buttered toast and thick bread and scrape ceased to exist as far as Susan and Anthony were concerned.

At last Susan heaved a sigh.

"Oh, I think that's all, but I'm not sure—only we must read it now— we really must. I can't bear the suspense any longer."

She put her arm through his and leaned upon his shoulder, and Anthony read, in a tone of protesting incredulity:

"To my sonne those matters broughte by me from the indies i thoughte to hide beneath the coldstone since all men feare to touch it but where i digged came up a blast that catched on fyre from my lanthorn i hardly escaping this beware after i layde them in the place will knoweth none else goe soe low as thou canst there is a stone that turneth harde by the wall presse where is the shield and with thy foote presse harde upon the second shield these two shields i cut for alle men feare merlyn's sign."

"Some of it doesn't make sense," said Anthony. But his face had flushed.

Susan tore the paper from him.

"It does. You must put in the proper stops. It's frightfully exciting. Listen!" She read aloud in her turn. Her voice trembled with excitement. "It goes like this, don't you see—'To my sonne. Those matters broughte by me from the Indies I thoughte to hide beneath the Coldstone, since all men feare to touch it. But where I digged, came up a blast that catched on fyre from my lanthorn, I hardly escaping. This beware. After, I layde them in the place Will knoweth, none else. Goe soe low as thou canst. There is a stone that turneth harde by the wall. Presse where is the shield, and with thy foote presse harde upon the second shield. These two shields I cut, for alle men feare Merlyn's sign—' There!" She paused, panting a little. "And the shield is the mark on the Coldstone—two interlaced triangles. They called it the Shield of David, and it was used as a charm. I found a cutting from a newspaper all about it—frightfully learned—I'll show you "

Anthony flung his arm around her.

"Don't be uppish!"

"I'm not uppish—I'm just very clever. I'm Sherlock, and you're Watson!"

"I'm not!"

"You are! I shall buy a violin and learn to smoke a pipe, and tell people everything they've ever said and done just by looking at their cigarette ash or the dust out of a pencil-sharpener. And you shall be Watson and knock villains down for me whenever I want them knocked."

There was an interlude.

When it was over, they drank the stewed tea and ate some of the less arid portions of the so-called buttered toast.

"When you get a dry bit, you wish they hadn't skimped the butter so, but when you do get a buttery bit you're not so sure," said Susan.

"It's pretty foul," said Anthony cheerfully.

It was after tea that things began to go wrong. The Daimler wouldn't start. Anthony cranked until he streamed, but after one cough she gave no further sign of life.

Passers by began to offer helpful advice. The boots of the hotel had a brother who worked for a gentleman who had a car that stopped dead "just like that car of yours, sir—and would you believe it, when they come to take 'er to bits, the 'ole of the engine was that wore out it fair come to bits in their 'ands. A very rich genelman 'e was, but 'e 'ated new things like poison. 'Old things is best,' 'e says, 'and old cars is best. Give me a good old friend,' 'e says. And that's 'ow 'e was served."

Anthony looked at him ungratefully.

A fat man leaning on a bicycle proffered the suggestion that he might have run out of petrol. He had an uncle in a good way of business who was towed ten miles and "never found out till he got to the garridge that he'd run her bone dry, and if the mechanics didn't half have the laugh on him."

An elderly female with a shopping basket and a nondescript dog on a string hoped that no one was hurt—"Shocking things these accidents—and I'm sure I do hope and trust—"

Anthony pushed back his hair and straightened his back for a moment.

"It's *not* an accident," he said in tones of polite fury.

Susan giggled.

In the end the car had to be man-handled to the nearest garage, where the expert opinion was not very encouraging.

"Isn't hardly safe to go on the roads with a car like this—not what I should call *safe*. She's been a good car, of course, but in a manner of speaking that's the trouble, sir. Anna Domminy—that's about the size of it—she's been a car too long. But I dare say we can patch her up for you to get home in—but I wouldn't like to say how long it'll take."

It took three hours.

They dined at the hotel, watched with interest by the red-headed girl, who held firmly to the opinion that they were both "batty"; whereas the boots diagnosed them as " 'oneymooners."

It was dark when they drove away.

Chapter Thirty-Five

THEY DROVE THROUGH the dark. The clouds were lower than they had been. The night was black, and still, and very warm. Rain might fall before morning. The old car ran well enough.

They talked all the time, saying the same things over and over, as people do when their minds are so full of something that they cannot leave it alone.

"He must have meant the cellar when he said, 'Go soe low as thou canst.'" That was Susan, as excited as if it were the first time she had said it.

"Yes, he must have." Anthony had stopped being incredulous. He couldn't say when he had stopped, but all of a sudden the adventure had him. He said, "Yes, he must have meant the cellar," and added, "And that's what those fellows were after—though how in the world they knew—"

Susan's heart gave a little jump. How much had Garry known, and how did he know it? And had he strung together all those blotted letters in the July eclogue and read Philip Colstone's message? No, he couldn't have done that. She murmured,

"Anyhow we've stolen a march on them."

"Yes."

Her shoulder touched his in the dark. A little shiver ran over her. Suppose Garry were to steal a march on *them*. Suppose he were there before them. Suppose they were to find the adventure rifled. Suppose... She spoke quickly:

"You've got the key safe?"

Anthony nodded.

"In my inside pocket. That's what I really came up for to-day."

"You *said* you came up to find me."

"I had to have a decent excuse. I did the key first anyway. I don't suppose they'd have sent it for days. I wonder if—the others—have got theirs yet."

Susan shivered again, and Anthony took his left hand off the wheel and put it on her shoulder.

"Cold?"

"Oh no—boiling."

"You shivered."

He heard her laugh and felt her press against him.

"I only want to get on. I want to be sure we get there first."

His astonishment was plain.

"You think—"

"I *know*," said Susan. This time the shudder was in her voice. Garry never gave up. He always went on until he got what he wanted. She spoke in breathless haste. "Can't you go faster?"

"Why? What's the hurry? We can't do anything to-night, anyhow."

He was aware of an abrupt movement.

"Not? Oh, but we *must*! You don't meant to say—"

"We shan't get down till after eleven."

"But that's just our very best time."

"You mean to look for the secret place to-night?"

"Yes—*yes!* They'll try and get in first—they will—I *know* they will."

She heard him laugh, a dry, short laugh.

"It would be a lot easier for me if I knew a little more about it all."

"Yes—but—I—can't. But we've got to be quick. Don't you see it's quite easy to do things to-night? Nobody will know we're back—nobody will know anything."

Anthony considered this in silence. He couldn't get in without rousing the house, unless... And then there was the car. Of course he could run it into the field at the corner. It would be quite safe there.

Susan was speaking again, softly, eagerly:

"You could come in with me, and we could go through the passage."

"I thought we agreed that you weren't going to come through the passage any more."

"Anthony! You don't imagine you're going down into that cellar to find things all by yourself?"

He abandoned the idea.

"Well, how are you going to get in, anyway?"

"Gran gave me the front door key. I told her I might be late, and she promised to go off to bed."

After a pause Anthony said, "You oughtn't to."

"I'm going to."

After another pause, "I could back the car through the gate into that field just before you come to the corner."

Susan hugged herself.

"Yes, you *could*!"

Her spirits began to soar. Garry wasn't following them. He wouldn't follow them. He'd just give up. He'd be bound to give up once they'd got the book. There wasn't anything he could do, really.

All at once she felt as if someone had dropped a little burning piece of ice down the back of her neck. She made such a quick movement towards Anthony that the car swerved right across the road.

"I say, don't do that! What's the matter?"

"I'm frightened," said Susan.

"What on earth have you got to be frightened about?"

"I don't know." (She saw Garry's eyes.)

"Darling—don't! I can't unfrighten you and drive the car."

"Sing!" said Susan. "Sing something nice and loud, so that I can stop hearing myself think."

Anthony risked another swerve by putting his arm round her and giving her a shake; after which he kissed her and began to sing at the top of his voice:

" 'Adam and Eve could never believe
That Peter the miller was dead.
Shut up in the tower for stealing of flour,
And never could get a reprieve.
They bored a hole in Oliver's nose,
And put therein a string
And drew him round about the town
For murdering Charles our King.'

Does that make you feel better?"

"'M—" said Susan. "You've got a nice loud voice." Then, in the middle of his burst of laughter, "Anthony, what do you suppose we shall find?"

"Dunno. We shall know when we find it. Suppose it's a spoof. You know, if it isn't, I don't see how your grandfather Philip, who was a younger son, ever got away with the book. I mean if there had been anything in it, somebody would have found out about it long ago, or anyhow the book would have been considered a valuable heirloom."

Susan broke in eagerly:

"I asked Gran about that, and she knew Philip had the book, but she said his father didn't care for any of the old things, and Sir Jervis didn't care either when he was a young man, and they let Philip have the book because of his name being Philip too. And I asked her if she thought there was a message in it, or anything of that sort, and she said the Bowyers always said there was, but they didn't speak about it, and, the Colstones didn't believe it, and whether it was a Colstone or a Bowyer, they were all for leaving well alone and not doing anything to stir up things that shouldn't be stirred up. So that's how Philip got the book."

They came down the hill into Ford St. Mary, and backed the car into the corner field nearly half an hour after it had struck eleven on the grandfather clock in the library at Stonegate.

As the car left the road, the man who had been standing at the corner looking up the hill turned and ran down the road towards the village. He made no sound as he ran.

The village street was as black as the inside of a chimney. You could just see where roof left off and sky began; and you couldn't see that unless your eyes had been long enough in the dark to catch the very faintest break in it. Every house was asleep, and every window except one was fastened and unlit. In just one window there was a little faint candlelight, enough to show that the casement stood ajar. The blind was down. The light showed where its edge fell short of the sill.

The man who had run from the corner stopped dead in the middle of the street. Someone moved towards him; a hand fell on his shoulder. He said, in a toneless whisper.

"They've just come. They've put the car in the field at the corner."

The hand on his shoulder was lifted. There was a whispered answer.

The man who had run went forward. When he was a yard away no one could have seen him. His footsteps went on a little way and then stopped.

The other man went back into the darkness from which he had emerged. One or two minutes passed very slowly. Then there came to his straining ears a very faint sound. It became less faint as it came nearer. Two people, walking however softly, make enough noise to reach anyone who is listening for just that very thing. Garry O'Connell stood and listened; and if his mind had been less fiercely concentrated on the present moment of time, he might have been taken back eight years and remembered other nights, when he had stood in some Irish lane or behind the loose piled stones of an Irish dyke waiting, in a night as dark as this but soft with rain, for the moment that would give him an enemy's life. He had taken life, and that not once or twice, with the extraordinary callousness of that time, but he had never waited for any of the men whom he had killed with the cold, fierce, bitter hatred which possessed him to-night.

Susan and Anthony came down the street without a light to guide them. They walked in the middle of the road, and went softly, having no desire to present Mrs. Smithers with a thrill.

Susan put her mouth to Anthony's ear and breathed, in a faint little whisper that tickled him,

"I can't see anything, but I can smell Gran's Virginia stock. We're here. Let me feel for the gate."

Anthony kept his arm round her, and they went through together and up the paved walk to Mrs. Bowyer's front door.

When it had closed behind them, Garry O'Connell took a step forward and lifted his eyes to where the square of Susan's window stared, unseen and unseeing, into the black dark. Garry stared back at it. There was a black darkness within him. His thoughts moved in it, and the dark was troubled, but not broken. If it broke, it would break in flame. He watched the window steadily. If a light went up behind that curtained square, if it were only the glimmer of a match, he would see it. If there were no light—if they were there, murmuring to each other in the darkness, shut in from all the world, it came to him that he would know that too. He waited. There was no light. There was no sound.

The room behind the unseen casement was empty. It was a dead room. Susan wasn't in it.

Garry's frightful concentration relaxed. If they were not in Susan's room, he could think again. When he thought, he knew where they were—they had gone through the passage into Stonegate. And if they had done that, it meant—Garry knew very well what it meant. He whistled, just under his breath, the first line of "Robin Adair," and then walked across the street and some paces along it until he came to a garden gate. He opened the gate and went through it, and on until he was standing immediately under the one lighted window in Ford St. Mary. Standing there, he took a pebble from his pocket and tossed it up against the glass. The window, which was ajar, was pushed open.

Garry O'Connell once again whistled: "What's this dull town to me, Robin Adair?"

Chapter Thirty-Six

SUSAN AND ANTHONY went down the cellar steps with the library lamp to light them. The lamp was Susan's idea.

"I will not look for hidden treasure with an electric torch! It's an anachronism."

Anthony held the lamp high and went first.

"I don't see why a Victorian anachronism is any better really than a neo-Georgian one."

"It doesn't keep spotting off and on, and it doesn't just make little holes in the dark and leave most of you soaked in inky blackness. Electric torches make me feel exactly like Guy Fawkes blowing up the Houses of Parliament."

"Who's being an anachronism now?" said Anthony.

But when they came to the heavy door that shut off the old cellars, he was glad enough of the lamp. The key that he had had made turned stiffly in the disused lock; he had to take two hands to it. Susan, behind him, uttered an exclamation. The lamp which he had set down at his side shed a still, yellow light upon the door, all scored black oak and rusty iron bands. It shone on the old lock, and the new key, and on Anthony's straining hands.

Susan uttered her exclamation, leaned between Anthony and the lamp, and touched the lock with the tip of her finger. She brought it away wet. The lamplight showed a dark smear.

"Anthony—did you put oil in the lock?"

"No." He looked up with a startled jerk of the head.

"Who did?" said Susan breathlessly. "Do you think—one of the servants?"

"Not by my orders." When he jerked his head up, a monstrous shadow jerked on the cellar roof.

Susan had a frightful feeling of recoil from what lay behind the door, and at the same moment it swung open and the lamplight went a little way into the darkness that lay beyond, and there stayed. An indescribable smell of mould and old used air began to flow out towards them like stagnant water.

Anthony picked up the lamp and stepped over the threshold. A dark passage with a very low roof was all that they could see, but half a dozen paces along it brought them to an open doorway on the left. It gave on an empty space. A similar opening on the right showed more emptiness. And then the floor began to slope downwards. They came to a door that blocked their path, running right across the narrow passage. It was held by a rusty staple and a broken chain.

Anthony held the lamp lower. Simultaneously he and Susan saw the bright marks on the broken iron—bright deep scratches where a tool had slipped and scored through the rust to the sound heart of the metal. He lifted the staple and pushed open the door. Three steps led down into a small vaulted room. Ceiling, floor, and walls were of stone. The air was very close, and the lamp flickered.

Susan bent as she passed down the steps. From the lowest tread she picked up a small wooden match with a bright green head.

"Anthony—" she said, and then stopped.

"H'm—" said Anthony; his brows drew together. But all of a sudden he laughed. "That's an anachronism if you like!" He looked at Susan with a hard, straight look. "I think they got their key first after all," he said.

Then, as he swung round with the lamp in his hand, Susan cried out and pointed with her left hand. On the wall at the farther end of the room, at about the height of her shoulder, there was cut upon the stone the figure of the interlaced triangles which she had seen at the head of the newspaper cutting in Garry's room—the sign of the Shield of David.

"Look!" she whispered. The finger with which she was pointing trembled a little. Her voice quivered with excitement as she spoke Philip Colstone's words:

"Goe soe low as thou canst. There is a stone that turneth harde by the wall. Presse where is the shield, and with thy foote presse hard upon the second shield. These two shields I cut, for alle men feare Merlyn's sign."

Her voice failed. She caught his arm, and shook the lamplight into a wild pattern of leaping light and dancing shade.

"Anthony—"

"Where's the second shield? Take care of the lamp!"

There was some broken rubble scattered here and there on the floor of the chamber. He set the lamp down and began to shift the débris with his hands, feeling over each patch of stone as he cleared it. He stopped a yard from the wall on a level with the first sign.

"Got it! Got it in one! Bring the lamp!"

He was dusting away a little white powder and some small pellets of chalky stuff. Some of it had lodged where the point of the second shield showed faintly about a yard from the wall.

"That's it!" He scrambled up. "Stand clear with that lamp! You'd better go right over by the door—I don't quite know what's going to happen."

Standing close to the wall, he pushed with all his might against it just where the two triangles crossed. At the same time he thrust hard with his foot at the second shield. There was a creaking, groaning sound. The stone under his foot moved so suddenly that he came near to losing his balance; only the thrust of his hand on the wall saved him. He drew back his foot and jumped, to the sound of a soft cry from Susan.

He put his arm round her, and they stood looking at the flagstone which had given under his foot with a forward tilt. And before their eyes it was moving now—moving slowly, tilting more and more, until its raised side almost hid a square black cavity.

After a moment Anthony went forward and looked over the edge.

"That's the place," he said in rather an odd voice. "It's a beastly black hole. I wonder what he hid there. Bit of a practical joker our ancestor Philip."

Susan said, "I hate it."

"Would you like to go back?"

"No, of course I wouldn't."

"Well, wait here anyhow. Give me the lamp."

"What? Wait here—with ghosts and bogles positively oozing out of the walls?"

She heard his unwilling laugh.

"Sherlock would have loved to meet a ghost. But you can keep the lamp—I've got a torch."

"Oh! I simply won't be left! Anthony—*Anthony!*" She spoke to a pair of hands gripping the sides of the opening, and the top of a brown head that hung below them.

Then the hands let go and the head disappeared. She could see nothing but a square black hole. There was a thudding sound, and then Anthony's voice:

"I'm all right. It's only a seven-foot drop, but I slipped, like a mug. Come on—it's quite dry. Wait a moment—give me the lamp first."

Susan stooped to pick it up. Still stooping, she bent over the hole, and saw Anthony's hands come up to take the lamp. She uttered a sharp exclamation and very nearly dropped it.

"What's the matter?" His voice came out of the darkness with a note of alarm in it.

She moved the lamp until the light shone on his upturned face and full on his outstretched hands. She said with a gasp,

"Your hands!"

"What's the matter with them?"

"They're black—they're coal-black—you look like a sweep." She began to laugh, and the lamp shook.

"Give me that lamp," said Anthony. And, then just as he was going to take it, he saw his own hands and laughed too, an odd excited laugh.

Susan saw the lamp go down into the hole. She heard Anthony laughing, and looking down, she saw that the light was filling a space about seven feet square—a black space, all black. She did not wait to see anything more.

"I'm coming down. Give me a hand," she called, and came down with a rush, fetching up in Anthony's arms.

He was still laughing.

"Coal-black's the word!" he said. "It's coal all right, and we shall both be like sweeps before we're through."

"Coal?" she said. Then, slowly, "That's not what Philip Colstone meant."

"It's coal all right. And it's what J. E. W. found. He came to Stonegate, and he reported coal under the estate. Sir Jervis said he'd be hanged if he'd have the place ruined. He tore up the report, sent West packing, and then, I suspect, Master J. E. W. tried to do the dirty on him and got together enough financial backing to make a bid for the place, and a pretty high one too. Only the old man wouldn't play—and by gum, I respect him. Coal was coal in those days, and he might have simply raked in the cash, instead of which he destroyed the report and went on refusing fancy prices."

Susan shook him by the sleeve.

"Anthony, stop! My head's going round. What has all this to do with Philip Colstone?"

Anthony said, "I don't know."

She shook him again.

"Darling Watson, you're mixing up two stories—you really are—and I'm not sure whether you're in one of them and I'm in another, which makes it frightfully muddling. We began by being in the 'Adventure of The Shepheard's Kalendar and the Matters Philip Colstone brought from the Indies,' and now all of a sudden you've switched off into the 'Adventure of the Hidden Coal and the Deceitful J. E. W.' And I like my story best—it's much, much, *much* more romantic. And I want most desperately to know what Philip Colstone brought from the Indies."

"I am *not* Watson," said Anthony. "If I've got to be Watson, I won't play—I shall go off into the other Adventure and be Sherlock all on my own." After which he kissed her, and left a rich black smear on her cheek.

"Let's do this Adventure first. You know you said yourself that—" She hesitated and then came out with, *"They* weren't breaking into the house and forging keys just to steal lumps of coal—especially now when coal's about as dead as mutton. The only awful thing is—did they get in here, and are we too late?"

Anthony shook his head.

"What would they want with *The Shepheard's Kalendar* if they'd found what they were after? I don't think it was coal either, though it beats me how on earth they got on to old Philip and whatever he stowed away here in—whatever year the Armada was. No—I'll tell you what I think. I think they knew there was some secret place—or perhaps they only guessed it. Anyhow they knew there was something hidden, and they knew it was in the old cellars, so they broke in and got away with an impression of the lock. Then they had to wait whilst they were getting a key made. But they must have hustled their man, because they evidently got their key before I managed to get mine. They've been into the old cellars, but they didn't find anything, because even if they knew this place existed, they didn't know how to get into it. So they buzzed off to town and annexed *The Shepheard's Kalendar*. And how they knew about it, or how they managed to collect it, has me beat—but I expect you know."

Susan turned away.

"We ought to be exploring," she said.

"There's not very much to explore."

She looked round. The place was just a hole in the coal. There was a thick soft dust under their feet. The lamp filled the small space with its steady light, and except for themselves it was empty. She stared at the emptiness.

"What could he have hidden?"

"Anything—or nothing."

"I'm sure there's something. I believe they did get in—I believe it's been taken."

"Not by them, whoever they are. But of course someone—anyone—a Colstone, or a servant, or in fact anyone—may have strung those letters together like you did, and found whatever there was to find, any old time in the last three hundred and fifty years or so."

There was a dismal common sense about this. In a depressed silence Susan picked up the lamp and looked about her. All of a sudden she cried out, ran a couple of steps forward, and threw the light low down upon the wall. About a foot above the floor, just where the dust and chips of the excavation had been swept into a loose pile against it, there showed, deeply scratched, the sign of David's Shield.

Anthony began to push aside the loose rough pieces with his foot. Susan set down the lamp and shovelled with her hands. After about a minute he stubbed his toe, and she a finger, against hard metal, and in a moment more the lid of a blackened box came into view. It was about eighteen inches long by a foot wide. It had ornamental hinges which came right over the top of the box, and a large hasp. Box, hasp, and hinges were all as black as if they had been carved out of the coal around them, but when Anthony scratched with the point of his knife, a yellow line threw back the yellow light.

Susan asked, "Is it brass?"

"I don't know."

"It's yellow."

Anthony said nothing. He drew the point of his knife along the curve of an embossed leaf.

"Brass is yellow," said Susan.

"So is gold," said Anthony. They were both speaking in whispers.

Anthony pulled at the hasp. It moved stiffly. And then, with a jerk, up came the lid. And the inside of it was a raw pale yellow, very strange to see in the midst of all that blackness. It had an ornamentation upon it of curving leaves and strange-headed birds beautifully engraved.

They looked in silence. Anthony's word seemed to hang on the silence—*"Gold!"*

The box stood flush with the floor, dust of coal and pebbles of coal scraped back from it on three sides. The lifted golden lid caught all the light there was and reflected it upon the heaped-up contents of the box. There was more gold, and there was the undimmed sharp sparkle of a great red stone half buried under the gold. There was a string of pearls long dead and lustreless. And right across, from corner to corner, a golden band holding a dozen flat green stones into which the light sank down, as it sinks into deep green water.

Over their heads in the dark cellar above them Mr. Garry O'Connell spoke. He said,

"Good-bye, Susan."

The turning stone fell into its place with a thud.

Chapter Thirty-Seven

They had been kneeling in front of the box, with the square opening in the roof a little behind them on the right. The stone fell with a thud and shut them in. There was just one horrid moment in which the realization of what had happened caught hold of them like cramp, and then Anthony sprang to his feet with an inarticulate sound of anger.

"Who was that? Who the devil was that?"

It was another moment before Susan could move. Something in her was quivering and crying breathlessly:

"It can't be true! It's too horrid to be true! It's like a bad dream. We shall wake up. Oh, *please* let us wake up quickly!"

Then she began to get up, and as soon as she moved she knew that it wasn't a dream at all. Garry had shut them in. And while she was thinking this, there was Anthony straining up towards the stone—pushing, straining, and making no more impression on the trap that had opened so easily to let them in than if he had been pitting himself against the impenetrable walls of coal. She began to say in a frightened whisper, "It's no use—it's no use—oh, darling, it's no use!" and all at once Anthony let his arms fall.

"It won't budge. I can't move it—I can't get any purchase. *The swine!*"

Susan came closer. He was panting with the effort he had made; his forehead was wet; the moisture began to trickle down into the coal dust which smeared his face. He had a most curiously disreputable appearance. His voice was hot with anger.

"What fools we were to leave the cellar door open behind us—what damned fools!"

"No—no—he's got a key—he'd have got in anyhow—that's why I was frightened." Her voice shook pitifully, and Anthony caught her in his arms.

"Darling—don't! Don't be frightened. Susan—*darling*—it's just a beastly practical joke. He can't keep us here, the swab!"

Susan drew a faint, quivering breath.

"You don't know Garry."

"Oh, it's Garry?"

"Yes"—with another quivering breath.

"Don't you think you'd better tell me who Garry is? I'm a bit in the dark, and it seems to me—if it isn't a practical joke, he's trying to do us in. Why should you screen him? Susan—who is he?"

Susan leaned against him.

"He's Garry O'Connell. He's Camilla's son."

"Your brother!" His voice was horrified.

"No, no—Camilla was a widow. Garry was ten when she married my father. He—he's always been rather troublesome—we've often never known where he was and what he was doing."

"What's he doing here? What brings him into this?"

"I think—I think he must have heard my father say something about Philip Colstone's book and the story. Gran says my grandfather Philip was the only one of the family who '*held* with it.' My father may have heard something from him. Garry was old enough to remember, but I never knew my father." The colour rose to her cheeks, and she stamped her foot. "He tried to make me believe he'd come down here about some treasure his grandfather, old Major O'Connell, found when he and Sir Jervis were young men together in the Mutiny."

Anthony spoke quickly.

"There's something about it in the diary I found—Sir Jervis' diary."

"It was all a delusion really, but Garry pretended that was what he was looking for. I thought that was why he hated you—and—and because of me. He has always wanted me."

"He's in love with you?"

"Oh, I didn't want him to be—I didn't. He frightens me."

Anthony looked grim.

"I suppose he's trying to score us off. If it's a practical joke, it's a perfectly beastly one, and by gum, I'll make him pay for it! I say, darling, don't shake like that."

"I'm n-not," said Susan very untruthfully; and then, "But it's not a joke, Anthony—it's not."

From overhead there came the sound of someone laughing. Then a voice said, "No, it's certainly not a joke—for you." The voice held a quality of cold enjoyment. It seemed to come from the trap over head. Looking up, they could see a crack at the edge of it; and through the crack came the voice of Mr. Garry O'Connell.

Anthony pushed Susan away and put out all his strength against the stone. The crack immediately disappeared. He strained once more against an immovable weight. After a while he gave it up. Then, as he stood away, the crack appeared again. Garry O'Connell addressed Susan this time:

"As there are things I'm wanting to say, will you keep that blockhead from interrupting. It's not the slightest use, because I've got my weight on the stone, and I've only to shift it the least thing in the world and you're just as much shut in as if you'd one of the Pyramids on top of you. And what's the sense of pushing up against a block of stone like this? If I wasn't here at all, he'd never be able to move it."

Susan steadied herself against the black wall.

"Let us out at once!" she said.

Garry O'Connell's voice changed. It sounded bitter cold as he said,

"Didn't you hear me say—good-bye?"

Susan wasn't trembling now. She put a hand quickly on Anthony's mouth and said in every-day tones,

"That is a very stupid joke."

"And do you think I'm believing that you think it's a joke?"

Anthony pushed Susan's hand away. He was very angry, but for Susan's sake he would hold his tongue.

"Let us out at once, Garry!" said Susan.

The crack opened a little wider.

"*You* can come out if you like," said Garry. "You can come out any time that you will—if you'll come on my terms, and if you'll tell me whether there's any oath in heaven or earth that I'll take from you or trust you by."

Susan stopped leaning against the wall. She stood up straight and came a step forward. There was only a voice for her to speak to, but she turned her face up to the inch-wide opening. Her own voice was steady.

"If you let us out at once, we'll both hold our tongues," she said—"and that's more than you've the right to expect."

Garry laughed.

"And I'm to say thank you and send you a wedding present! I suppose he *is* marrying you!"

Anthony broke his silence at the sneer, but before his anger had taken words to itself Susan was gripping his arm. He choked on what he was going to say, and was furiously silent.

"Garry," said Susan, "you're making a most awful ass of yourself. Come off it and let us out!"

"*You* can come out, as I said before."

"Then I'll come."

"On terms, my dear. And you'll have to find that oath I spoke about—something that'll hold you, and damn you deeper than the devil himself if you break it. And there isn't any oath in the world that I can think of that I'd trust to shut your mouth if I let you go now. So you must stay, Susan, you must stay—and if there's air enough, you'll starve, and if there isn't, you'll suffocate, and whether you take the long way out or the short, it'll be all the same a hundred years hence."

"Not for you," said Susan. Then she stamped her foot. "If you think you're frightening me, you're not. Do you suppose no one will look for us?"

"Why should they? Who knows you're here?"

Susan's heart struck against her side with a sickening throb. Who knew that they were here? No one knew that they were here. No one in the whole world knew that they were here.

Garry went on speaking:

"I'd be hating to think you were buoyed up with false hopes. If it's the car you're thinking of, it'll not be found here." His voice darkened in an indescribable manner.

Susan, still holding Anthony by the arm, pressed close against him, whilst a shudder ran over her.

"That car will be traced," said Anthony. "We came through Wrane, and as soon as we're known to be missing you'll find there are people all up and down the road who will remember passing us."

From first to last Garry O'Connell took no notice of Anthony. He continued to speak to Susan as if they were alone. In his own mind they were alone—isolated in a cold space where every kindly thought he had ever had for her was frozen and dead, and other thoughts, like wolves without pity or mercy, ringed them round, waiting to rush in and make an end. His lips moved stiffly and his voice came low:

"There's no way out," he said. "There's no way out for you or for me, for if you took an oath on your soul, I'd not believe you. And if you swore you loved me—and put your hand in mine at the very altar itself and swore, I'd not believe that either. I'd believe what I saw in your eyes this day—and it's because of that we've come to the end."

Susan shuddered again under the bleak, cruel misery of his voice. She remembered Garry teaching her to ride, Garry running upstairs three steps at a time with a laughing, screaming child on his shoulder, her hands deep in his hair, and Camilla scolding them both. She remembered a hurt finger, and Garry kissing the place to make it well. But that was before the change. She was Susan to him then, not something he must have and would smash rather than give it up— something to be held, possessed, and broken. She felt a mingled rush of pity, terror, anger. She said gently, "Garry—" And there was a long, long silence.

Perhaps he struggled. Perhaps he only looked into the eyes of the wolves and saw them closing in. Susan waited, her hand upon Anthony's wrist, her face raised, colourless, eager, her eyes darkly blue, her left hand at her breast. After a long time there was a sound. She thought it was a groan, but instantly upon it came Garry's voice, quiet and bitter:

"You may be interested to know that the car will be found at the foot of Crayling Cliff. It will be plain to everyone that a regrettable accident has occurred, and the tide will have come up and gone down again, and I'm afraid that Mr. Colstone's body will never be recovered."

"I see—" said Susan. She spoke quite softly. "I see. And will my body never be recovered either?"

This time she did hear a groan.

"Will you leave him and swear—and swear—Ah, what's the use of it now? Aren't you dead already, the way you could look at me when I touched you? Could I lose you more than that if you were ten times dead? And could you be gone any farther away from me than when I had you in my arms, and all the ice of hell between us?"

Anthony held Susan close. With his lips at her ear he said, "He's mad," and she made some answering movement, but whether it meant "Yes" or "No" he could not tell. He released her abruptly and measured the distance to that crack above their heads. If he had anything to wedge it with.... His coat would do at a pinch, but if they had an iron bar.... They hadn't, so what was the good of wishing for it? He had his coat off and spoke again, soundlessly against her ear:

"Get him to lift the stone a little more—somehow—anyhow."

She nodded, looked up again, and called his name:

"Garry—are you there? I want to see you. I can't talk to you like this."

Silence.

"Garry—don't you remember—when you used—to carry me upstairs?"

Silence.

Anthony felt her shiver. She looked half round at him and made a helpless gesture. He put his face against hers.

"Go on," he breathed.

"Garry—won't you just look at me?"

The stone moved, tilted. Anthony stepped back and braced himself. The opening was an inch wide—an inch and a half—two inches—The longer he waited, the better he could wedge the stone, but it was moving so slowly, so horribly slowly. And then, in a single flash of time, there was a square, all dark, and Garry's face looking out of the darkness. The lamplight struck on it, showed it ghastly. And then in the same instant it was gone, and even as Anthony thrust upward with all his strength, the stone fell.

Chapter Thirty-Eight

Just for a moment Susan stood quite still. She saw Anthony's hand with the coat wrapped round it strike the stone, and she heard him call out. And then a most terrible wave of panic swept over her. Garry had gone away, and these four black walls and the fallen stone were between them and all the world they knew. It was a cold and dreadful thought. The colour went out of her face and the courage out of her heart. The place was full of mist.

She went unsteadily to the wall and sank down beside it. Garry—Garry had done this—Garry had gone away and left them here—he wouldn't come back—no one would come, because no one would know. She put her face in her hands and bowed her head upon her knees. There was a rushing sound in her ears like water—black water—carrying her away. Very dimly she thought that she was fainting, and after that she did not think at all.

It seemed like a long time afterwards that she heard Anthony's voice. She heard his voice before she felt that his arms were round her. His voice was very near—very near, and sharp with distress.

"Susan—darling—my darling! Susan! *Susan!*"

Susan opened her eyes. Her cheek was against the rough cloth of Anthony's coat, and she must have been crying, because her face was wet. And Anthony was kissing her, and his face was wet too. She opened her eyes, and the mist was gone. There were only the four black walls and the open golden box filled up with its useless treasure—and she and Anthony like creatures in a trap.

She put up her hand to his wet cheek and said, "I'm all right," and then, "I'm sorry I made such a fool of myself."

Anthony choked a little.

"You didn't."

"Oh, I did!"

She sat up and looked at him, and almost at once she knew that he was wondering whether it wouldn't have been better to have left her in her swoon. His face was set in lines she had not seen before. He controlled his voice with an effort and said,

"Susan—"

"What is it?"

"I think—we ought to put the lamp out."

A horror of the dark brought a little panting cry to her lips.

"Oh—*no!*"

"I think we ought to. You see it's—using too much air."

Susan hid her face against his shoulder. What was it Garry had said? Something about the long way out or the short. She pressed her mouth against Anthony's sleeve, because she wanted to scream and it was no good screaming, because nobody would hear. She felt him hold her close and, holding her, lean sideways. There was a clicking sound, and when she opened her eyes the light in the lamp was shooting up, shooting up and falling again, whilst the black walls seemed to rock and the shadows rushed in upon the failing light. With a last shooting flame it was gone. A smooth, even darkness, as impenetrable as the coal itself, filled all the little space from end to end.

Out of the dark Anthony's voice came quite cheerfully:

"Don't be frightened, darling—I'll hold on to you. It's only I think we ought to save the air a bit, because there's not much ventilation in this beastly hole. We can always light it again presently. You don't mind sitting in the dark for a bit, do you? I don't suppose it'll be for very long." It was astonishing how much easier it was now that the light was gone and he couldn't see Susan's eyes.

Susan shook her head. And then she remembered that he couldn't see her, and said "No" with a sigh that put a leaden weight on to the word.

The little chamber was very hot. The air in it felt still and dead. She wondered just what Anthony had meant when he said that perhaps it wouldn't be for very long. She shivered and said,

"Can't we do anything? Can't we call out?"

"I don't think it would be much use. I don't see how anyone could possibly hear us unless they were in the cellar just overhead—and if they were, we should hear them."

Susan pressed closer to him.

"Anthony—do you think we've got a chance?"

"Of course we have."

She moved impatiently.

"I don't want fairy stories—I want what you really think."

A tingling anguish ran over her in the moment that she waited for his answer. If he thought they had a chance, he would say so quickly, he wouldn't hesitate or keep her waiting. It was really only a moment before he said,

"I think O'Connell's mad. But there was another man before—there were two of them the night they knocked me out."

"Yes—yes."

"Well, I think the odds are that the second man's somewhere about. He won't want to do us in—he'll want the swag—he isn't in this for his health, or to score us off like O'Connell."

"You think—"

"I think we might be able to do a deal with him. He can't get away with the stuff while we're here."

Susan's breast heaved. Words came that she hadn't meant to say.

"He might—wait—" And there her breath failed her. She had a horrible picture of what he might find if he waited.

With a violent shudder she wrenched away from Anthony and wept. Only a few hours ago life had been so sweet, so dear. There had only been one single cloud in all her sunny sky, and now that cloud had blotted out the sun and covered the sky with a blacker darkness than night. She felt Anthony take her in his arms, and she wept there without comfort. Yet presently her weeping spent itself and she was still. She did not know that at the very height of her anguish the first spark of hope took hold upon his thought.

The chamber was small and contracted, the air was hot and dead, and time was passing. Minutes had passed—ten—fifteen—and for half that time the lamp had wasted their precious air. Yet now the dead, close atmosphere seemed no closer and no deader than before. To be able to go on breathing seemed a wonderful and a hopeful thing. It meant a respite, and it meant time. The spark of hope flickered into a pale flame.

Chapter Thirty-Nine

OLD MRS. BOWYER opened her eyes. She was lying on her back with her head low and her hands folded. Her coverlet and the sheet that was turned over it were as smooth and unwrinkled as when she had herself smoothed them down before falling asleep. Out of that light sleep she wakened lightly. It was as if she had been in the next room with the door open. She had been dreaming a pleasant dream in which she walked in a field by the river and saw her children at play, threading buttercups and daisies to make garlands. The sun shone on Susie's hair.

She opened her eyes, and felt a little bewildered. She had waked to the sound of a closing door. She lay in the dark and considered. The sound was certainly not one that had come with her out of her dream, because no orderly person would dream about hearing a door shut in an open green meadow. She lay and listened.

If the sound had been made by her own door, there would be other sounds. If Susan had come home, she would hear her moving in the next room. She lay quite still and listened, but no one moved at all. Then it came to her that the sound had come from below and not from the kitchen door, for that was towards her feet, nor from the front door, for that was away to the right of her. No, the sound had come from right underneath where the head of her bed stood hard against the wall, and that was why it had waked her. She folded back the coverlet, sat up, and struck a light. It was just half-past eleven—a most ungodly hour for anyone to be astir in Ford St. Mary.

Mrs. Bowyer got out of bed and put on the black stuff dress which she had taken off when she undressed. It did not quite cover her nightgown, so she fetched two safety pins from the patchwork cushion on her chest of drawers and pinned up the long white folds. Then she covered her unruffled hair with a cap, slid her feet into slippers of crimson wool, and put Susan's large white shawl about her shoulders. It took her some time to dress. Her face all this while was set in the lines of a deep displeasure. She was quite sure now that she had heard the click of the door in the kitchen chimney—"the old chimley door" she called it to herself—and that meant nothing in the world but that Susan had come home "unbeknowst" and was away through the passage to Stonegate.

Mrs. Bowyer was very highly displeased. Promised, or not promised, it was no way to go on, nor no way to make a man think the more of you. Susan should ha' known better, and if she didn't know no better along of having been brought up by that crazy Moll of a stepmother, why then she'd got to be learned, and Susan Bowyer was the woman to learn her. She'd a piece on her tongue for Anthony too. If he didn't know when he was risking the good name of the girl he was going to make his wife— well, he'd know a deal more about it before she'd finished what she'd got to say to him.

She took up her candle and came down the stair with a high spirit and a muffled tread. She went first into the empty living-room, and then to the kitchen, where she lighted the wall lamp. Then she opened the "chimley door" and stood looking down the dark steps and listening.

Susan Bowyer had still the keen hearing on which all the Bowyers prided themselves; she could have heard a mouse run across the far end of the passage. She heard something now, and what she heard brought a deep puzzled line to her forehead. It was the click of the panel at the

Stonegate end. It puzzled her a good deal. If Susan had gone into the passage when she had heard the sound that waked her, she must have reached the other end some time ago. There would be nothing to keep her in the dark underground place. The click must mean that she was returning. The lines about her mouth relaxed. If she had not stayed, Susan Bowyer would not be so very angry—"though I'll not pass it over light even so," she said to herself.

She waited eagerly for the footsteps that ought to be coming towards her now. But there were no footsteps; a dull, unbroken silence filled the passage like stagnant air. Mrs. Bowyer felt the weight of it on her mood; her quick anger sank to a close-packed dread. She was afraid, though she would not, either now or at any time, acknowledge fear. She was afraid, but she did not herself know why. She had a sense of something that threatened Susan.

She went back into the kitchen, set her candle down on the table, and stood with her back to the open door in the chimney. She stood there for a quarter of an hour. She was still listening. A cold breath and an earthy smell came up from under the ground and through the open door. "A right-down churchyard smell," was Mrs. Bowyer's thought. It seemed to sweep between her and Susan. She took up her candle with a steady hand, turned and went through the door, and closed it behind her, all but an inch-wide chink. It was somehow pleasant to look back and see the lamplight.

When she reached the fork, she looked sharply to the left, but did not stop. She held up her skirts with one hand and her candle with the other, and when she came to the panel which carried Patience Pleydell's portrait she opened it with a firm touch and stepped out into the library.

A lamp burned on the table, but the room was empty. Mrs. Bowyer shut the panel behind her. It was midnight, and the lamp stood burning in an empty room. Where were those whom it should have lighted? She stood there with the dread heavy at her heart and the minutes ticking away on the old clock with the silver face. The dread became more than she could carry in silence. A sort of groan passed her lips. The candle-flame shook with her shaking hand. With an effort that took all her strength she forced herself to move and break the spell. "If I'd ha' stood another moment, I'd ha' dropped," she said half aloud; and then, "Lord ha' mercy, where's my maid?" And with that she came to the library door and opened it.

The hall was dark. It was like her fear. Why was the hall dark if Susan was here? Why had Susan gone into the darkness? Where was she? Mrs. Bowyer thought the dark an evil sign. And now her sharpened fear drove her. She had to find Susan wherever she was. She opened three doors in succession, only to see black, empty rooms. Then she took her skirts in her hand again and began to climb the stair.

She climbed slowly, holding on to the oak rail. Every now and then she stopped and took her breath. The last time she had come up this stair it was to sit for an hour at Sir Jervis' side before he passed. The first time—no, she couldn't remember the first time; it lay so far back behind the barrier which separates the child who thinks and remembers from the infant whose days are just a pleasant coloured pattern that shapes itself and is gone. Between the first time and the last there lay nearly a century.

She passed the turn of the stair and stood for a while looking down into the black hall. There was a strange feeling about the house to-night. It was hushed and silent, but it was not asleep. It made her think of times when she had laid awake as a child and been afraid to move, or stir, or even breathe, for fear of something that was hidden in the darkness. She thought that was how the house was to-night—keeping terribly still, and holding its breath.

The sound at the door did not take her unawares. It was just as if she was expecting it—the faint sound of a door opening and closing again—and as she heard it old Susan Bowyer turned her head a little to the right and blew out the flame of her candle as composedly as if she had just said her prayers and made ready for bed. The end of the wick glowed, and she pinched it out with a dexterous thumb and forefinger. Then she stood listening. Someone had come into the glazed passage through the door that opened from the village street. Someone was coming into the hall through the second door, and there was no sound of a turning key. The doors had not been locked—had not been locked?—or had been unlocked?

Mrs. Bowyer could see the hall door moving; because outside darkness is never quite so dense as the darkness in a house, and the door looked blacker than the passage beyond it. She could see the black door move, but she could not see who came through it; only she knew that someone had come through it, because there was a sound of stealthy movement. She stood quite still. The person who was moving must know the house. The faint sound passed the library door and was cut short by another sound, the falling to of the baize door that led to the kitchen wing.

Mrs. Bowyer began to come down the stairs with surprising agility. She left her useless candlestick on one of the oak steps and held up her skirts with both hands. What did she want with a light, when all was said and done? There wasn't anywhere in all the house that she couldn't have walked blindfold either by night or day and never have to stop to think whether she might stumble.

She went through the swing door with just enough of a pause to make sure that there was no one in the dark on the other side of it. The passage had an empty feeling, but, as Susan had done before, she stopped just short of the housekeeper's room, and heard voices coming from the other side of the door; only where Susan had found the door open, Mrs. Bowyer found it closed. She came up to it cautiously and listened. The door was closed, but not latched. The latch had a trick of slipping these fifty years.

Mrs. Bowyer pushed the door with the tip of one finger. It moved about half an inch, and she could see that there was some sort of light in the room beyond—dim lamp or lantern light, or perhaps a candle like her own. There were two voices in the lighted room, and one of them she knew. There was a man talking to a woman, and a woman answering a man.

Mrs. Bowyer let go of her skirts, dratted her trembling knees, and held on, with one hand at the handle of the door and the other at the jamb. The man was speaking now. Even in a whisper, there was something precise about the way in which he said,

"I entirely fail to see why he should think himself in a position to give me orders."

"Oh, but you ought not to have come in!" The woman's voice shook and was very much afraid.

"Where is he?" said the man contemptuously.

"He went down—oh, a long time ago. I don't know what is happening. Oh, I *wish* he'd come back!"

"Then I'm going down too."

Mrs. Bowyer's knees stopped trembling.

There was a wailing cry of "Oh, don't leave me!"

Mrs. Bowyer shut the door gently but firmly upon the man's reply and slid home the stout bolt which was just above the lock. Thirty years before there had been a burglary scare in the neighbourhood, and Sir Jervis had had a bolt fixed on the outside of every door on the ground floor. The bolt creaked a little. She picked up her skirts and ran to the corner, round it, and up to the second door. She reached it and slipped the bolt just as the handle of the first door was turned and shaken.

Mrs. Bowyer stood back breathing rather quickly. "Won't break down that door in a hurry, the rumbustious robber," she said to herself. "No one won't break down that door in a hurry, let alone not daring to make a noise." She heard the second handle tried, and chuckled. The window opening into a small closed courtyard did not trouble her at all. The robber was caught, safe and sure, and there he could stay until she found her maid and Anthony Colstone. The robber was Anthony Colstone's affair, and not hers. "Both of 'em's his affair if it comes to that—sure and certain they are. And oh, Lord help us, where's my maid?"

She was standing away from the bolted door, her mind so much taken up that it was only when she turned that she became aware of the door at the head of the cellar steps standing ajar and a faint glow of light coming through the opening. It should have been locked and bolted at this hour of the night. She turned from the vague sounds which came from the housekeeper's room and opened the cellar door. The steps ran down into the light—not a bright light, but just enough to make a world of shadows. The dark lay on the steps like splashes of ink.

Mrs. Bowyer blinked once or twice as she descended, treading softly. When she was still three or four steps from the bottom she stood still. The place was the central hall into which other cellars opened. A lantern stood on the floor a little to the right of where the steps came down. There was an old mowing machine beside it, and a broken ladder. The light fell on a packing-case or two and some sacks. The light fell on a man lying face downwards in the middle of the stone floor, his arms thrown wide. His face was hidden, but Susan Bowyer knew at once that this was a stranger whom she had never seen before.

The black sleek hair, the curve of the ear, the long delicate hands were all quite strange to her and to Ford St. Mary. She gazed at him without emotion. It was plain that a judgment had overtaken him, and she considered it extremely proper that, as she herself would have put it, "such should be the case."

She was about to turn and mount the steps again in order to rouse Lane, when the man groaned.

Chapter Forty

AFTERWARDS MRS. BOWYER said that her flesh "creepst" all over. At the time she remained commendably calm. The man obviously wasn't dead. If he wasn't dead, how nearly dead was he, and could he do anyone a mischief, or couldn't he?

The groan was a low one, but somehow or other it did not sound to Susan Bowyer like the groan of a dying man. " 'Tis more like as if he was in mortal pain and not wanting nobody to know," she said to herself. And as she said it, the man groaned again, and she saw the hand that was nearest her contract as if in some spasm of agony. The deep groan and the fingers that made as if they would dig themselves into the unyielding stone meant pain.

Mrs. Bowyer came down another step. A judgment was a judgment, but she had nursed too many sick people to be able to stand aloof when pain called to her. As she moved, the man moved too. His hands beat the stone. He raised his head with a choking sob. Mrs. Bowyer thought that he said "Susan," but he didn't say it to her. He got up on his knees, and showed a white face streaming with sweat, and the eyes of a man in torment. He took his head in his hands and swayed, and groaned, and muttered. He certainly did not see the cellar or old Susan Bowyer standing at the bottom of the steps; he saw only the wolves that were tearing him, and would tear him for ever. He said, "What's the use? Susan—what's the use? Susan—*Susan!* What's the use, I say? I can't reach you—I can't touch you, but you're mine—you've always been mine—you don't know it, but you're mine—*always.*"

He stumbled on to his feet, and he looked right past Mrs. Bowyer with those tormented eyes.

"Oh, my God! What have I done?" His voice sank groaning to a whisper. "Susan—what have I done? They'll be together—it doesn't hurt them. Susan, I haven't killed you—I've killed myself! *Susan!*"

Old Susan Bowyer took the shock of his words with a steady front, but inwardly they were like blades of ice cutting into her. She thought the man was mad, and she thought that he had killed Susan. If his words meant anything, they meant that. With a deadly cold at her heart she went up to him and put a hand upon his arm.

"Where's my maid?"

Garry O'Connell stared at her. He was in one dream, and she was in another. His brain reeled with the distance between his dream and that of any other living soul. He was alone. He had killed Susan.

Mrs. Bowyer shook him slightly.

"What ha' you done with Susan?"

"I've killed her," said Garry O'Connell.

Mrs. Bowyer's hand tightened on his arm. She did not believe him, but just to hear it said was like the clap of thunder that leaves a man dazed and silly. She said, in a loud, shaking voice,

"You ha' *not!*"

"I've killed her," said Garry O'Connell. "She's dead and buried, and a stone over her head." He broke into a terrible laugh. "The stone that Merlin blessed!"

"An' I saw it just so clear as I ever see anything in all my born days— just so clear as I ever see anything. An' if it wasn't the Lord a-showing it to me, who was it? That's what I'd like to know. I see it in the twinkle of an eye." This was Mrs. Bowyer afterwards. At the time she held Garry O'Connell firmly by the arm, looked in to his wild eyes with a dark, steady gaze, and said, "Don't you talk nonsense, my lad!"

Something penetrated the dream. Perhaps it was the tone of brisk authority, perhaps it was the courage and faith behind the tone. He trembled under her hand and repeated,

"She's under the Stone."

"Then we'll get her out."

Garry dropped his voice to a dreadful whisper.

"The treasure's there—Philip Colstone's treasure—and two dead Colstones to guard it."

The hand on his arm was clenched.

"What ha' you done with them?"

He laughed again and wrenched away from her.

"I? Nothing—nothing at all. But—there's no air. The stone is shut, and there's no air." With the last word his voice rose into a scream.

He snatched up the lamp, crossed the cellar running, and disappeared through the open door at the end. Mrs. Bowyer followed the light which swung and wavered ahead of her. In all her years she had never seen the opening of the low, heavy door. Now it stood wide. The lantern light went dancing along the passage behind it and down into a vaulted room. When she came down the steps, Garry O'Connell stood in the middle of the floor with the lantern hanging from his hand. His head was a little bent, as if he were standing by a grave. The light shone on a flagstone deeply cut with two interlaced triangles.

"*Hic jacet*—Susan," he said. And then all of a sudden he let the lantern fall with a jangling crash and threw himself down over the stone, calling aloud, "Susan—Susan—*Susan!*"

The lantern rocked and steadied. The light still shone. From the other side of the stone there came the sound of knocking. Mrs. Bowyer spoke in a deep harsh voice which she did not know for her own:

"Open that stone! Open it at once!"

The knocking ceased. Another sound took its place—the muffled, hollow sound of someone shouting in a confined space.

Mrs. Bowyer put a commanding hand upon Garry's shoulder.

"Now, my lad, look sharp!" she said. "There's no sense in calling through a stone. You look a bit lively and open what's got to be opened."

Garry O'Connell lifted his head with a jerk, looked her in the face, and sprang up. With a sort of convulsive energy he struck the wall with his hand and drove with his right foot against the sign that was cut upon the turning stone. The stone turned, tilted, showed a black square, and Mrs. Bowyer, picking up the lantern and looking, as she herself would have said, "down over," saw the light strike on Anthony Colstone's upturned face. What she really saw first were his eyes, unnaturally light because his forehead and cheeks were as black as a sweep's.

She said, "Lord, ha' mercy!" and then, in a sharpened voice, "Where's my maid?"

As Anthony stooped, his voice started an echo.

"She's faint. Get out of the way, and I'll lift her up."

Then he raised himself with Susan in his arms. Her eyes were open, and the tears were running down her cheeks. When her head came above the opening, she drew in her breath with a gasp and caught at the edge of the stone to hold herself up. Her eyes passed in blank surprise from Gran, with the lantern in her hand, to Garry, still thrusting at the wall as if his arm were rigid and he unconscious of it.

Mrs. Bowyer saw their eyes meet and Susan shrink away. She frowned and issued another order.

"Anthony'd best come up first. Put her down, lad, and come you up."

"Yes," said Susan shuddering—"yes." She let go of the stone and slipped back into the darkness.

Garry O'Connell laughed. A sound of whispering came up from below. Then Anthony Colstone swung himself up and clambered out of the hole. He had far more the appearance of being the villain of the piece than Garry, who leaned now against the wall, his smooth, pale face almost expressionless. There was just a hint of mockery in the set of the upper lip. Mrs. Bowyer, watching him with the same alert, compassionate gaze with which she would have watched a fevered child, saw the hand which hung at his side close and unclose continually.

Anthony knelt and reached down for Susan. He took her under the arms, but when he had lifted her, he knew that it was not going to be easy to get her up alone. She was a dead weight. Her eyes were half closed, and her breath came in gasps. Garry's face—and then to go down into the dark again.... She felt as if she was still going down, slipping down, down into a deep black well. Over her head Mrs. Bowyer spoke sharply:

"You there, my lad, come and give a hand! The wall don't need you to prop it. The maid's fainting. Give him a hand."

Susan came back to consciousness to find herself leaning against Anthony's shoulder, whilst Garry held her by the arm. She looked from one to the other, a puzzled, piteous look. And then, as Anthony's arm closed about her, she burst into tears and hid her face against him.

Garry let go of her and fell back a pace. His voice cut through the sound of her sobbing breaths:

"It wasn't he who saved you—it was I. What is he to you anyway—*Susan?*" Susan turned a little and looked at him with wet, frightened eyes. "What has he got to give you? I've given you everything. He'll never give you half as much. I love you so much that I'd have killed you. He'll never love you enough for that!"

It was like a conversation in a nightmare. Susan stamped her foot.

"I don't want him to! Why don't you go away?"

"That's enough, O'Connell!" said Anthony roughly. "We'll get out of this."

"And bed and a drink of good hot milk is what she'll be the better for," observed Mrs. Bowyer. She made a determined move towards the door, and there made a pointed gesture to Garry to precede her.

They came out through the old cellar door. Anthony stopped to lock it, and as he pocketed the key, Garry laughed again.

"Yes," said Anthony, "you've got a key too—haven't you? I hadn't forgotten that—I was just going to ask you to hand it over. The game's up, O'Connell."

"Yes, the game's up," said Garry. He balanced the heavy key in the palm of his hand; it looked raw and new in the lantern light. He tossed it suddenly to Anthony. "The game's up. But it wasn't your game—it was mine. Perhaps you'll be thinking of that later on. It was my game, and I gave it away to Susan—not to you. You'd be under that stone for good and all if it wasn't that I'd give Philip Colstone's treasure a dozen times over for Susan—and that's a thing she'll not forget. And when she's had her fill of stagnation, and her fill of being the squire's wife, and her fill of your enlivening society, she'll come, maybe, to wish in her heart that I'd left you there. And now"—he threw back his head and struck an attitude—"what are you going to do with me?"

"See you out of the front door and bolt it behind you," said Anthony.

Chapter Forty-One

ANTHONY DROVE HOME those bolts with a will. If Garry O'Connell ever came messing round here again, he'd get his face pushed in. If he had touched him to-night, he'd have killed him, the murdering, play-acting swab. He turned from the door to find Mrs. Bowyer at his elbow, Susan in the background, sitting on the bottom step of the stair with her head against the newel-post.

"There's two more in the housekeeper's room," said Mrs. Bowyer.

Anthony's jaw dropped.

"In the—"

Mrs. Bowyer nodded in a businesslike manner.

"In the housekeeper's room. I turned the key of the door upon them—both doors."

"Two of them!"

"In a manner of speaking," said Mrs. Bowyer.

Anthony was turning towards the door again.

"Then I suppose I'd better get Smithers. Lane's no earthly."

Old Susan Bowyer's hand was on his arm.

"Well, lad, I shouldn't do that."

"Why not?"

"Least said, soonest mended, my dear."

Anthony felt very much as if he had put a finger on an electric wire; the shock tingled all through him.

"What do you mean?"

"You'd best to come and see," said Mrs. Bowyer. "And I'd take a poker or something along with me if I was you—there's one in the libery that'll settle him easy if he gives trouble."

She led the way. As Anthony passed Susan, he bent down and said in a low voice,

"Are you all right, darling?"

"Yes—quite. Where are you going?"

"There's someone in the housekeeper's room. You stay here."

She pulled herself up at once.

"Oh no, I must come too."

Mrs. Bowyer turned impatiently.

"Come, or stay, but make haste about it or we'll none of us get to bed to-night!"

She went on through the baize door, still carrying the lantern.

Anthony went to the library for the poker. It seemed strange to see the lamp burning there in the empty room. He hurried back to Susan with the feeling that she might be spirited away if he were to delay.

As they came through the swing door, Mrs. Bowyer drew back the bolt and threw open the door of the housekeeper's room. Anthony sprang forward, but she was already advancing into the room, holding the lantern high. The room had been dark. An extinguished lamp stood on the table. A man who had faced old Susan Bowyer as she came in had now wheeled about and stood with his back to the door. Perhaps he had expected Anthony when the bolt shot back. Perhaps he had thought that he could rush him and get away unknown. Sitting at the table, with her head buried in her hands and her face hidden, was a woman, dressed as Patience Pleydell was dressed in her portrait, in a blue petticoat and a flowered gown, and a cap that covered her hair.

Mrs. Bowyer set the lantern down upon the chimney-piece, and there was a moment in which the silence weighed heavily on the five people who were in the room. Then, defiantly, the man flung round.

It was Bernard West.

Anthony stared at him. The silence went on. Bernard West broke it.

"Well, I suppose you're surprised."

"Good Lord!" said Anthony. "Surprised? *West!*"

"If you had ever accustomed yourself to think, you would not find it surprising at all."

"Look here, West—"

"None of your family ever have thought, as far as I can make out. They were given a clue over three hundred years ago, a clue which any intelligent schoolboy could have unravelled in half an hour, and during the whole of that time I don't suppose any of them ever so much as looked at it. I only wonder that the book survived. And are you going seriously to advance the theory that three hundred years of stupefied ignorance entitles the family to something which they never did an honest day's work for?"

"I don't know that I was going to advance a theory at all," said Anthony drily.

Mr. West snorted.

"On what theory, or what notion of ethics, do you base any claim? Your Philip Colstone was, on your own showing, nothing in the world but a high-class pirate. Whatever it was he got, I suppose you're not going to contend that he came by it honestly?"

Anthony began to wonder if he was light-headed.

"I'm not contending anything," he murmured.

Mr. West hit the table.

"He took it by robbery and murder, and he got what he deserved! And where's your claim to what *he* hadn't the shadow of an honest claim to?"

"Aren't you assuming a good deal? Anyhow I don't quite see where you come in."

"He come in," said Mrs. Bowyer, "along of his grandfather that he's the spit and image of, the one they called Jew like I told you—that's how he come in, and just such another interfering piece of goods, to listen to him. The grandfather he come down here at Sir Jervis' bidding, and sick, sore and sorry he was about it when it was too late."

Bernard West struck the table again.

"My grandfather would have made Sir Jervis' fortune if he hadn't been so infernally pig-headed!"

"You mean he found coal on the estate," said Anthony.

The woman who was sitting at the table lifted her head. Miss Arabel's little ravaged face was turned towards Anthony. She had been crying for the last half hour. The tears kept running down as she spoke in a weak, choked voice.

"Papa never thought about anyone but himself. He never thought about us. He didn't care if my heart was broken. He sent John away. He found the coal, and Papa sent him away. There would have been plenty of money for us all. Papa would have been a very rich man. He only thought about himself."

"Cousin Arabel!" said Anthony, in horrified tones.

Miss Arabel felt for her pocket handkerchief, and failing to find it, sniffed helplessly.

"I ought to have had my share. Bernard said I should have my share—he and the other young man. They said it was only fair."

"What did you want it for?" said Anthony. This was rather horrible.

"I wanted to travel," said Miss Arabel. "I wanted to travel and see the world—I always did. And we never went anywhere—we never went anywhere at all. Agatha didn't mind, but I wanted to go to San Francisco—and Rio—and Nova Zembla—and—and—Japan—and Tasmania—and the Fortunate Islands. But Papa only thought about himself." She sniffed piteously and said in a whispering voice, "I can't find my pocket handkerchief."

Susan knelt at her side.

"Here's one. Don't cry. You shall travel if you want to—only do stop crying."

"I pulled back the bolts and let them in," said Miss Arabel, dabbing her eyes. "I came through the passage, and I pulled back the bolts—I had to climb on a chair. And I made myself a dress like the picture—I had to lock my door whilst I sewed at it. That was after I saw you in Agatha's old dress which she gave to Susan Bowyer. You see, I thought—if anyone saw me—they'd think—" She broke off with a sob. "Anthony did see me once, and I hid in Susan Bowyer's kitchen till he went away. Oh dear, oh dear, I shall never see any of those places now! I'm too old!"

Susan patted her.

"You're not a bit too old. We'll give you some of the treasure, and you shall travel all round the world."

Miss Arabel stopped crying with as much suddenness as if a tap had been turned.

"You're Robert's granddaughter," she said. Her voice had sharpened.

Mrs. Bowyer had come up to the table. She leaned on it with both hands and fixed her black eyes on Miss Arabel's tear-stained face.

"Ha' done with Robert's granddaughter!" she said, in a strong, forcible voice. "She's no more Robert's granddaughter than she's yours. Robert never had no granddaughter. She's Ralph Colstone's daughter, and Philip Colstone's granddaughter. She's just so much a Colstone as you are, my dear—and Anthony Colstone's promised wife into the bargain."

Miss Arabel looked sharply from one to the other. Then she pressed Susan's hand.

"Did you find anything down there? Will he give me my share? I ought to have my share, you know. Papa wasn't fair to us."

Anthony did not catch the words. He saw Susan whispering something back. He saw old Mrs. Bowyer straighten herself up with a sardonic smile. He spoke with an effort to Bernard West:

"I think you'd better get out. O'Connell's gone."

Mr. West actually appeared aggrieved. As he preceded Anthony to the front door, he delivered an aggressive lecture on the subject of brains versus an obsolete law of inheritance. He was still talking when he stepped into the street.

227 | THE COLDSTONE

Anthony was moved to sudden laughter. What a colossal nerve! What a colossal gas-bag! You caught the fellow red-handed in a burglary and he lectured you on the ethics of property! He heard himself shouting with laughter.

"You're too damned long-winded, West," he said. "I can put it in a sentence—a talk in a tabloid, and a good old English proverb at that—'Findings is keepings.' Only, unfortunately for you, I've done the finding, and I'm going to do the keeping."

He slammed the door, and felt better.

Chapter Forty-Two

THEY MADE TEA in Mrs. Bowyer's kitchen, after Anthony had seen Miss Arabel to the end of the passage which opened into the Ladies' House.

She sent him away before she opened the door, because even Susan Bowyer, who thought she knew everything, didn't know the trick of the catch, or just where the passage came out. The opening had been very cleverly planned, and only Miss Agatha and Miss Arabel knew the secret. Nobody would have guessed that the back of the left-hand china cupboard was really a door. Some day, perhaps, she and Agatha would tell Anthony; but not at present—not until they were a great deal older than they were now. So she sent Anthony away, and watched him out of sight before she opened the door.

In the kitchen, Mrs. Bowyer talked over a cup of sweet, hot tea. She liked four lumps to the cup, and on great occasions five. This was a great occasion.

"Bowyers have always known as there was something hid. 'Twas Colstones that didn't believe. By all reckoning some of 'em didn't believe no more than what their own eyes could see. Stubborn, hard folk some of 'em were, and none too easy to live with. Jervis wasn't none too easy to live with—Miss Arabel was in the rights of it there—he didn't think of nothing but himself and his land. He'd ha' thought more of his daughters if they'd been young filly horses 'stead of yuman beings. Miss Arabel was in the rights of it there. Mind you, I don't say as he'd ought to let her marry that Jew. His grandson's the very moral of him, and why she wanted him, Lord knows. I wouldn't ha' taken him myself if I'd never seen another man and didn't know there was one. Give me another cup of tea, my maid, and leave the sugar in the bottom of the cup. Wilful waste makes woeful want."

Susan had set out gingerbread and currant cake. She and Anthony had washed off the worst of the coaldust. His hair was wet and dark. Her cheek was pale. They sat side by side on Gran's old Windsor chairs, and felt very young and happy—tea and currant cake in the middle of the night, and Gran in her woolly shawls drinking cup after cup and emptying the sugar basin.

"I'm *frightfully* sorry for Cousin Arabel," said Susan.

Mrs. Bowyer sniffed.

"Not but what I'm glad she got her letters," she said.

"What letters?"

"Oh, there was letters passed. And when it all come out, Jervis took 'em away, and he kept them for a stick to beat her with, and after that she didn't give no more trouble. I dunno what was in them, but she fretted something cruel, poor little toad, and I'm glad she got 'em in the end."

"How do you know she got them, Gran?"

Mrs. Bowyer stirred her tea and sipped from the spoon.

" 'Twas a few nights ago, and I woke up same as I woke to-night and along of the same reason. 'Twas the click of the chimley door waked me. I'd have to be sounder asleep than I'll ever be this side the grave not for to wake if so be anyone lays a hand on the chimley door."

Susan looked at Anthony, and Anthony looked at Susan. Mrs. Bowyer nodded and stirred her tea.

"I come down and I set the kitchen door ajar. And 'twas all dark, but 'twasn't all still—there was a kind of a fidgeting and a kind of a rustling, and a kind of a sighing sound like someone taking their breath in a hurry. And then I heard Miss Arabel say 'Oh dear!' once or twice as if she was frightened. And then she fetched out one of they 'lectric lamps, and turned it on, and I could see as she'd got her skirt held up with a heap of letters in it. And she set the light down on the kitchen table and picked up a two three of the letters and held 'em where she could see the writing, and she cried a bit and kissed the paper—Lord knows what was on it, poor soul."

"Oh—" said Susan.

"And after a bit she opened the chimley door and went away. And when she'd gone I went in and down and along to have a look, and right by the end of the passage behind the picture, on the left-hand side, I see a bit of the wall open—a kind of a cupboard it was. Did you find it, lad?"

"I found it open," said Anthony. "Sir Jervis' diary was inside. And I'm afraid I startled Cousin Arabel. Her letters must have been there too. She left the door ajar, or I'd never have found it."

Mrs. Bowyer nodded.

"That would be the way of it. Put a little water in the pot, or we'll run dry."

Anthony jumped up and fetched the kettle. He wondered how many cups of tea Gran was good for.

"What'll you do with what you found down under, lad?" said Mrs. Bowyer when her cup was filled. "There's plenty of milk—don't stint it."

Anthony laughed.

"Sell it, and live happy ever after."

"Look here, Gran," said Susan, "this is what I don't understand. You told me a story all about Philip Colstone telling Will Bowyer he'd raised the devil, and a fire up by the Coldstone, and how frightened Will Bowyer was, and how nobody would ever go near the Coldstone afterwards."

Old Susan Bowyer's black eyes became intent.

"Well—and what if I did?"

Susan leaned across the table.

"*Because* in the message in *The Shepheard's Kalendar* Philip Colstone says he put the treasure in a secret place—'Will Bowyer knows, none else.'"

Mrs. Bowyer clasped her fingers about her cup.

"What did he mean?" said Susan. "First he says he was going to bury the treasure under the Coldstone, only fire came out. I suppose there was gas or something, and it caught fire from his torch. And then he says he put it in the secret place and cut Merlin's sign on the stones to keep people away."

Mrs. Bowyer nodded.

"The tale I told you was true enough. Will Bowyer ran out in the night like I told you, and he met Mr. Philip, and that's what he said to him, just the way I told you. And if he told the tale like he did tell it, maybe it was by Mr. Philip's orders. Bowyers never did tell Colstone secrets unless they were bid, so I'll be bound he said what Mr. Philip told him to say—and more than that no one never knew. But I think they put the treasure away together safe and sure before they went off to the fighting. Mr. Philip would tell Will what he wouldn't tell his own wife, for they'd fallen out, as I've heard tell, and a six months after he was killed she took and married a cousin of her own that she and Mr. Philip had had words about—so he wouldn't tell her nothing. And his boy was only a matter of six years old, so, as I read it, he told Will Bowyer, and he wrote his message in the book where you found it, and he give it to Will to take to his son."

"But what happened?" Anthony was leaning forward too.

"Give me another cup of tea," said Mrs. Bowyer firmly—"and only four lumps this time."

"What happened?" said Anthony. "If Will Bowyer knew, why didn't he tell the boy?"

"Will Bowyer never come home," Mrs. Bowyer's voice was as solemn as a knell. "He never come home because he died by the way, of his wounds that he got fighting with the Spaniards, and when those that was with him brought the book to Stonegate, there wasn't no one that could read the message right, only Bowyers always believed as there was something hid."

"How did they know, Gran?"

"Maybe Will Bowyer talked in his sleep afore he went away. Maybe he said a word to his wife—maybe he didn't." She pushed away her cup and got up. "It's time we all went to our beds. Susan, when I knock on the floor, you'll come up."

She took Anthony by his hands, and as he bent down to her, she kissed his forehead.

"God bless thee, Colstone," she said, and turned to Susan. "God bless thee, my maid," and kissed her too.

She went up the stair and left them together.

With his cheek against Susan's cheek, Anthony asked,

"*Will* you be bored—living down here—with me?"

"No, I won't."

"That blighter said—"

She put her hand over his mouth.

"I won't be bored—I shall love it. I like everyday things, and being happy, and having a garden, and driving in a car, and—and puppies and kittens—and Gran just across the road. I do love Gran."

"Do you love me—*Susan?*"

"Yes, I do—you know I do—*Anthony!*"

They kissed and were silent, and kissed again. The clock ticked and the wall lamp shone on them. The darkness outside was beginning to thin away. In half an hour the birds would be calling to each other.

Old Susan Bowyer leaned out of bed and knocked three times on the floor with the heel of her shoe.

THE END

Made in United States
North Haven, CT
03 March 2024

49526584R00134